TO LOSE THE SUN

TO LOSE THE SUN

A NOVEL BY
DON LUENSER

To Angie

Don Luenser

TATE PUBLISHING & *Enterprises*

Published by Tate Publishing & Enterprises, LLC
127 E. Trade Center Terrace | Mustang, Oklahoma 73064 USA
1.888.361.9473 | www.tatepublishing.com

Tate Publishing is committed to excellence in the publishing industry. The company reflects the philosophy established by the founders, based on Psalm 68:11,
"The Lord gave the word and great was the company of those who published it."

Book design copyright © 2008 by Tate Publishing, LLC. All rights reserved.
Cover design by Stephanie Woloszyn
Interior design by Lindsay B. Behrens

Published in the United States of America
ISBN: 978-1-60462-968-2
1. Fiction: Action & Adventure   2. Fiction: Science Fiction: Series
08.04.18

To my wife Sharon and my son Marcus.

ACKNOWLEDGMENTS

I would like to first and foremost thank my sister Mary. With encouragement and help, she showed me how to reach further than I knew how to alone. She spent many hours reading and editing but most of the help came in her support of me and my story.

Thanks also to Jean Ann for her support and for her help with story editing and consistency.

FOREWORD

I have great pleasure and pride in writing the foreword for this book, *To Lose the Sun*, by Don Luenser, and congratulate him on sharing with us the world he created.

It is difficult to categorize this, his first book. It is science fiction, but as a lover of science and good fiction I often find that science fiction is neither good science nor good fiction. Don's book is both good science, in that his world obeys the known laws of the universe, and good fiction, in that his characters are people I want to know and spend time with.

To Lose the Sun is a book about a catastrophic change in the world of an unsophisticated farming community. Don weaves a tale of disaster befalling these engaging people on this planet from their own perspective. It is the reader's knowledge of science that adds to the building sense of foreboding and suspense.

Drel knows that the planting season will come late this year. The shadow dial, erected by his father many years ago to predict and track such things, has clearly indicated a change. For some time, the number of days in a year has been increasing, but Drel has no explanation for the village, until the visiting moon reappears in the sky after a five year absence.

To help the farming village supplement its food, the leaders have asked Pred to re–learn the skills of hunting. The Hunter trains his son Jait, and to the surprise of the village, his daughter Tymber in those skills.

Tymber is a brave young woman with the curiosity and energy of a natural explorer. To the amusement of her family, she has a need to name all the places that they visit. As a family, the trio travels into the unfamiliar forest and venture far from the village in search of good hunting and fishing.

During their travels the visiting moon nears and the results on planet Adentta are far reaching. Their travels turn from hunting and fishing to a quest for survival.

Don is uniquely qualified to introduce us to the wild natural world of Adentta. He holds a bachelor of science in forestry, and his knowledge and love of nature runs deep. He literally grew up in a log cabin built by his father and grandfather in the middle of an oak and maple forest in Illinois. A forest preserve was on one side, Boy Scout camp on the other and wild woods and a swamp in between. He and his sister were the oldest of six kids, and the two of them spent every hour they could in the woods. As youngsters they took botanists to see the wild yellow violets and other rare flowers that grew in remote places in the woods.

Don has taught forestry in Louisiana and instilled his love of nature to his students by teaching a wide range of courses from practical trigonometry to tree identification. He is currently chief workforce development officer and assistant campus dean for the Louisiana Technical College. Don has spent years developing training curriculum to draw jobs into Louisiana by developing customized training programs for business and industry within the region.

—Mary Adams–Moe

ONE

He was sure that it couldn't be. At least he hoped that it wasn't. He had not felt a ground vibration for five years, the year of the Lost Moon.

Lying in bed and just waking, he wasn't sure if it had really happened. Something made him wake suddenly. Drel laid perfectly still, dreading that he might feel a vibration or hear the humming of one approaching.

It did not come. He was sure it must have been a dream.

He lay there as the memory of the ground vibration faded. His thoughts turned to the cold in the cabin and the stale smell of smoke that lingered in the air from the wood stove.

It was early morning, but still dark. He hated the thought, but he had to get out from under his blanket, run across the wooden floor to the stack of wood by the door and throw a couple of chunks into the stove.

When he finished that task, he lay back in bed and reflected on the duties of the day. He was sure of his observations but that wasn't going to matter much. He had to convince the entire village including the Leaders. The science behind the readings was incidental and to be honest, he wasn't real sure what the readings meant, but didn't like the trend.

Dawn came when expected ... at least that was good news. The dark in the cabin turned to shadows and then to dim light. It was time. He had to get up.

The cabin had warmed up somewhat, but still had a layer of cool lying on the floor. Drel looked outside through the window and was surprised to see no frost. He was sure by the coolness in the cabin that there would have been one. If it had frosted, he would have an easier time later in the day.

He didn't feel very hungry but he knew he would later, so he prepared his usual breakfast of grain cakes, hen's eggs, sausage, and hot root tea. The smell of the food cooking made him hungry and he ended up eating more than normal.

Unfortunately, the cold weather prevented him from eating his breakfast outside on the porch. By this time last year, he was enjoying all of his meals outside, sitting in his rocking chair. He looked forward to the warmer mornings of summer when he again could eat outside. It always seemed like such a wonderful way to start the morning.

After breakfast, Drel dressed in his normal brown pants and blue shirt. Since the morning is so cold, he slipped on his lined leather jacket and cloth cap that covered his ears. He grabbed his notes and was out the door to walk to the village center.

He lived at the very edge of the village by design and regretted it only when he had the long walk to the village center. Most people didn't want to live this close to the forest, which is why his single cabin was available when he needed it.

He was determined not to think about the meeting. Instead, he walked in silence and enjoyed the cool sunny morning.

The trail at this edge of the village was not well traveled since he was the only one that walked there. It was barely wide enough for one person and he had to duck under many overhanging tree limbs.

The sun was still low in the east but was shielded from view by the trees, even though the leaves were still in buds. He stopped to look at a low branch of a Swicka tree to examine the buds. They were still many days from leafing. This was the first time that he could remember the trees had not leafed by the first day of Plant.

One line equaled three days; two lines equaled twelve days, what did three lines mean? Who knows? He stopped thinking about it.

Ahead he could see the field that contained his shadow measurement dials. It was too early to take a reading now. He had to observe his shadow lengths near midday; he may have time to take a reading on his way back, if Leader didn't talk too much.

He had not realized until he entered the field that there was a slight fog lying close to the ground. A light breeze made little swirls in the fog that randomly formed, danced for a moment or two, and then disappeared. The dew on the grass sparkled like stars in the early morning sun.

On the left of the trail was the first dial. It was on a pole that stood around four feet high. It was a round disk laying flat about a foot in diameter with twenty etched marks around the outer edge, a vertical pointer in the middle, and eight circles of various diameters around the central pointer. His father installed that original shadow dial over twenty years ago.

Just past that dial, the trail forked. To the right were the other two dials that he had built identical to dial one, just in different places. To the left was the direction of the village center.

He wondered briefly if the village leaders would want to come and see the shadow lengths for themselves. He would have to explain the shadow dial to everyone and exactly the purpose of each line. To them, the readings would have no meaning and he hoped that they would not want to view the dials.

After watching his father observe the shadows for years, and reading the shadows on the dials himself for eight years, he knew what the readings meant, but was not sure of why they were unusual these days.

Through the small line of trees ahead, he could see his nearest neighbor, Shodder's double cabin. Shodder has a double cabin even though there is only one family living there; after all, he did have six kids. It seemed to Drel that even a double cabin would not have enough room to house all of their kids.

As he passed where the trail forked to the left up to Shodder's cabin, he could see movement through the trees. He could barely make out the outline of Shodder's wife Marta. It appeared that she was sweeping off the front porch. Drel turned his head back to the trail and hoped that she would not see him.

"Good morning Keeper," Marta shouted, as she waved her hand.

She had seen him. He was hoping to get past without having to take the time to stop and exchange chitchat, which seemed to be all the conversations he and her ever had.

"Good morning Sl … Marta," Drel said. He almost called her by her nickname, Slippers. She hated that name. She insisted she does so much more to help Shodder than make slippers. Drel thought the nickname suited her, whether she made slippers or not.

"How is Shodder this morning?" Drel asked, as he stopped to acknowledge her. He could hear the kids in the cabin having what sounded like a scream and tag game, but it appeared that she didn't even notice.

"He's fine," she said. "He's left for the meeting already. I'm surprised you're not there by now. I guess if you hurry, you will be on time. Personally, I would rather not go anywhere if I'm going to be late. Just hate to be late. I thought about going to the meeting. Everyone is going to be there. When the women meet I get … "

"Say, I need to get moving Marta. Hope you have a pleasant day," Drel interrupted, with the hope that it would end the conversation.

"…Oh okay, I know you have to get going and you probably have a lot on your mind these days."

"Yes Ma'am, talk to you later." Drel left quickening his pace. He wanted to show her how much in a hurry he was, or a least, how much in a hurry he should be.

Drel was not much for socializing. It wasn't an accident that he lived at the end of the village in a cabin by himself. That's what he preferred, the nice quiet loner life, to the dismay of more than a couple of young ladies in the village.

Of average height and build, with dark hair and bright blue eyes, at the age of twenty–four he was considered to be a smart young man, although a little strange because of his desire to live at the edge of the forest. He of course thought of it more as living on the edge of the village.

Not having married seemed to him as an advantage, but the people in the village frowned on anyone who didn't marry and have offspring to train and carry on their family crafts. Being the Keeper of the history/records of the village was one of only a few crafts that didn't produce food or other products. Shodder had so many kids he could borrow one of his to train to be Keeper. The village would never need that many boots anyway, or slippers. Drel smiled and realized it was probably the first time that day he had smiled.

In the distance, he could hear the tower bell chime announcing the meeting of the village leaders. Most of the leaders lived close to center so they didn't have far to walk. As usual, Drel would probably be a little late.

He shook his head as he thought about most of the village being there today and he was going to be late. As Keeper, he was invited to the village Leaders meeting whenever they had one. In fact, he was expected to take notes during the meeting if there was something important said or decided. Drel seldom took any notes.

The trail headed into the south vegetable field. As Drel looked out on the field he could see that it had been plowed and rowed and was awaiting planting.

"It's not time yet," he said out loud to himself. The ground even looked too cold for planting.

At the top of a small rise, Drel could see the fish pond on the right. The pond had a blanket of fog over its surface and the water could only be seen in a few places. Lake Simpton, which was only the clear lower end of Lowland Swamp, came right to the edge of the trail, but the water was very low for the time of year.

The past winter was hard on the village. The weather stayed near freezing most days and a snow covered the ground on occasion. The fish in the pond and the herds took losses because of the cold. The people of the village were anxious for spring and warmer weather.

As Drel neared the village center, the number of cabins increased along the trail. Zeplip, the village Builder, built them mostly of the same design and with the same type of cone wood. He didn't want to vary his design, except in size. Most people said it was because he didn't know how to change the design.

Builder's father, Fendal, built some of the older cabins and other structures such as the center hall. He was a man of imagination and when he was Builder he would build differently just so things wouldn't be the same. Everyone wished imagination was a trait that had been passed down to his son.

The smoke coming from the cabins' chimneys looked eerie as it moved up and overhead and then lay down on the trail to appear to block the way of the traveler. Drel could have taken that as a sign to turn around and go back, if he believed in such things.

He walked through the archway entrance to the center of the village. The center buildings were arranged in a square around a beautiful garden, well it was beautiful in the summer. In the winter it was mostly various shades of gray and brown. No leaves or flowers have bloomed yet this year.

People often stopped to rest on the benches in the square after their walk to the center. Large shade trees offered protection from the hot summer sun and there always seemed to be a breeze blowing through the square. On this cool morning, however, the breeze was not welcome.

The buildings around the square were places of craft. One building was where Shodder crafted his boots, one was a craftery for shirts and pants and another building was for crafting tools. The far corner was where Storer kept the grains, meats, and other things not of immediate need. People knew that if they didn't have it, Storer probably did.

One of the main attractions to the center was the bakery. It seemed at any time of day, Baker would have something cooking that made the whole square smell delicious. This morning the square smelled like bread. People often picked up a loaf of Baker's bread on their way home.

Drel could see the doorway to center hall a few doors away. With its ten steps up to the door, it was easily the largest and tallest building in the village. Like all buildings in the village, it was constructed of wood but was unique that it stood tall with large windows on all sides.

When Builder's father built the hall, he was criticized for making a structure that would not be able to stand up to the storms, but after standing for fifty years, everyone now considers it of monumental design and expert construction.

There were groups of people gathered around the entrance to the hall. As Drel approached , he planned a route around the groups so he would not get caught up in their small talk. It looked like he was not going to be successful, when they heard the gavel pound for the start of the meeting. Luckily, a simple wave was then a sufficient greeting as they walked up the steps of the hall.

The meeting was about to start, so he slipped into the meeting room, quietly closed the door behind him, and sat down in the back.

TWO

The meeting room was large enough to hold a hundred people, which was most of the people in the village, and it was packed. The meeting was the last one prior to Plant and was always popular. Villagers were excited about the start of replenishing the food supply. They also were anxious to work outside their cabins. It had been a fairly cold winter and not much outside activity had taken place. Digging in the soil and planting crops seemed like a fun thing to do after sitting inside and waiting for the weather to warm.

The village leaders sat in the four chairs on the opposite side of the long table in front of the room during the meetings to discuss the topics of the day. There were four other chairs on the side of the leaders for people they asked to the table. Down the middle of the room and on the far sides were aisles and between the aisles were small wooden chairs. The side walls had large windows that looked out onto the village center. In between two of the large windows, sat the wood stove that had just been lit to help warm the cool air in the building. People naturally stood around the stove as they visited with each other to help get warmed.

Two lanterns were lit in the front of the room and two in the back, but the windows with the bright sunlight shining in provided all the light needed. In fact, on the east side of the building, the curtain was partially closed to block the direct sunlight.

The room was surprisingly noisy with chatter even though the gavel had sounded, but the four leaders were still chatting amongst themselves so everyone assumed that was a signal that talking was still permitted.

The talk Drel heard from people around him was about tomorrow being the first day of Plant. Everyone seemed anxious to get the new growing season underway. Drel did not care to enter into the conversation. Nobody in the room would like to hear what he had to say, and nobody would believe him anyway.

To Drel's far left, he saw Shodder who slightly waved to him, and next to him was old man Shirts, who ran the clothes craftery. It looked as if almost everybody in the village had come to this meeting. Drel avoided making eye contact whenever possible. If he got the opportunity to speak at the meeting, he was not going to be a popular person. They did not want to hear what he had to say, however, he was convinced it needed to be said.

Today's meeting was a little unusual by having children in attendance. They were present so their mother's could also attend. Drel thought it was good that Slippers wasn't there, or her kids would probably be playing scream and tag.

Bam! The gavel sounded again so hard and loud that it scared everyone into silence. Some of the children screamed, and after a short silence everyone laughed at the children that had screamed, even the Village Leader.

The Village Leader sat in the middle, on the opposite side of the front table, and looked out on the audience. His heavy gray beard and moustache almost hid his smile at the children. His eyes were dark and not easy to read but one could tell a wise man was sitting there. His face and hands were wrinkled and weathered from a lifetime of hard and strenuous work.

Maclend, or Leader, as he was usually addressed, has been the leader of the village for as long as most people could remember. He was highly respected and people usually did as he wished.

He looked into the faces of the people of the village and was pleased by the large crowd in attendance. He smiled down at the little girl in the front that screamed the loudest. The little girl was embarrassed and hid behind her mother.

"Welcome," he said in his deep gruff voice. "Thank you all for coming today. With the first day of Plant being tomorrow, we are all anxious to get another growing season underway. I think everyone here will agree that we are glad that the winter has passed."

Everyone cheered at the declaration that winter was over. Keeper abstained.

The four main leaders in the village, Leader, Crafter, Farmer, and Builder were the elder men sitting at the front table. Leader organized many of the village projects, kept organization, and settled disputes.

Crafter trained and led various craftsmen in their trades, which included everything from baking to smithwork. If it didn't have to do with farming, or building, or the village center, Crafter was the leader in charge.

"First," Leader began, standing up, "My fellow leaders and I would like to take this time to dedicate this great hall." Leader raised his arms in a gesture of pointing out the hall.

"This hall was built fifty years ago today, when I was just a lad, by Builder's father, Fendal Betalum.

"Under recommendations from my fellow leaders, and if there are no objections, from this day forward this hall will be named the Fendal Betalum Community Hall."

The Hall erupted with applause with most of the audience clapping, except for Builder. He just sat there with a wide grin. He knew how proud his father would have been to know that the building he was so criticized for became such a monument in the village.

The Hall was built long before Zeplip was born but his father often told him the story of its construction. How he had used all the boards produced for that whole year to build the hall.

The leaders around Zeplip gave him pats on the back in acknowledgement. He just smiled at them and whispered thanks.

When the clapping died down, Leader glanced at his notes and announced the next item. "Would Storer come to the table please and report on our food reserves?" This of course was on everyone's mind since the village had such a severe winter.

At first Drel could not see Storer, but then his head rose slightly above the seated people as he walked up to the table. He was a very short man and it did not help that he was bent with age. He wore tattered clothes for being a master storer, kept a pipe in his mouth whether lit or not, and wore an old brimless hat. Regardless of what he wore, the village people greatly respected his knowledge in storing foodstuffs and at having most items on hand when needed.

When Storer sat down at the table, he again disappeared from Drel's view, however he could still hear what was being said.

He started talking about the very successful year in the storing of the fall harvested vegetables, fruits, and grains. The cold weather was definitely an advantage when storing food stuff and the quantities that remained should be enough to last till next harvest if people didn't waste.

Storer continued to talk about storage concerns.

"At present our supply of meats are plentiful," he said, looking for approval from the crowd, but there was only a slight acknowledgement.

"We had a very cold winter," Farmer chimed in, "and we needed to harvest more of the herd than usual. The cold winter had put a strain on the herd's grain and graze. The reduced herd may reduce our meat supply during next fall and winter, unless we have a bountiful birth rate in the herd. We have to maintain a minimum number in our herds in order to harvest them."

Farmer asked one of his helpers, Herder, to come to the table and talk about the various bulls and cows needed to maintain enough herd for the village. His voice disappeared into the background of Drel's thoughts. Drel was considering how he was going to address the Council and the village people with his information. Nearly everything he was going to offer will be counter to a speedy plant and the beginning of the growing season.

Drel thought about the consequences of not telling his information. What would or could happen? Then he came back to the reality of why he was Keeper. The past does the present no good in silence.

" ... of course if we had to we could reestablish hunting."

Drel snapped out of his thoughts to hear Leader's suggestion.

"We have not had a Hunter in decades and that would help supplement our meat supply, if we need it."

Leader turned to Farmer and asked, "Do you think we need to plan to have a Hunter?"

"Herder could probably tell you exactly," answered Farmer, not expecting this question and stumbling over the answer. "But we had to slaughter more cattle than we usually do during the winter because of the lower supply of grain and the scarce grass. There simply wasn't enough in supply to feed them all, so we harvested them. The future supply of meat may be under stress. To be safe I think that the answer should be, yes, we need a hunter."

"We have just been told that we have an oversupply of meat!" Builder blurted out. "How can you even suggest that we take people away from their jobs and train them to hunt?"

"I am just saying that this next autumn we may experience a shortage on meat," replied Farmer. "It's a hard thing to predict. I do know that ratios in our herds are not very stable. Too many bulls are born. We need more cows and fewer bulls. If our summer ratios do not improve, the future herds could run low as early as autumn. We could actually run very low on meat."

"We will prepare to be ready if necessary," said Leader. "Keeper, do you have notes from the last Hunter?"

Drel just sat there for a couple of moments until he realized that the question was directed to him.

He quickly stood up and stammered while thinking of an answer.

"I do have the notes of the last Hunter at my cabin. I believe the duties of hunting were given to the Trelop Family and Foster was Hunter."

"Is there anyone from the Trelop family here?" asked Leader, standing up and looking around.

There was no response. The Leaders conferred among themselves for a few moments and announced that they wanted to talk to Pred, Hunter's eldest son.

"Messenger, please send a runner to request Pred to come so we may talk with him."

Messenger signaled for one of his runners to go get Pred. The runner was a young boy that Drel had never seen before, but was fairly certain he was Messenger's youngest son. He was short and thin and looked well adapted to moving at a fast pace.

As the runner left Fendal Betalum Community Hall, the meeting room became loud again as people discussed the need or lack of need for a Hunter. Judging by what Drel heard, there were as many people that welcomed the idea as were opposed to it. Then the discussion unexpectedly turned a little heated. Many people said nobody could be spared to hunt, others said the skill of hunting needed to be reestablished and that the craft should have never been forgotten.

Drel used this time of confusion and unrest to approach the table to confer with Leader. He would rather meet with the leaders on an individual basis instead of in front of the entire village.

"Leader, I would like to speak with you for a moment if I could," he said, in a voice only Leader could hear. "I would like to recommend postponing the planting."

Leader looked at Drel with eyes of dismay and disbelief. He stood up, turned to the audience and proclaimed a recess until the return of the runner. Leader remained silent for a few moments as he decided his next action. He leaned over close to Drel's ear so only he could hear.

"Certainly you must know how important Plant is to the village. Please come with me and try to convince the leaders with such a notion."

Leader turned to the men at the table.

"Leaders, please follow me, we need to confer about a matter. Keeper, Storer, and Herder, please come as well."

They left by a door at the front of the room and went to a smaller room that was only large enough for a medium sized table and eight chairs. They sat down and Leader addressed the group.

"Keeper has told me that he wishes to recommend postponing planting again this spring. I thought that this would best be discussed in private before bringing this news to the village."

Farmer chuckled at the notion and shook his head.

"On what basis do you make such a request?" he asked. "This is the second year in a row now that you have requested postponing Plant. It was outrageous last year and it still is."

"The Time of Planting has not yet arrived," replied Keeper. "If we plant now we could endanger the seeds or the crops to freeze or frost."

"I'm no Keeper," said Farmer, "but hasn't it been three hundred days since last Plant? For generations my family has organized the planting to be three hundred days between Plants. I remember that last year you wanted us to wait eight days. It is a good thing we did not listen to you; we were running out of everything at harvest as it was. How much time do you propose we delay planting this year?"

"Eighteen days," said Keeper.

The room broke out in laughter.

"This must be some sort of joke," said Farmer. "We can ill afford to wait five days much less eighteen days. The fields are ready; we have plowed and rowed them. The seed must be sown before the rains set in. Surely, you can understand. As Storer had already pointed out, we will just have supplies to last until harvest, if we plant now."

"Tell us Keeper why you wish us to delay Plant?" asked Builder, in front of the whole Council. "Certainly he must have a good reason."

"I do have a good reason," explained Keeper. "If we plant now, I am afraid that the plants will be hit with a frost and we will lose them all.

"Twenty years ago, my father, as Keeper, erected a dial that indicates the position of the sun at various times of the year. You all know of this dial. The pointer's shadow direction tells the time of day and its length indicates time of year. It had worked well for many many years. The shadow clearly indicates when the sun is high enough and it is time for Plant. The shadow is now still many days away from the Plant line."

"Obviously your dial is in error," Farmer said. "We cannot still be eighteen days away from Plant. I count the days from Plant to Harvest and then from Harvest to Plant. Tomorrow is three hundred days since last Plant."

"The dial is not in error," said Keeper. Five years ago, at the time of the first slight change, I erected a duplicate dial and it also reads like the first. Last year I erected a third since there was a great change and it too says the same as the first two. We are about eighteen days from the sun being in position for Plant. We plant when we do because of the position of the sun. It is when the sun becomes high and warms the air and soil enough for the crops to grow. It is not yet high or warm enough. We may still have additional frosts or maybe even a freeze."

Keeper looked around the table at each person individually. He wanted to make eye contact with everyone in the room to try to plead his case.

"Have you not noticed that the trees have not leafed and how cool the air was this morning?" he asked.

"It is only a cold snap," said Storer. "Tomorrow and the next may be warm and sunny and the leaves will bloom. Do not judge things by weather. I remember when I was young we had a cold Plant and the plants took longer to mature. It just happens at times."

"How do you explain the low sun?" Keeper asked.

Keeper had a sudden regret for asking that question.

Farmer leaned over the table to look Keeper straight in the eye.

"How do *you* explain the low sun?" he demanded.

Keeper sat back in his chair and looked down at the table. He knew he did not have the answer to that question.

"I am working on it," was his answer.

There was a knock on the door. Messenger came in.

"Forgive me Council for intruding, but my runner has returned with Pred Trelop,"

"Thank you, Messenger," Leader said, as he stood and announced. "I'm sorry Keeper, without more information we cannot delay Plant. We all know the importance of a prompt Plant and Harvest. Let us go back to the meeting and talk with the son of Hunter."

The large meeting room was loud with talking when the Council reentered. None of the talk seemed to be of any importance. Storer and Pred sat at the table with the Council.

Keeper could not get back to his seat in the back of the room quickly enough. He had said his say. The rest was up to other people. He did, however, understand why Leader decided not to delay Plant.

"Son of Hunter, Pred," Leader began, "I am sure you know why you were summoned to this meeting. We have been told by Storer and Farmer there may be a shortage of meats in the autumn and throughout next winter. It has been many years since we have needed hunters, but it has been suggested that we should again have that craft. Your father was Hunter and if I remember, you had made hunting trips with him. We would like you to lead the hunters."

Pred looks like a hunter. He is tall enough to easily be seen from Drel's seat. Wearing camouflage colors and a hat to hold his long curly blonde hair out of his eyes; he looked very uncomfortable sitting in front of the village with the leaders.

"I will be glad to lead the hunters, Leader," Pred said. "But I am in the middle of helping Builder with additions to a craftery here in center."

"Don't concern yourself with that," said Builder. "It will be longer to finish … but we will."

"I think the time is now for you to brush up on your hunting skills Hunter and start planning," said Leader. "You have one son. Is that correct?"

"I have one son and three daughters," he replied. "My two oldest will make good hunters."

Complete silence filled the room. People could not believe what Pred had just said. His two oldest children would be hunting? Did he really intend for his daughter to hunt?

For the moment, Leader ignored what Pred indicated.

"After we all have helped Farmer with the Plant, please begin planning and constructing your hunting equipment," he said to the entire meeting room. He then turned to Pred, so just the table could hear, "You and I will have further conversation about your daughter being a hunter."

Leader signaled to Hunter that he was free to leave the table. Pred got up and left the meeting room.

"There is one more item I would like to bring to the attention of the Council," said Farmer. "Fisher has notified me of a reduced number of fish in our pond. He has said it was because of the cold winter and the deep freezing of the pond. We may want to decline in our fish harvesting until this is better understood."

"Very well Fisher, Leader responded, "let us put a twenty day hold on fish harvesting. Storer, when the fish storage runs out, we won't replenish the supply for twenty days from now."

"Please keep us informed as to the quantity of fish in the pond," Farmer told Fisher. "We can lengthen the twenty days if we need to."

"Yes sir."

"Farmer," said Leader, turning to him but saying it to the entire room, "Please organize the crews you will need to begin planting. I'm sure the other leaders will let you borrow the people that are needed to help you accomplish this."

"Is there any other business?" Leader asked.

No one responded.

"Thank you all for coming this morning," he said.

Leader ended the meeting with a *bam* from the gavel.

As Drel walked back to his cabin, he thought about the meeting. He was unconvincing to the Council in his bid to delay Plant. The only way the Council was going to be able to respect his decision was if he was able to explain the problem. He had clues about what was happening, but certainly no proof. He also knew he would probably never have proof.

It was nearing midday so he would stop by the dials to take readings. As he left the shadows of the trees by Shodder's cabin and entered the sunlight, he realized how warm it was getting. Was he wrong about delaying? Since they were not going to delay, he hoped that he was.

Dial three was the closest so he stopped there first. He stood by the dial for a few moments before the sun came from behind a cloud. Still almost three lines shy of Plant. He found the same at dial two and at dial one. They all showed nearly three lines shy of the start of Plant.

Back at his cabin, he decided to pull the notes from his father, the last Keeper, to see if the sun had ever been slow to raise high in the sky in the past. He doubted if it had. The construction of the dial and its measurements were based on the consistency of the sun. Nevertheless, maybe it is written in the Keepings of a time the sun was slow, and hopefully, an explanation.

He started with the notes labeled Keeper Lundley Year One. There was nothing in the history of that year that would indicate a slow sun. It did show it was very cool that year at Plant, but nothing that indicated that it was due to the sun's position in the sky.

Year after year, he looked through the Keepings of the village, but found nothing that indicated any sun position issues. Drel did find where his father wrote about the idea for the shadow dials to indicate time of day. Predicting and tracking seasonal cycles seemed to be an afterthought to the dials.

In year fourteen, he found where the Council advised after the death of Hunter, it was unnecessary to continue the hunting craft. Herds were plenty and Herder was providing enough meat for the village.

Drel could barely remember Hunter, but he could remember the day when Hunter did not come back from the hunt. Pred was twenty–two and wept for days. Exactly what happened was never discussed, at least not around him. Drel was only seven years old at the time.

What happened to Hunter? And why it was not recorded in that year's notes? That was another mystery he would save to solve for another time. All births and deaths were recorded in the notes of each year and if the cause of death was known, it was usually recorded as well.

It was dark before Drel finished his search for any information about the sun. He never found anything, except for years of cooler and hotter, wetter and dryer seasons, nothing that helped him in his search for information.

It had grown cold since the sun went down. On his way to bed, he threw an extra chunk of wood in the burner. He didn't want to get up during the night because of a cold cabin.

The next morning when he woke up, he did not bother to worry about the cold in the room. He ran to the window but it was fogged up and he could not see out so he ran outside. Immediately he knew Plant would be delayed at least one day. The ground was frozen.

THREE

Pred and his family gathered around the table on Plant morning for breakfast. There was an air of excitement in the Trelop double cabin. They shared in the excitement of Pred becoming Hunter— everyone except his wife Sella.

Sella finished cooking a marvelous breakfast of grain cakes, syrup, and hen eggs. She brought the meal to the table without a word. She had not spoken much this morning about the change in craft; her feelings were made known last night. She was not in favor of Pred becoming Hunter.

At first glance, Sella might appear delicate, but actually she was very strong with energy that men envied. She was always able to take care of the family, do all the chores, garden, weave for the village, and be able to smile at the end of the day. But, today she didn't think she had much to smile about.

She sat at the table and looked down at the food she had prepared as the rest of the family discussed the changes that being a hunting family would bring.

Sella pushed her long light–brown hair over her shoulder and pretended to be concentrating on her meal. She occasionally looked up at Pred with sad blue eyes. Pred and Sella have been married for many years. She always supported him in the things he thought to be important. He knew she was uncomfortable about the change, but that she would soon accept it and support him in his work. The kids were anxious to learn the chores of hunting. Pred decided that only Jait, his son and Tymber, his oldest daughter, would actually be involved in hunting activities. The other two daughters were to continue with their training as clothiers, but could help with hunting preparations if needed.

Jait, the oldest of their children, looked to be growing into a copy of his father. At nineteen, he is as tall as Pred, just not quite as broad. He has curly blond hair like his father too, but he has his mother's blue eyes.

Tymber is a pretty girl. Everyone says she looks just like her mother did at that age. She is a little shorter than her mother and has a thin athletic figure. She usually keeps her light brown hair pulled back into a ponytail, tied with a blue bow.

Tymber is not like most girls of seventeen in the village. She likes to do things mostly done by boys and was always by her father's side helping build every chance that she could. Pred did not encourage or discourage Tymber in her desire to learn how to build. His way of thinking was to let her learn what she desired to do.

Making clothes, cooking, and other women's crafts did not interest her. To be part of hunting for the village was almost more than she could have wished. However, her biggest job may be convincing Leader, and her mother, that she should go on the hunts.

As they sat there, Pred watched his wife. He understood her feelings, but wished she felt differently. She had to know that hunting is what he always dreamt of doing, ever since he went on hunts with his father when he was Tymber's age.

"It's a cold day for first day of Plant, don't you think?" Pred asked, looking up at his wife hoping to start a conversation.

Sella tried to smile but it didn't come out quit genuine.

"Yes it is," she said, avoiding his eyes. "I think Keeper was right to ask for Plant to be delayed."

"Well he was right to ask for one day," Pred said. "The ground is frozen. I bet Farmer is pacing back and forth in his cabin just itching to get the seed in the ground. It feels more like a good day to go hunting than it does planting."

Sella looked up at him, and by the look in her eyes he knew he should not have said that.

"Jait, go get the hunting knives. We must sharpen them before we will be able to use them. "Tymber, check on our supply of string. We will need five spools by our first hunt and I'm sure we will have to make some."

Sella asked the two youngest daughters to start their household chores. They complained briefly and then went about their tasks.

"Pred, why did you agree to become Hunter?" Sella asked. "I will worry whenever my family is in the forest. No one has entered it since your father's disappearance."

"No one has entered the forest since my father's disappearance because the need had not arisen till now. We have had plenty of meat for the village without the hunt.

"Besides, we are still not sure if the hunt will be needed. It will depend on the size and condition of our herds. The herd had to be reduced during the cold winter because of the lack of food for them. If we think that will be necessary again, we will need to hunt."

"You have not hunted since you were a child. Why do you think you still have the knowledge to hunt? You don't even have the maps of the forest that were made by your father. To do this is foolhardy, especially to involve your own children."

"Sella, we are only preparing for hunt if needed. There is a good likelihood that one will not be necessary. The village needs to be able to hunt, if not this year, then maybe for the future. We were wrong to let the hunting skills fade."

"But why you?" asked Sella. "I married a builder, not a hunter."

"Why me?" asked Pred rhetorically. "I'm the only person who has ever been on a hunt, or in the forest for that matter."

"The forest has been banned since your father's death, and rightfully so. It's a dangerous place to go. There are things and animals out there of which we have no knowledge."

"We will be well prepared. The first hunt will not be until the first of autumn. I will visit Keeper to find any maps of the forest that are in his keepings and map what is not now mapped. Before the hunt, I will have markers to show the way to and from all the different areas of the forest. You will see that it is not as bad as everyone has imagined."

Jait returned with the hunting knives in their wooden case. He moved the dishes aside and laid the case on the table. Pred hesitated opening the case. He had not looked at the knives since his last hunt. These were the knives Pred's grandfather made for his father when he became Hunter. He turned the latch on the case and opened it. Three beautiful knives sat familiarly in the case. All three with the handles expertly crafted with the horns of forest animals.

As Tymber entered the room, all she could say was *wow*. She continued to stare at the beautiful knives when her father asked her about the string.

"We only have one spool of string," she said. "I will go to see Storer this morning and get flax, if he has any, to make more." The whole time she talked she never took her eyes off the case of knives.

"You need to go to the swamp and cut and soak the flax if he doesn't have any prepared for twine," Pred told Tymber, not knowing if she had heard his request.

"After Jait has sharpened the knives, he will have first choice to which knife he will carry."

"Thank you, Father," Jait responded.

"Tymber, I will give you second choice."

At that, her eyes lit up with excitement. She didn't care which of the three knives she would carry, each of them seemed equally special.

"Tymber, when you're at Storer's, bring back a sheet of pounded leather so you can make new sheaths for these knives. These old ones are in bad shape and would probably not survive a hunt."

"Gladly, Father," she responded.

After a few chores, Pred put on his leather jacket and started his walk to Keeper's cabin. He wanted to see what maps were saved from past hunts in the forest. He knew his father had made maps, and hoped that they had been saved and stored with Keeper. If not, he had no idea where they would be.

Drel lived across the village from Pred, and also where he was considering entering the forest. If he remembered correctly, it is close to where his father started his hunts as well.

It was approaching midday so Pred knew where Drel would be. He would be in the field with his dials.

Pred was one of the few who agreed that the sun did not seem right for the time of year. As a youngster while hunting, he would track the sun to judge the movement of the animals. The leafing of the trees would also signify the end of rut and the time to plant. The trees had not yet leaved; therefore, it was not time to plant.

Pred was right—Drel was standing by dial two, writing notes.

"Hello Keeper," Pred said, as he approached. "How are you today?"

"Doing well," Drel responded, not looking up from his notes. Drel and Pred have been friends for years and he recognized Pred's voice. Even though Pred was about fifteen years older than Drel, they had instruction together in Builder's school of measurements and quantities.

"And how are you Hunter?"

Pred hesitated for a couple of moments because he was not used to being called Hunter. He thought of his father as Hunter.

"I'm doing great Drel. I came to see if I could find maps of the forest in your keepings. I'm hoping that my father had saved them with your father. When I go into the forest, I would like to know as much about it as I can."

"I think I have writings by your father about the forest," answered Drel. He glanced up at Pred. "There may be information in them that you would want, perhaps some maps as well. It has been years since I looked at those writings.

"If you give me a few moments, we'll go and see. It's nearly midday and I would like to take a reading before we go."

"I'm not in a hurry," said Pred. "Since I've been released from building, I'll have a lot of time on my hands to plan for hunts.

"Tell me, what do you see on this dial that indicates the sun is slow at rising this year? I agree it seems lower than on most Plants."

Drel looked at Pred for a moment and decided that he was serious in understanding the dial, so he began to explain.

"The sun shines on the pointer and it casts a shadow on the dial. The direction of the shadow indicates the time of day. If you look, the shadow is almost on the middle line that divides the dial. That is midday. The shadow moves toward the east as the day progresses.

"Now look at the length of the shadow. It is long and reaches to this line that circles the pointer." Drel pointed to the line that indicated shadow length. "As the year progresses, the shadows become smaller because the sun is higher in the sky."

"The shadow is too long for this time of year?" asked Pred, thinking he understood the concept.

"Yes it is," answered Drel, looking a little surprised that Pred understood. "The shadow should be as long as this line at Plant." Drel pointed to the Plant line on the dial. "As you can see it is a little less than three lines away from Plant. And no, I'm not sure how many days that is. It is many days from plant however. I told Leader eighteen days. That was just a guess.

"This line indicates the longest that the shadow gets, and this line is the shortest shadow line. When the shadow reaches either of those two lines, it begins to move back in the other direction. So the inside line indicates midsummer and the outside line is midwinter."

"I want you to know that I believe the Plant should be delayed this year as well," said Pred. "Have you noticed that the trees have not yet leafed?"

"Yes I have. I even mentioned that to the leaders. It didn't seem to matter to them. Of course, I don't blame them for their decision. They have to try and protect the village and I can't explain why the sun is not as it should be, or at least not as it has been in the past."

"Well, Drel, I think this morning showed them that they at least needed to delay one day."

Drel looked up from his dial long enough to smile.

"If it stays sunny all day today, it will freeze again tonight," said Pred.

"I believe you're right."

Drel and Pred looked at the dial and the shadow was exactly on the midday line.

"The good news is that it looks like the shadow is a little closer to the Plant line today. The bad news is that it is still a long way away from it.

"Let's go to the cabin and see what we can find in the forest writings. We can stop for a second at dial one and check the reading, however I already know what it says." Drel gave a little half effort at a grin as they started walking to the cabin.

"It is midday and the ground is just now thawed," Pred said. "I hope this is a warning to Farmer. Even if it doesn't freeze tonight, there is nothing to say that it won't freeze sometime in the next few days."

"I think the danger exists for more than just a few days," Drel answered. "We don't need to ruin our seed by planting too early."

Drel invited Pred into his cabin and brought the writings to him at the table by the window.

"This is all I have from your father." Drel handed him a few sheets of writing. "I do see that there is a sketch with forest features; however, it does not appear to be much to hunt from.

"You also need to remember that these writings are from many years ago. One of the sheets was actually written by your grandfather. Unfortunately, Hunters and Explorers have not been the most cooperative in writing down their experiences and bringing them to the Keeper."

"The first thing I need to do is try to relearn my way around the forest," Pred said, as he looked at the sheet that looked like a sketch of the forest. "I will use anything that we find here as just an indication of what may be in the forest. I plan to map the forest this summer and place markers to show location. I don't plan on getting lost."

Drel paused for a moment. He knew or suspected that Pred and others thought that Pred's father didn't return from the hunt on his last day because he had gotten lost. He was glad to see that Pred had no intention of doing the same thing.

"Before autumn and the first hunt, I will know the forest very well."

"What will you do if a hunt is not needed? All your work will be wasted."

"I don't think this work will be a waste of time even if there is no need for a hunt," answered Pred. "We need to have knowledge of the forest. I need to show that it is not a place to fear. Our village is surrounded by forest, therefore surrounded in fear.

"It is time that the people understand the forest for its beauty, and not just its dangers. We have had too much superstition about monsters and curses."

Drel and Pred studied the writings and the sketch of the forest well into the evening. The map indicated that the ground rises behind Drel's cabin and then drops down to a small stream. The stream can be followed south down to a river. The river continues to flow south but that is where the map ends.

Pred pointed at the map's end and told Drel that was probably the farthest he and his father had gone into the forest. His father may have gone farther, but he did it alone and didn't tell anyone.

The writings told of the animals that lived in the forest. The wild pigs seemed to be the most hunted. They had poor eyesight, but good sense of smell and had to be hunted downwind. There were writings about antelope that had great meat value but were as fast as the wind and easily spooked. They were very hard to hunt but were worth the effort should the hunter take the time. The village was occasionally visited by antelope that wished to eat from the planted fields.

A large fowl that roosted in the trees at night was the hardest to find and hunt and was Pred's father's favorite wild meat. There was also mention of a field with herds of large field beasts. There was no mention however of the location of the field.

A page of writing told of seeing a pack of wolves. Pred's father had seen them traveling in the distance. They each were carrying a part of a previous kill. He said in the writing he was lucky they were distracted and were not hunting at the time. They never saw him. The page also told of seeing a bear moving away from him on a distant ridge.

One thing that occurred to Pred as he looked at the sketch of the forest is that he could possibly netfish in the stream or river this summer to try to help restock the fish pond.

"I will ask Fisher for a couple nets to use on our travels to the river. I think fishing is where I need to concentrate on learning for the time being. I know that the animals of the forest will need to drink water, so they will be near the river. We can fish while we are there."

Drel was wondering who exactly Pred meant when he said we.

After the two thought they had learned all they could from the writings and the sketch, they quit.

"I had not realized that it had gotten dark," Pred said, looking out the window. "Sella will begin to worry if I don't leave soon. Of course, she is not happy with me right now anyway. She wants someone else to be Hunter."

"Will Jait hunt with you?"

"Yes, and so will Tymber."

Drel knew Tymber to be a girl that liked the outdoors. He knew she even helped her father with building, but to go into the forest and hunt? Drel wanted to question Pred with that decision, but didn't.

"Well now I know why Sella is so worried," Drel said, instead. "Her husband and two of her children will be going off into the forest."

"I know, I will try to be patient with her," replied Pred.

Pred decided to change the subject, "Drel, I know that you had said you don't know why the sun is slow this spring, but certainly you have an idea what is happening."

"Well," Drel hesitated to continue. "It is not just Plant that has been slow to come." Drel looked at Pred with pleading eyes and said. "Please don't repeat this because I don't know why, but the entire year has been longer than ever before."

Drel could see the confusion in Pred's eyes.

"It is true that Plant was every 300 days," Drel continued. "That is how everyone judged a full cycle, by counting days. Plant, count days until 300 and plant again. That worked out well for a long time.

"My father constructed the dial with that cycle in mind. He marked the lines to signify time of day and the lines to show the time within a cycle. Every 300 days the pointer shadow was at the same line, Plant line.

"This continued for all the years he was Keeper and well into the time I have been Keeper.

"But something happened five years ago when the Lost Moon appeared. The cycles were taking more days than expected. It took

301 days between plant lines that year. That didn't seem odd at the time. I assumed that the dial had accidentally moved so I built the dial that you saw me at today. Four years ago, it took 303 days, three years ago 307 days, two years ago 312, last year 318, and this year, I don't know yet. I am guessing 323.

"Our years are growing in days," continued Drel. He stood up and retrieved a sketch of the dial. "If you look at the dial, going from the top line or the longest shadow line, moving to the shortest, and then back to the top, took 300 days. Last year it took 318 days.

"Why has Adentta slowed down going around the sun?" asked Pred.

"Well, I don't think that is what is happening," answered Drel. "I think that we are drifting farther away from the sun and therefore taking longer to go around."

They both sat silent for a few moments thinking about what all that could mean.

Pred finally spoke. "You need to tell the Council your theory."

Drel started laughing. "What are they going to do, order Adentta to move closer to the sun? Any talk about this would be bad. And, I may be very wrong."

"Why do you think Adentta is farther away and not just slower?" asked Pred.

"Each year since the Lost Moon entered and left our skies five years ago, the summers have been getting cooler than normal and the winters are getting worse. I think we are getting farther away from the sun's warmth. I just don't have anyway to prove it."

They decided to call it a night.

They stepped out of the cabin and into the cool dark night. Pred hurriedly put his leather jacket back on. It was so cold they could see their breath as they talked.

"I will get you a lantern for your return," Drel said. He turned to go back inside to get one.

Pred shook his head and said, "Not necessary for tonight. The moon and stars are bright and I'll be able to see my way."

"Have a safe walk and a good evening, Pred."

"Thanks for your help."

Drel stood at the door and watched Pred move down the path and out of sight.

FOUR

Because of the cold spring weather Leader requested Farmer to delay planting crops until there were three days of no freeze and no frost. Therefore, the crops were not planted for twelve additional days. To Drel, that was still too soon but he did not say anything to request additional time. He was glad Plant was being delayed as long as it was. Now he just hoped that the freeze was over and no more frost after the plants emerged.

The air was becoming warm during midday, but was still cool at night. It will take an extra amount of time for the seeds to sprout because the ground was still cool.

Pred and his family, like most of the families in the village, helped Farmer with planting. Each family helped with a field that was close to their cabin. Farmer had the field close to the Trelop family listed as potato this year. It was one of the harder crops to plant because of the deep hole needed. A couple of families came and helped the Trelop's with their field when they had finished planting their own.

It took everybody ten days of very hard work to plant the fields.

When finished with the plant, Pred got busy constructing his hunt tools. He got a lot of help from Crafter's crew. They made three bows and twenty–one arrows to take with them into the forest and nine practice arrows.

After days of practice, both of his children were shooting the bow slightly better than Pred was. But they were only shooting still targets. Pred made a rolling target from an old wagon wheel. He drew a circle in the middle for them to hit. It was quite a challenge at first to try to hit the moving wheel.

Unfortunately, after practicing with a moving target, they quickly lost or broke the nine practice arrows and had to have Crafter make more. After that, they were much more careful with their arrows and became very good at shooting.

Fisher didn't have a spare fishnet so Sella used her weaving skills and weaved a couple of fishnets. She said it was simple to do using her weaver. Pred could then begin net fishing to help restock the fishing pond. He thought that would give him enough reason to go into the forest and to the river.

Tymber had finished the sheaths for the hunting knives. They were very nice looking with designs along the edges. Each was sewn together with different colored leather threads and she burned their names on the sides. The pride she had in the knives was obvious.

Jait asked Tymber which knife she wanted before he chose his. All three knives were very nice and it didn't matter to him which one he had. She thanked him with a kiss on the cheek, something she had never done before, then picked out her favorite to carry and Jait picked the one he wanted.

Pred smiled when he saw which knife was left for him. It was the same knife he carried on hunts with his father. When he picked up his knife, it seemed natural for him to hold that knife. He wondered if Jait and Tymber had known to save that knife for him.

He looked at which knife each had chosen. Tymber picked Pred's father's knife and Jait had picked Pred's grandfather's knife.

Pred decided to make an exploratory trip into the forest to mark the trail to the river before actually bringing his nets. He didn't really know what to expect in the forest and wanted it easy to explore.

Jait and Tymber were also anxious to go into the forest. They wondered what was beyond the borders of their village. There had never seemed to be any need for them to enter the forest in the past.

Along with being anxious, Jait was a little nervous as well. All his life he had heard that the forest was a dangerous place and was not permitted to enter. Jait knew his father was younger than he was when he hunted with his own father, but could not put the stories of the monsters in the forest he had heard as a child out of his mind. Certainly, those stories were created to keep children from going into the forest. Nevertheless, the stories seemed to be clearer now than they had been for years.

Pred entered the kitchen and saw Sella sitting at the table sewing two cloths together. He sat down beside her and sat silent for a little while. She looked up from what she was doing and looked Pred in the eyes.

"So tomorrow you take my children into the forest."

"Yes," he answered. "How did you know it would be tomorrow? I have not even told Jait and Tymber, yet."

"I could hear it in your silence," she said, with a little smile.

"We are well prepared for our trip."

"I know you are, Pred." She looked back down at the work she was doing. "I know you would let nothing happen to yourself or to Jait and Tymber; however, you have to realize how worried I am going to be."

"We will go tomorrow and mark the way to the river. I antici-pate that just taking one day; however, it may take more. We will make sure the way back is well marked for all to easily see. We will be back before nightfall whether we get all the way to the river or not."

"Pred, I'm afraid of what will happen, but I'm very proud of you." She looked up at him and smiled brightly. "Not many men in the village would do what you're going to do."

"Thank you, Sella, it means a lot to me for you to say that." Pred got up, gave her a hug. "We will leave at first light."

He left to tell Jait and Tymber of his plans for in the morning.

Pred found both Jait and Tymber working on packing the nets and tent. They were trying to decide the best way to pack them to make them easiest to carry.

"We will work on packing the nets after we get a trail to the river," Pred said. "We leave for our first trip into the forest tomorrow."

"Woohoo," they shouted.

"We have been waiting for you to say it was time," said Tymber.

"We will take our bows, our knives, and a couple of hatchets with us," Pred said, looking at the growing pile of necessities. Your mother has finished sewing our backpacks to carry many of our sup-plies. We will hang our water sacks from our belts.

"I have drawn the sketch of the forest that I got from Keeper for each of you. I want you to keep track of where we are and make notes on it of things that we pass. We will get up early. Your mother will make a big breakfast for us, and we will leave just before dawn."

"We are ready to go, Father," said Tymber smiling brightly. "I have been ready since the day you said we could go with you." She tapped the knife strapped to her leg. "We will make the village proud of us and thankful."

"Remember, tomorrow our purpose is solely to investigate, learn, and record," said Pred. "We will have time in the days to come to prepare for our fishing and hunting trips.

"As cold as the weather has been, the fish have not yet spawned and I would rather bring back finger fish and let them grow here. Of course, we may get some big fish to bring back to eat."

They all smiled at that thought. They have not been able to eat fish for many days due to the fish harvest ban that had been extended.

Jait picked up one of the fishing nets that his mother made.

"When I saw Fisher yesterday, he said he was not sure when fish will be available again. He said that maybe not at all this summer. He did wish us luck when we go on our fishing trips."

"Father?" asked Tymber. "I have hesitated asking you this, but how did you convince Leader to let me go into the forest and hunt?"

"Well Tymber, I really didn't convince him. He still doesn't think I should take you with me. He knows that he can't keep me from taking you if that is my wish. Like he said, he has no control over the forest.

"He understands why I want you to go. We need people trained to hunt and since I have only one son, he could see why I wanted you to go. And besides, Leader knows you, Tymber, and he knew you wouldn't let me go without you."

They both smiled and Tymber hugged her father's neck.

"Okay you two, it is getting late and we need to get up early. Off to bed with ya. I'll see you in the morning."

There was not much sleeping going on in the Trelop cabin that night. Everyone's thoughts were on the next day. To Tymber, it had seemed like she had just lain down when her mother came into her room to wake her. Sella laid the lantern down on the table and sat down on the edge of Tymber's bed.

When she sat down Tymber turned over to look at her.

"Its time to get up now honey," her mother said softly. "I've made hens eggs, fried potatoes, and a slab of ham for breakfast. You need to eat hardy this morning so you won't grow hungry before lunch with all the walking you'll be doing."

"Mother, I want to thank you for letting me go with Father and Jait."

"That was your Father's decision, Tymber. You will have to thank him."

"I have, Mother."

Tymber lay next to her mother for a few moments trying to decide how to explain her desire to be a hunter.

"Mother," she began, "to go with them is important to …"

"Tymber, you need not explain. I understand the need to pursue your desires. I hope this trip will be all you want it to be."

Sella stood up.

"Now get out of bed and come eat breakfast before it gets cold."

Sella opened Jait's door to find his bed empty. She went in the kitchen and found him with his father sitting at the table. He was already dressed and ready to go. Sella thought about how much he looked like his father sitting there at the table about to go off with him on an adventure. She had to force herself not to tear.

Sella and Tymber sat down at the table and began to eat. Not much was said during their meal except that Pred told them that he had put their equipment on the porch last night so they wouldn't wake up the girls when they left.

"It will be dawn soon, let's get our gear and head out," Pred said, after they finished eating.

At the door Sella hugged each of them.

"Please be careful. I will prepare a feast for you when you return this evening."

They smiled and began their walk to the forest. Pred had decided to enter the forest near Drel's cabin, which was no short walk in itself.

Pred noticed how pretty the stars were, even though the sun's early morning glow already had an influence on the morning sky.

"Look at that large star on the horizon," he said, entering a planted field. "I don't remember ever seeing such a large star before. It shines as bright as any I have seen."

By the time they got to Drel's cabin the sun was well up. They passed by Drel's cabin without stopping. They didn't see any activity and saw no need to wake him. They just silently passed by the windows as they headed to the back of Drel's land and to the beginning of the forest.

The farther they walked towards the forest, the more trees they passed. They all expected a definite edge to the forest, but the only sign they saw that they were about to enter the forest was a very old downed wooden fence, probably built during the time Drel's cabin was built.

"This is a good place to sit and rest for a few moments," Pred said, finding a log to sit on. "Tymber, tie a ribbon around that old tree as our first marker and take out your maps. Let's mark on the map the tree where we placed the ribbon."

They each got out their maps and sat side by side on the log. After agreeing where they were, they each marked their sketch with the red ribbon tree. The start of the forest was at hand.

"From now on we will move slowly and investigate along the way. We will mark some of the trees we pass with a hatchet scar using three hacks at eye level. We will follow the marks back when we return.

"Our first objective will be to go to the top of the rise that's on the sketch. Once we're there, we'll decide where to go next. We are in no hurry. If we don't reach the river today, then we will tomorrow or the next."

He smiled and looked at his children for the first time as adults.

"Let's go into the forest."

They each took a sip from their water sacks, and started their journey into the forest.

FIVE

Drel sat straight up in his bed when he heard the knocking. He was confused as to what just happened. First off, it was light out and he was still in bed, something that seldom happened, and secondly, he thought he heard a knocking.

He heard the knocking again. It was the door. Drel got up, put his pants on, and went to the door. Farmer and Bistinolapta, Farmer's helper, stood at his doorway. Drel thought that certainly he was still asleep. He had never had a visit from Farmer, or any village leader for that matter. In addition, Bistinolapta, nicknamed Crops, was one of the people in the village he very seldom saw, much less expected to see at his door.

The first thing Drel thought was that he had done something extremely wrong and they were there to have it out with him. However, as he thought more about it, he couldn't think of what that would have been. Asking for a delay in planting certainly didn't deserve a visit, particularly since they did delay and had completed planting days ago.

Apparently they saw the confusion on Drel's face because quickly they smiled to show that everything was all right.

"Good morning, Keeper," said Farmer. "I hope we didn't wake you up."

"No not at all," Keeper lied. "I've been up awhile."

He opened the door fully to let them in. He directed them to the table by the window and asked them to have a seat.

"I was just about to make hot root tea, would you care for some?" he asked.

"No, we have had our fill all ready this morning," said Crops, "but please feel free to go ahead and make your morning tea."

Drel decided to use that time of making root tea to try to figure out why he would have visitors so early in the morning and one of them a village leader. Nothing that he came up with could explain it.

When the root tea was ready, he put it on the table with three cups.

"Please help yourself if you would like some. I have plenty."

There was a moment of uncomfortable silence as Keeper poured a cup of tea for himself.

"So to what do I owe a visit from such busy men this morning?" he asked, as he finished pouring the tea.

Farmer and Crops looked at each other and then looked at Keeper.

"Did you see it this morning?" asked Farmer. "It was as plain as daylight, just as it was five years ago."

Keeper looked at the two men sitting at his table and again was as confused as ever. He was getting tired of being confused.

"Gentlemen," he said. "I obviously have no idea why you are here or what you are asking me. It is early in the morning and I guess I have slept through something very important. Could you please fill me in on what I don't know?"

"If you would have been up prior to dawn this morning," Farmer began, "you would have seen a very bright star in the east. It was as bright as any star that I have seen."

Are these people here this morning to talk about a pretty night sky? Keeper shook his head visibly and disregarded that as the reason for their presence. His visitors thought he shook his head because of the negative answer to their question.

"Well we have seen a star nearly as bright once before," Crops said, waiting for Keeper to finally understand. "Five years ago, the year of the Lost Moon. We are concerned that we will have another year like that one. It was a very cool summer that year and we had a very late and low yield harvest. If we had not had reserves that year, we would not have made it through the winter.

"I'm sorry to say that we no longer have that kind of reserves. Any repeat of a year like that will be very bad for the village."

"A star is not going to decide whether or not a growing season will be good or bad or if the weather will be warm or cool," replied Keeper.

"We know that," said Farmer, shaking off Keeper's response. "But, we know that you had predicted that we should delay planting because it was going to be too cold. As it turns out, you were right. We are wondering if your dials can predict if the growing season will be cold or warm as well."

Keeper looked down at the table hoping that they did not see the disappointment in his eyes. After all the times he has explained his dials they are still thinking of them as weather predictors. He sat there for a second trying to find the proper words. He didn't want to offend these farmers but had to tell them the truth.

"I wish I could help you but my dials are not able to predict the weather. They simply indicate the time of day and the time of year. I have no way to foretell what the weather will do.

"I do however have some guesses that I will share. Not because of the star, but I do believe we will have a cool growing season this year. I also think that the growing season may be longer this year than in past years. I believe our years are growing longer and therefore every season will be longer, summer as well."

"Keeper," said Farmer, "I can see that you may be able to predict the sun and the seasons, but why do you think it will be cooler this growing season. You just said you could not predict the weather."

"I am not predicting the weather. I am recognizing a pattern in the weather from the past couple of years. Each year for the last several have been cooler than the last. Like I said, it is just a guess."

Keeper did not want to go into the distance Adentta is from the sun—not at this time anyway and not with them.

"Do you have the records from five years ago so we can look at the production of grain?" Crops asked.

"We could also use the records from the years since then as well," added Farmer.

Keeper got up and got the keepings labeled Drel Year Six and handed them to Farmer. "As you know," he said, "I can't let you leave with these notes but please take your time and look over them and copy all that you want."

"At times I may need help with this Keeper," said Crops. "I never had time to learn to read all words."

"I will help all that I can," Keeper replied.

For a long time the farmers studied the harvest notes. They then asked for all the records from each year for the past five years. They found that there was definitely a decline in harvest yields each year.

In the past, there were ample grain reserves. Those reserves were now depleted.

This worried the group around Keeper's table, which was added to by Herder, Storer, and Fisher.

Keeper stayed out of the discussion for the most part, except when he had to explain something or read one of the words for them.

At midday he left to read his dials. When he returned, he prepared a meal for his visitors. He made a sandwich and a bowl of vegetable soup for everyone.

While the others ate, he sat on his porch, drank a glass of root tea and thought about what the others had seen earlier that morning. Was that just a coincidence that the moon visit was the same year that the years started to get longer? He knew that if he was going to explain that as being the reason for the longer years, he would have to assume it was the cause.

But how could it be? How could a moon from another world pass by Adentta and change the length of the years. If Adentta was moving away from the sun, then the Lost Moon had to have moved Adentta somehow.

Adentta's moon has always been here in the sky and hadn't seemed to change the length of year. Why would a Lost Moon that passes by, cause the change?

He knew he just didn't have enough information. How was he to figure this all out? One thing for sure, he knew he was going to have to be up before dawn and see the star. He wondered if the appearance of the star five years ago had anything to do with the appearance of the Lost Moon five years ago and would that happen again.

About that time, his company opened the door and came out onto the porch to leave. Drel got up and went to meet them at the door.

"Have you gentlemen finished?"

"Yes, Keeper," said Farmer, shaking his head, "and it is not good news. It appears that we are in a food decline and we have been for some years."

"It has been decided that the extra fields need to be planted," added Crops. "I think there will be enough seed. We will need to pull some of Builder's people to help with farming."

"Well that will be a decision for Leader to make," added Farmer quickly. "That is just what we will recommend."

"And we will need people to help see that each cow is bred to increase the herds," Herder was quick to add not to be outdone by the plant growers.

"The only way to increase the fish is to feed them more grain," said Fisher.

"People need the grain more than the fish do," Storer replied.

"Keeper we wish for you to watch and record the sky," said Farmer. "Let us know about the sun and the morning star. We do not understand the day and night movements of our sky objects as well as you. I will inform Leader and we would like you to report to the leaders any 'guesses' that you have concerning things that might affect our crops or herds."

"I will be glad to do that for you," replied Keeper. "But as I have said, I think only the sun's movements will control the seasons and temperature."

Keeper's guests said farewell and left down the path towards the village center.

SIX

The travel through the forest was hard at first because of the underbrush. They used their hatchets to clear a narrow path, both to go through the brush and to mark the way back. But, the farther they walked, the heavier the tree canopy became, and the less dense the underbrush, so walking eventually became easier.

As they broke through the heaviest of the underbrush, they decided it was time to take a break. Pred had not seen his children work so hard and he was very happy that they were still in such good spirits. They all knew that at times this travel would be difficult, and at least, it looked like they were out of the thorn vines. They all had small scratches on their legs from the thorns.

"I don't know about you two but I have worked up an appetite," Pred said, taking off his backpack.

"So have I," said Jait.

Jait and Tymber laid down their tools and took off their backpacks. They each took out the lunch that Sella had prepared for them. They didn't realize it until then, but she had prepared each one a different lunch with their favorite food.

They sat on a log and ate.

"I'm not sure I've ever tasted jam this good," said Tymber, with her mouth full.

They laughed knowing it was just because she was so hungry.

"It looks like it will be much easier travel ahead," commented Jait. "I'm about ready to make up some time we lost hacking at the brush and vines."

"We are not having a race, Jait," Pred said, looking over his shoulder in the direction they're traveling. "It may take us longer to get to the river than we thought. The distances on the sketch that we copied from Keeper were not known. It would seem like we will not make the river nor maybe even the stream today."

Tymber stood up, looked around, and sat back down.

"So far the forest doesn't seem much different than the wooded areas in the village. I have seen only a couple of plants that I didn't recognize."

"I saw a tree that I'm not sure I've seen before," said Jait. "It may be just larger than any in the village."

"Father, we have worked hard to get this far today," said Tymber. "Will we have to go back to our cabin tonight? It seems like we will be working too hard just going back and forth to the forest."

"I know, Tymber. But we are going to go home at night, at least until we get a trail made to the river.

"We know that we are sitting here, enjoying our lunch, but as far as your mother knows, we are in the forest fighting off monsters. It is mostly for her peace of mind."

"I can understand that. I was just wishing we could get farther in a day."

"Well tomorrow we won't have to hack our way through the brush," Pred answered. "We'll be able to walk right through it. That will save a lot of time and the trees we've passed are well marked.

"Let's put this end of the brush on our sketch and continue. I certainly would like to get at least to the top of the ridge today. We won't have the time to go farther than that I'm sure."

They progressed at a faster pace after lunch, stopping along the way only to hack the three marks on the trees they passed. Tymber agreed to carry Jait's backpack if he would make all the hatchet trail marks on the trees. That arrangement seemed to work well for both of them and made things go quicker. The slowest time was when they needed to mark a thick barked tree. In order to be able to see the marks, they had to chop deep into the bark.

When they were nearing the top of the ridge, they found something completely unexpected. Pred stopped in his tracks while looking ahead.

Jait and Tymber stopped too and looked in the same direction as their father.

"Father, is that an orchard?" Tymber asked.

"I believe so. Sheath your hatchets and draw your bows."

They approached the orchard cautiously, working their way around and through the bushes and vines. The orchard didn't appear to be tended; however, after they were under the orchard trees, they found not much growing under them.

"This orchard has been here a long time," said Pred. "The trees are old and the forest has grown up to its edge."

They stood behind the first few trees of the orchard peeking around them. They could not see any danger.

"I think it is safe," Pred said. "But be ready just in case."

They put their bows away and Jait and Tymber began investigating the orchard.

Pred decided to look around at the orchard edge. The forest trees close to the orchard were small and they steadily were larger going away. It made it look like the orchard was gradually attended to less through the years.

"What type of fruit trees are these?" Tymber asked her father, after he rejoined his children. "The trees have a very pleasant sweet smelling blossom."

"I'm not sure," answered Pred. "The leaves are not fully out and I do not recognize the bark. I don't think I recognize the blossom either."

He looked around the orchard for signs of something in the trees that would give him a clue as to what kind of trees they were. It was obvious that they were fruit trees, but the way they branched seemed different from any he had seen before. He looked on the ground for leaves that had been there since last fall, but there were none that he could say for sure that were from the fruit trees.

"We may not know until we see the fruit, and we may not even know then."

They walked through the orchard, looking up at the trees and in all directions, still somewhat nervous about this unexpected find. Jait kept his hand on his sheathed hatchet and Tymber kept her hand on her knife strapped to the side of her leg.

"Did you not come to this orchard before in your hunting travels?" Tymber asked her father.

"No, I've never been here before. I'd remember this. In fact, I don't think my father had ever been here either. He would have told me of it and had it on the sketch.

"This may be a very important find for our village. It doesn't appear that the orchard has been tended to for a long time. If it had, the trees of the orchard would not have been allowed to grow so tall. It is too hard to harvest the fruit on tall trees.

"But actually the orchard is not the biggest mystery here," Pred said, stopping and pointing towards a corner of the orchard.

Pred started walking towards the corner of the orchard. Jait and Tymber followed but could not see what their father saw. When they approached the corner, they stopped in their tracks. They saw an old cabin hidden by the overgrowth of bushes and trees. Unlike the cabins in the village, it was made of stone.

"Wait Tymber," Pred said, as she was heading for what appeared to be the way to the door. "We need to be careful. We don't know what kind of animals have taken up residence in and around that cabin. Let's chop these bushes away from this side of the cabin; it appears to be the front."

"Father," Tymber said, "that cabin is made of stone."

"I have never seen a stone cabin before," said Jait. "I wonder where they got all the stone. In the village, we are lucky to find enough to make a chimney."

"If I remember correctly, the banks of the river and some of the streams are lined in rock. They must have gotten the rock from the stream and carried them back."

"Who do you think lived here?" asked Tymber.

"That I have no clue about."

They finished chopping a way to the door and stood there for a moment looking at the large cabin that stood before them. It stood tall and almost majestic so deep within the forest. They could now see the front door with two windows and either side. Vines climbed up the walls and it looked like it appeared to have had a wooden porch at one time; however, it had long since collapsed and mostly rotted away.

They looked at each other as a sign to proceed, but with caution.

Pred pulled out his bow and strung an arrow to it. Tymber pulled out her knife and Jait had his hatchet in his hands. Jait stood on the ground where the porch had been and reached up and pushed on the door to open. At first, it did not want to and he had to push harder. Then it slowly opened. Jait stood back so his father could be the first to go in with his bow in hand.

Pred climbed up to the doorway and took one step inside the cabin and stopped. His eyes were trying to adjust to the dark interior. He strained to see what was inside. Slowly his eyes adjusted from what he could see just inside the door, to what was in the whole room.

He took a couple of steps and called for the others to come in.

"Stay there by the door until your eyes adjust to the dimness."

The cabin smelled dank and dusty with stale air. Even without seeing, Jait and Tymber could feel the immense size of the cabin. When their eyes adjusted, they were as amazed as their father. They expected the cabin to be empty but found wooden furniture instead. Through the dust, they could tell that the furniture was well crafted. In the front room, by the door, they found very nice comfort chairs and a couple of small side tables. On the walls, were small shelves with old dusty candleholders and a number of small–carved wooden objects that looked like decorations. To the right was the kitchen, straight ahead was what Pred called the main living area. To the left was a bedroom. With some investigation, they found five bedrooms.

In the main living area, there were two large sofas that looked as long as beds. At the end of the sofas were a couple additional small tables. What was the most outstanding thing in the room was above the fireplace, a head of a great beast. It had the ears, eyes, and teeth of a cat, but with a little longer nose. It was mostly dark gray with darker gray and black patches and three thin white streaks starting at its eyes and going towards the back of the head.

The three travelers simply looked at the head of the beast and found it at first hard to speak. Finally Tymber was able to glance away for a moment.

"What a beautiful animal," she said.

"Maybe from a distance," Jait responded.

"From the size of the head," Pred said, "it would appear that the animal may have weighed a couple hundred pounds. I have never seen an animal like it before.

"It was definitely a meat eater judging by its teeth."

After looking at the head for quite awhile, they all wondered if they would see one during their travel. They hoped that they would see one, but only from a distance.

"It would take more than one arrow to knock down that beast," Pred said, breaking the silence. "It would take all of us shooting at him."

"And then run," added Tymber.

"I wonder if they can climb trees," Jait asked Tymber, who was not able to take her eyes off the beast.

"Thanks Jait, now I'll be looking up in the trees instead of watching where I step."

"Actually," Pred said, hesitating, "it looks like it might be a good idea to look up occasionally."

"It would be so hidden with its coloring," Jait said, "we would probably not see it if we looked right at it."

"Do you think it was male or female?" Tymber asked.

"I hope it was a male," Jait answered. "I would not like to think that this one is female and that there is a larger one of those out there."

Pred moved out from that room and was looking at shelves along the wall of an adjoining room. On what looked like a desk, he found sheets with writing on them. He looked at them for a time but could not read everything on them.

Tymber came into the room and Pred handed the sheets to her. She could not read all of the words either.

"Put the sheets in your backpack, I will want to look at them later and show them to the leaders. Maybe Keeper has seen such writings before."

"Who were these people, Father?"

"I don't know, Tymber. There have been stories of people that lived on their own outside of the village and stories of people that lived in other villages. And to tell you the truth, I never believed them. I guess I never saw a reason to live anywhere else."

"I wonder what happened to these people?" Jait asked, as he entered the room. "It appears as if one day they just didn't come home."

As soon as Jait had finished his sentence, he wished he had not said that. He looked at his father for a reaction. The very same thing happened to Jait's grandfather. One day he just never came home.

Jait's father gave no outward reaction. He had lived with his father's disappearance most of his life and any such reactions were long in the past.

"Tymber, I believe these are map sketches. Put them in your backpack, they may be helpful."

Pred and Tymber took more time to look around and investigate each room. Pred kept to the living areas, but Tymber favored investigating the bedrooms. She thought she could tell more about these people by looking in those rooms.

She went from room to room and found many nice things, including some nice clothes in the closets; at least she was sure they were nice when newer and still being worn. On a couple of dressers, she found boxes with necklaces in them. They were mostly made from pretty rocks and pounded metal pieces. She thought that they were very pretty, so she tried a few on but quickly put them back into the boxes.

In one of the bedrooms, she found a leather case with a wooden stick inside. It was about ten inches long with holes in it every so often. She didn't have a clue what that would have been used for. They had lanterns on a couple of walls in each room with shelves that were full of carved decorations and candles. She used the striker lying there and lit one of the candles. It had a very sweet and pleasant smell. She never knew a candle could have a pleasant smell.

Entering one of the small rooms, she nearly tripped over an area on the floor that was very uneven. It surprised her but then realized it was a very old cabin and the floor must have become uneven with age. She decided it was time to stop her investigating.

Jait had gone back outside and looked around the cabin. He found a couple of fruit and nut trees that he did recognize. In the distance, he could see where the tree line ended to begin a large cleared area. He was sure that area was for their garden. It was now of course grown up in vines, brushes, and small trees.

Jait walked over to the water well and cranked up the rope that ended in an empty bucket. He picked up a stone and threw it in the well; there was no splash, the well was dry. He was very disappointed. He was looking forward to sitting down with a nice cool drink of water.

Pred and Tymber left the cabin and walked up to Jait.

"I see why they moved away. Their well went dry."

"That may be why they left, but I think it was a more sudden move. One not planned for."

"Look over there, "Tymber said.

They walked over to where Tymber was pointing and found a small cemetery surrounded by a mostly downed stone fence and a rotted gate at the front.

"This must have been the family burial site," said Pred. "Some of these graves look very old indeed."

"This grave only has a very plain marker and looks like it may be the most recent," said Jait. "I wish I could figure out what those words on the plaque means."

"It is probably a name."

"Some of these words are the same as those," Tymber said, looking around at other graves.

Pred motioned to Jait and Tymber to follow him out of the graveyard.

"We could stay here for days looking around," he said, "but we have stayed too long in the forest for our first day. We are going to have to hurry to get out by dark. We can go back to our cabin and study the writings and sketches."

The return was a much easier trip than it had been earlier that day. All they had to do was follow their markings back.

The sun was nearly set when they got back to Drel's cabin. Jait commented that they must have gone farther into the forest than originally thought and that they needed to adjust the map sketches.

"We need to stop at Keeper's cabin and let him look at the writings," Pred said. "I hope that he'll be able to make more sense of them than we can."

They saw Drel sitting on his porch. He was so occupied in thought that he had not heard them approach.

"Hello there, Keeper," Pred said, hesitantly.

Drel was so startled he almost fell off his rocking chair.

"Sorry if I startled you Drel. I saw you deep in thought and didn't know how to get your attention without scaring you."

"That's okay, Pred," he answered, "It's not the first time I've been startled today. I have had more visitors today than I've had in a couple of years put together.

"I'm glad to see that you made it into the forest and back in one piece. Did you meet up with any monsters?"

"Only the head of one," answered Jait.

Drel looked quickly at Jait in shock.

"Well I'm not sure it qualifies as a monster," Pred said. "However, it was very large. I have never in my life seen an animal like it before. It resembled a large cat with a longer nose. It was dark gray with darker spots and three thin white stripes going back from its eyes."

"You said you just saw the head?"

"Well that's the biggest reason why we decided to stop and talk with you. We have found something very much unexpected."

"Come inside and tell me about it."

Drel took them to the table and asked them to sit down.

"Does anyone want some root tea?"

All three were very tired and thirsty so Drel made some tea.

"So what did you find in the forest that was so unexpected, beside the head of a would–be–monster," he asked, while making the tea.

"Well, we found a cabin—a rock cabin—that has been abandoned for years."

Drel stopped what he was doing and came back to the table.

"You found a cabin outside the village?" he asked. "How far from here is it?"

"A little more then a half day's walk," Jait answered.

"It is huge," added Tymber. "It has five bedrooms."

"Above the fireplace was the head of the beast," said Pred. "It is an awesome, beautiful animal. It looks to be large and powerful and it may be a tree climber. It looked like it was displayed as a trophy. We will have to watch for that animal on our travels.

"An odd thing about the cabin is that it seemed to have been deserted in a hurry, with everything left as it was and all the furniture remains. We even found sketches and writings there."

Tymber got the papers from the stone cabin out of her backpack.

She smiled at Keeper as she handed him the pages. He flipped through the first few and looked up at Pred.

"I can't make out some of these words," he said, "many of them are not written as we write them."

"I thought the same thing. I can read most of the words but some are strange to me. Towards the end of the pages are the sketches. I have not looked at them in any depth, but they look like they may be maps."

Drel flipped past a few pages and found the first sketch. "Yes, I believe this sketch is a map. It will take quite awhile to figure this stuff out."

Pred glanced out of the window and saw that the sun had set.

"Jait and Tymber, go back to our cabin and tell your mother of our adventure and that I will be there soon. She will be very worried. I'm going to stay here with Drel for awhile and see what we can find out." With a slight protest, they agreed. It had been a long day for them and they knew that it would be good to be at the cabin.

Jait and Tymber got up to leave.

"Also, tell your mother that we will probably not be going back into the forest tomorrow. Instead, we will come back here and study the writings and sketches. There is no need to go back until we learn all that we can.

"Oh—and, eh—your mother need not know about the beast right now."

"Goodnight, Keeper," Tymber said, as they left his cabin.

"Do you think there are other cabins in the area?" Drel asked, after Jait and Tymber left the cabin.

"I did not see any signs that would indicate other cabins, but we saw that cabin by accident. We saw the orchard first and the cabin was in a corner."

"An orchard?"

"Yes an orchard of what looked like fruit trees of a kind I have never seen.

"There was also an area that was once cleared for a garden. If we would have had more time, I may have been able to tell what they grew there from what was growing there now.

"So tell me, Drel, what do you make of all of this?"

"I don't know. We both have heard stories of people that lived in the forest by themselves. Of course, I thought they were just stories."

"Now I am wondering about the stories of other villages," added Pred.

"This definitely looks like a map of some sort," Drel said, looking at one of the sketches. "I'm not sure what all the symbols mean but some of them seem to be obvious."

He laid the sheet on the table so Pred could also look at it.

"This symbol is probably the cabin, this is a stream or river, and this may be a trail that ends at the stream."

"There is much to learn here," said Pred. He stood up to leave. "I will be back in the morning to study these more. It has been a very long day."

"Come before dawn tomorrow."

"Before dawn?"

"I will be up to see the morning star."

"Oh yes, I was going to tell you about it. We saw it on our way to the forest this morning. It certainly didn't last long in the sky. It was there, then it was gone."

"I was not up that early this morning. Farmer, Crops, Herder, Storer, and Fisher were here telling me about it today. They asked me to watch the sky and report to them what I think it all means.

"They worry that we will have another very cool summer like we did the last time a bright morning star appeared. As it turns out from the records, we have been harvesting less and less now since the last morning star, five years ago.

"We can watch the sky together and make our guesses," Pred said, as he went out the door.

They both smiled and waved good-bye.

SEVEN

"It's cooler this morning than it was yesterday," Pred said, warming his hands on his cup of tea.

"This hot root tea is just what's needed on a cool morning like this," responded Drel.

They were sitting on Drel's porch, in nearly complete darkness, waiting for the morning star to rise in the east.

"What exactly are you going to observe and measure with the star?"

"I'm not sure. I have set up a dial of sorts with moveable pointers so I can record where on the horizon it rises and how far it is away from the sun. I am hoping those are the only measurements I need.

"They think that I will have some answers for them, or rather more accurately, some weather predictions. Somehow they think that all I have to do is look at the sky and tell if it will be hot or cold or a good or poor growing season."

"I don't have to look at the sky to know it's cool," Pred said, shivering.

Drel laughed as he sipped on his tea. He took another glance toward the east to see if the star was up yet. It was not.

"Do you think the Lost Moon will return since the morning star is back?" Pred asked.

"I don't know if the two are connected or not. It has happened only the one time as far as anyone can remember. It has not been recorded by any Keeper as far as I could find. I went back and looked at records that went back to my grandfather and could not find any deviation in the seasons. Of course, I wasn't exactly looking for the mention of the appearance of a large bright star in the east."

"How far away is the dial?"

"Its right over there," Drel said, pointing to his right. "I couldn't think of a good reason to go farther to set it up. I have a perfect view of the horizon from here and it didn't seem important for me to go a long way to do something I have no clue about.

"There's the star, Drel."

"Wow that is a bright star."

They got up and went over to the dial. Drel moved two pegs on the inner ring of the dial to line up the exact position of the star on the horizon.

"Now we have to wait for the sun to rise and we'll line up the outer ring to record the space between the star and the sun. Let's go back on the porch and finish our tea. It will take a little time before the sun rises.

"If I remember," said Pred, "the last time the morning star appeared it was only in the sky for a few days in the spring and then disappeared behind the sun. Later that year during midsummer, the Lost Moon appeared in the evenings."

They sat on the porch and gazed at the star in silence waiting for the sun to rise. Each reflecting about what the star could mean. Drel thought about the *maybe–groundshake* he felt while in bed the day before Plant. He had passed it off as a dream, but with the return of the morning star, maybe it wasn't. Nobody else had mentioned feeling a vibration that night, so it was probably a dream. It does seem unusual though that he would have that dream near the time that the morning star reappeared.

Many people in the village had superstitions about the star. They claimed that it caused sickness, and caused their hens not to lay eggs; they even say that was the cause for the lake to dry up that year. Slippers said that the star killed her flowers in the garden, made her cow give less milk, and made her children wilder. Nobody believed that the star made Slippers' children wilder. Everyone knew they couldn't get any wilder.

"How many of the stories of what happened because of the star do you think is true?" Pred asked.

"Little or none," Drel answered.

They sat in silence thinking about all that was said concerning the star. Pred was not as ready to dismiss the stories as Drel.

"It appears to be more orange this morning than it was yesterday," Pred said, breaking the silence.

"The sky at the horizon is lighting up, the sunrise will be soon."

Without saying anything, they both got up and went back to the star dial just as the sun rose. Drel moved the peg of the outer ring to the very inner edge of the sun.

"They rose at four marks from each other. I will check again tomorrow to see if there is a difference."

They went back on the porch and watched as the star's light was overpowered by the sun and disappeared from sight.

"What would a different reading tomorrow mean?" asked Pred, finishing his tea.

"I'm not sure. We will just have to see how it changes.

"Let's go inside and look at those sketches you brought back."

Pred agreed. That was the real reason why he came over to Drel's cabin; however, it was interesting to see the star and compare it to the sun. He just couldn't see how it was going to affect what his job was going to be, going into the forest to fish and hunt.

They sat at the table with the lantern lit and studied the sketches. They oriented the map to what they believed to be the correct direction, which led most of the map away from the village and towards the south.

"It looks like the map may start at the stone cabin," Pred said, as he tried to orient himself to the sketch.

"What we consider to be a river symbol must be the same river that's on my father's sketch, the river where he and I used to hunt. This must be the stream that runs into the river. I wonder what that '𝑤' means on the stream behind their cabin." He pointed at the symbol he didn't know how to say.

"It might mean that's a good place to fish."

"That's where I'll head to first to get an idea of what their symbols mean. Of course, it might indicate where one of those beasts live," Pred said, only half in jest as he halfway smiled. We really need to name that animal so we don't just keep calling it beast."

"Since you found it, I think the perfect name for it is Pred–ator."

"Very funny, Drel."

"I'm getting hungry. Would you like breakfast? I have eggs and I can make grain cakes with jam."

"That sounds good."

Pred continued to look at the sketches and the notes.

"I sure wish I understood these words," he said. "I think this could be very useful to us to have someone that lived in the forest teach us about the forest."

"Do you think there are other cabins in the forest?" Drel asked.

"Yesterday morning I would have said no, today I would think that it is quite likely. I can't imagine anyone living completely away from everyone else. There may even be other cabins close to the one we found. We investigated that one and didn't go any farther. On the other side of their garden spot there may be another cabin or even where that w is on the sketch at the stream."

Drel brought the breakfast to the table and the two men ate as they looked at the forest cabin notes.

"What do you think this dark filled–in circle along this line means?" asked Drel.

"I'm thinking that it's a pond along a stream, but who knows. I'm anxious to get back in the forest with this sketch and see what these things are.

"It looks like on the other side of the stream, there is a pond or something drawn of a large size. If we find a way to cross the stream, we may go see what it is."

"If you don't mind, Pred, could you copy that sketch on this sheet? I would like to keep these papers from the stone cabin here in the keepings."

"You're probably right, it could rain or I could fall into the river and ruin them."

"I will mark them as Stone Cabin keepings and maps and keep them here on the shelf if you need them if I'm not here."

"Drel, have you noticed that neither my father's map nor the Stone Cabin's map shows anything to the north? I know that the river flows south, but I wonder why they seem to never go north. I may go north just to see what's there."

After they were done eating, Drel took away the dishes and Pred copied the map sketch.

There was a knock on the door. Drel opened it to find Crops standing there. Drel invited him in.

"Good morning, Keeper," he said, walking in. Then he noticed Pred there as well. "Oh good morning to you too, Hunter." He turned back to Drel. "I was wondering if you observed the star this morning?

"Yes I did. Pred and I took directional readings of the morning star."

"So what do you think?" Crops asked.

"What do I think about what?"

"Well, do you think we are going to have another cool summer this year?"

Drel turned away from Crops and looked at Pred who was smiling as he quickly looked down at the sketch.

"According to the star, its going to be a great and wonderful summer," said Drel. "Just make sure you plant all that can be planted."

EIGHT

The forest trio left the next morning a little earlier than the last time from their cabin. This time they were going to stop at Keeper's and watch the rise of the morning star. For some reason, Pred had taken an interest in the star.

Last night they had talked about what they were going to do today and where they were going to go. The plans were to go back to the stone cabin as their first stop, possibly not even to enter, just to begin where the cabin sketch begins.

The next objective was to go to the ᚹ at the stream. Pred wanted to find out what it meant. They started calling the symbol a 'yuwt.' He hoped it was a good place to fish, however they only brought a small fishing net. They could go back to fish when other things have been discovered and explained.

They got to Keeper's cabin a little before dawn. Drel had four cups of root tea ready when they arrived. They each turned their rocking chairs to the east and sat to watch for the star rise.

It was only a few moments before the star rose.

"The sky seems to be a little lighter today than it was yesterday at star rise," Pred said, watching Drel put a peg in the position of today's star rise.

Not long after, the sun rose too.

"Its only three lines from the sun now," Drel said. "It was four yesterday."

"What do you think that means?" asked Pred.

"That we are going to have a great and wonderful summer," said Drel, grinning from ear to ear.

"But hunt and fish all we can," Pred added, smiling.

The Trelop family headed back into the forest as soon as it was light enough to see, but by midmorning the forest grew dark. There were storm clouds overhead and not much light was coming through the forest canopy. The small forest animals and birds appeared more nervous by their guests.

The feeling of an impending storm was in the air and the wind started to stir the treetops. The smell of rain drifted in and the Trelops quickened their pace. Ahead they could see lightning but it was yet too far in the distance to hear the thunder.

"Let's try to get to the stone cabin before the rain," Pred said, glancing to the sky as to measure how much time they had before the rain began.

As they neared the stone cabin, Tymber heard a roar in the distance. Well it wasn't exactly a roar nor even a growl, but more of a yawn of a large animal. She looked at her father and Jait who didn't seem to hear it, so she quickly dismissed it as her imagination. She must have been thinking about the predator above the fireplace.

A cold mist hit them in the face and made them shiver.

They reached the cabin in time to get inside before the downpour. The storm clouds made it dark inside the cabin so they lit candles they found on the mantle underneath the head of the predator. Tymber went into one of the bedrooms and brought out a lantern she saw on their first visit.

The sound of the rain on the roof was almost deafening. They were glad to have had cover during such a storm. The lightning started to flash near by and the thunder was so loud it shook dust from the ceiling.

They all looked out of the windows at the rain. The wind was strong enough to blow a few small branches out of the trees that hit the roof. Leaves on the ground were swirling in random motions. Luckily it didn't last long.

As the rain eased up, Pred, Jait, and Tymber took time to eat lunch and rest up.

"Let's store some of our water and supplies here in the cabin," Pred said, looking out the window at the softer rain. "That way we won't have to carry everything all day, only what we need until we return."

The rain finally subsided and it was growing lighter outside. They decided that they needed to get moving if they were going to reach the stream today.

"We will make better time if we walk under the trees and follow the edge of the overgrown garden area instead of heading through it. That will make us go a little farther, but the travel will be easier. Don't forget to mark our way. There may be more than one overgrown field."

They hesitated at the door as they were leaving. They knew that the rest of the travel that day was going to be wet and uncomfortable, but that was something that hunters had to do.

The rest of the trip to the stream took longer then expected, and it was well after midday before they started to head downhill and into the streams valley. Occasional rock outcroppings became evident on the way downhill and the tree canopy closed even further.

After a little while, they stood on the stream's bank. The stream was dry. All three stood silent not really believing what they were seeing. The hope to fish in the stream was gone.

Jait broke the silence.

"At least we know where they got their rocks for the cabin."

The dried streambed and most of the bank was made of stone and rock of all sizes. On both sides of the stream the flood plain was heavy timber with leaves fully out. The tree canopy was so dense that it looked like sun had never penetrated to the forest floor. Moss grew dense on both rocks and tree trunks.

"I don't see a yuwt," Tymber said, looking around with a little smile in her eyes.

Pred and Jait didn't feel like smiling, but couldn't help it.

"Maybe the way they write words, yuwt means dry stream," Jait said.

Pred didn't want to be outdone by his children.

"It probably means don't bother coming here," he said, shaking his head.

They all had to laugh about working so hard to get to a dried up stream. They knew that their ultimate goal was to get to the river, so it really didn't bother them too much.

"Let's go down into the streambed and have a snack."

They sat, talked, and ate. Their discussion centered on their next move. Tymber wanted to cover more ground by splitting up and going both *upstream* and *downstream*, or what would normally be those directions. Pred would not hear of it.

"We need to stay together until we know more about this territory. With possibility of cat beasts around, we may always stay together."

Pred looked around at the stream and then up in the sky to decide on time of day.

"I think we should head downstream toward the river tomorrow when we have more time. Today, we will walk upstream and see if we can find what that yuwt could mean, or simply to investigate. Mark this spot so we know where to leave the streambed to head back home."

As they walked in the direction that would be upstream, the terrain on both sides rose to the point of being hilly. The banks of the stream got higher as the stream cut deeper into the landscape. The travel upstream got more difficult when the rocks in the streambed grew in size.

The group was about to turn around when they came to a cave in the bank of the stream. The mouth of the cave appeared to be above the normal flow of water and was about as tall as Jait and nearly twice that in width.

Of course, the three couldn't resist climbing up to the cave from the streambed and taking a look at what they found.

The entrance to the cave was very sandy and the first thing they did was look for large animal tracks. They found many of the normal small animal tracks, but nothing that would look like it would pose a problem. Pred strung an arrow to his bow as they stepped inside.

The cave was dark with cool air, which was expected. However, what they didn't expect was the sound of flowing water.

After their eyes adjusted to the dimness, they could see that the cave narrowed to just a crawl space. Pred handed Jait his bow and took off his backpack. He asked Jait and Tymber to remain as he got on his hands and knees and crawled through the narrow opening.

Every couple of moments Tymber would call to her father to see if he was okay. He always answered 'yes.' The last time he answered, it sounded like he was quite a distance away.

"I'm coming back out," he said.

When he got back to Jait and Tymber, he stared at them shaking his head.

"You are not going to believe this," is all he said.

"What did you find, Father?" asked Tymber.

"What's in there?" asked Jait.

"Leave your backpacks and bows here and follow me"

Jait and Tymber got on their hands and knees and followed Pred back into the crawl space of the cave. As they crawled, the sound of flowing water got louder.

Pred stopped and turned around when he got to the end of the crawl space.

"We are going to drop down now onto a ledge and you will be able to see what's here."

Pred swung his legs around and stepped down onto the ledge. He could hear Tymber gasp as she saw the inside of the cavern. They both followed their father onto the ledge.

"Be careful not to go any farther than right here."

All three sat down and stared at the massive cavern in front of them.

Far below on the floor of the cavern was a flowing stream. To the right, coming from somewhere above, was a small waterfall splashing into the water below. It appeared that the stream flowed towards the left and then disappeared under a stone ledge in front of them.

Along the opposite wall of the cavern, was a faint silver glow, which shimmered in the ripples of the stream.

"This is the most beautiful place I have ever seen in my life," exclaimed Tymber. "That glow is giving us enough light to see."

"How did this place come to be, Father?" asked Jait.

"I'm not sure. I have heard of caves in stories, but I have never seen one. In fact, it is in stories that we all lived in caves at one time before we knew how to build cabins. But I had no idea they could be so large, or have a stream running through them."

"It looks like in places, liquid rock has been dripping from the ceiling and piling on the floor," Tymber said, as she pointed to the objects.

As they talked, a few small birds and animals scurried around not accustomed to hearing the voices of people.

Feeling a little braver, Tymber got on her stomach and scooted to the edge of the ledge to look down. She could see a series of ledges below them. With rope, she was sure they could reach the cavern floor and get to the stream.

"I know what you're thinking, Tymber. I'm not sure we have enough time today."

"Please, Father. We won't stay down there long. We can go down there, see where the stream goes, see what the silver glow is, and climb back up. Two measures of rope should be enough. I'll go back and get them."

"Very well, Tymber, but bring all three measures of rope."

Before the other two could blink, she was up and into the crawl space. In just a little bit she was back with three coils of rope.

As she entered the large cavern, she tied one end of a rope on a large boulder. She tested her knot going down on to the ledge with Jait and her father.

Before either of the others could say anything she was over the edge of the ledge and walking down the wall of the cavern.

"I guess she's going first," Pred said to Jait.

"So it would seem."

A few ledges down Tymber ran out of rope from the first coil. She tied off the second and began down. Jait took that as a signal for him to proceed down the first rope.

At the end of the second coil of rope, Tymber was on the floor of the cavern. She waited there, looked up, and watched Jait and her father come down the ropes. As she watched them, she realized that there was a silver glow coming from the wall that they had just come down as well. She hadn't noticed it on her way down.

When they all were down, Tymber pointed up the wall and showed them the glow.

"Wow," said Jait, "we went right by the glow and didn't notice it. We can investigate it on our way back up."

They all three turned to the stream at the same time. Tymber was the first to its edge. They were surprised to see the deep sand on the floor of the cavern. She knelt down and put her hand in the cool underground stream. She could tell that it ran swiftly, which surprised her.

"It's cool and tastes clean," she said, after a sip.

"I wonder if there are any fish in there?" asked Pred.

"Would you like me to get the net, Father?" asked Tymber.

"No, we don't have time enough to fish now."

From the floor of the cavern, they could now see that the stream did not start in this chamber but was added to by the waterfall. The stream entered near the waterfall through a narrow cave with a low ceiling and flowed out by a similar cave but with a slightly higher ceiling.

"Any guesses on where the stream goes?" asked Jait.

"I would think it goes to the river or to a lake," replied Pred, as he too dipped his hand into the water and took a few sips.

"Can I tie a rope off and see how deep it is?" asked Tymber.

"We don't have enough time today and we really should see if anything lives in there first, and if so, what it is.

"Have you two noticed how fresh the air smells in here and how easy it is to breathe? You would think deep in the ground the air would be stale and thin."

"Let's go back up and investigate the silver glow," she said.

The three took turns with the ropes and climbed back up the cliff to the third ledge where they plainly saw silver glow from down below.

"I no longer see the glow," stated Jait, as he picked up some rocks. "We must have stopped at the wrong ledge."

"I don't think we did, Jait," said Pred. "I think that all these rocks are glowing slightly and together they appear as a silver glow. Let's take a few of the rocks back with us and look at them closer."

They each gathered a few of the smaller rocks and climbed back up to the crawl space to leave. When they walked out of the cave they were nearly blinded by the mid afternoon sun.

"I had no idea we were in the cave so long," said Pred. "We are going to have to hurry to get to the village by dark."

"I don't think we can make it back that fast," Jait said, as he put on his backpack.

Energized by what they had found they hurried back to Keeper's cabin. It was after dark when they arrived.

They told Drel what they found and left a silver glow rock with him to look at. Pred told him that he would see him in the morning before dawn to watch the star.

When they got back to their cabin it was completely dark. They found Sella sitting on the porch waiting for them. They knew they would need a good reason why they were so late. They explained to her about the cavern that they found knowing that would explain to her satisfaction why they were late. It did not.

Around the evening meal, they talked of the cave and all its amazements. When they got to the silver glow rocks, Tymber wanted to bring the rocks outside in the darkness and see if they would glow. She got up and went outside and everyone followed her. She took out the rocks she had in her pocket and laid them on the porch step.

Sella gasped at what she saw. They were not bright, but the rocks definitely did have a silver glow.

"With enough of them we could replace the lanterns for rocks," Tymber said, as she gathered the rocks back into her pocket.

"I don't think they are bright enough for that Tymber," answered Sella, "but they sure are nice to look at."

Of course, Tymber took that as a challenge. She knew that she could collect enough rocks to eliminate the need for lanterns.

"It's bedtime for me," said Pred, heading towards his bedroom. Morning will come quickly after a long days travel. I will see you all in the morning."

NINE

Morning did come quickly for the three forest travelers. They sat sipping hot root tea on Drel's porch waiting for the star rise. They could feel the tired in their muscles. All three knew that if they were to go to the river during hunting and fishing, they would have to stay closer than what they did now. Too much time and energy is given to coming and going. Of course, as Tymber had mentioned on numerous occasions, the stone cabin would be the best place.

"I examined the glow rock last night after you left," Drel said, sitting back in his rocker. "I don't think that it is the rock that is glowing. If you look real close at the rock, it has very small plants growing on it. They are not much wider than a hair, but there are thousands of those plants on the rock that you gave me. I lightly scraped some off the rock and they glowed. They didn't glow long though. I think they died after I took them off the rock."

"So you're saying it isn't the rock that is glowing but very small plants growing on them?" Pred asked, looking at the rock he had kept in his pocket. "Now that you mention it, I can see the hairs. Why do they glow?"

"I don't know any of the reasons," said Drel. "I just saw it was those hair plants that were glowing."

Everyone sat there looking at their glow rocks, until it started getting too light to see the glow.

"The sun is rising," said Pred, as he got up off his chair. "Did we miss the star?"

Pred looked at Drel as Drel was looking at the sun.

"It must have moved enough to be behind the sun," he said. "It moved a lot in just one day"

"Oh well, maybe we will see it again in five years," Jait said, looking at Drel.

"Well one good thing about it," said Drel smiling, "I won't have to get up as early now to do my measurements."

Pred told Jait and Tymber it was time to get their things and they left for the forest, hoping at last to get to the river.

After they left, Drel sat in his rocker for hours thinking about the disappearance of the star. Something was bothering him about its coming and going. He didn't know exactly the movements of the sun, moon, Adentta, and the stars. Really, only what his father had told him about his thinking on such things.

The other stars don't come and go, at least not as pronounced. Some were visible only in the summer and some only in the winter, but that was a seasonal change. In addition, this star was larger and moved in just a matter of days.

What would cause it to show up after five years and then go behind the sun again in just a couple of days? It had to do with the motions of outer objects he was sure, if he could only understand them better.

He replayed how his father explained them to him. He held an apple up to a lantern and moved the apple around the lantern to show how he was thinking that Adentta moved around the sun. Drel knew it was not simply that Adentta was in position now to see the star; the star would be seen every year.

The star is moving around the sun? Drel thought to himself. *No, no, no, if my father was correct, a star is a sun that is farther away. It wouldn't be moving around our sun.*

A star wouldn't be moving around the sun; however, a moon might.

"For instance, a Lost Moon could move around the sun as Adentta does," Drel said to himself in a forceful voice.

The Lost Moon was much larger than the star but it may just have been closer to us at that time. The star and the Lost Moon did appear in the same year. Are they the same thing?

If it were going to happen again this year as it did the last visit, it would be moving toward us and grow larger in appearance. However, would that mean that it was on this side of the sun?

He glanced again at the sun, but could not see anything for its brightness.

Drel sat back and rocked in his rocker thinking of the possibilities. He couldn't track something if he didn't know where it was. He had to find out whether it was on this side of the sun or the other side. That would surely tell what it was—a star or a moon. Well at least it would tell what it wasn't.

He remembered a trick his father showed him to look at the sun when Adentta's moon was passing in front of it. He could see both the moon and the sun on a blank sheet.

The set up was easy. He just needed one sheet on a stand with a small hole in it and another sheet on a stand to see the image. When he completed the construction of the two stands, he set them up next to a window that had a view of the sun. To see the image he had to make the cabin as dark as could be with the stream of light from the sun as the only light.

After adjusting the heights and distances of the stands, he was able to see the image of the sun on the sheet. Looking closely, he could also see a small but definite dark dot on the sun. Whatever it is, it is on this side of the sun. So it was not a star. He would never be able to see a star in front of the sun. A star would be bright and not show up as a dark dot.

What a great discovery. Five years ago, they had it all wrong. It was not a large bright star but the Lost Moon at a great distance, at least, according to his theory.

Drel got excited about the prospect of seeing the Lost Moon again. Outer objects always interested him and this time he would take better notes and maybe even be able to predict when it would be back.

He took a few moments to think of the odd things that happened last time it was here, a couple of groundshakes, the overflowing lake when it had not rained, and the cool summer and cold winter. None of which could be from the Lost Moon. At least, how could it be?

Drel got another cup of tea. He couldn't help but think of the things that happened that year. And since then the years have been getting longer. There have been many coincidences that go back to the Lost Moon. Perhaps there is more to it than what he thinks.

The sun had moved above the window so he could no longer see it on the sheet. He didn't really need to see it anymore. In fact, he really didn't notice it was gone until he realized how dark his cabin had gotten.

He knew his best guess was that the Lost Moon was returning. It may not get as close and cause the things that happened last time, if it really was the cause.

He wished his father were here to help him to understand the outer object movements. He might have been able to tell him what to expect with the moon moving in front of the sun. His father should have written down his thoughts on their movements. Drel had searched during the last Lost Moon appearance for writings of his father in hopes to find writings on the outer object movements, but found none.

His father was the smartest man Drel had ever known. It seemed like he always had the right answer for things. Unfortunately, he didn't always write them down.

With that thought, he got a blank sheet and started writing what his thoughts were on the Lost Moon. Maybe if he wrote it down, it would develop into something that made sense.

"When I was young it was a rushing river full of water," Pred said, as he looked down at the river from above, "but now it's barely a stream with knee–deep water and only in the middle."

They had followed the dried streambed south to the river where it ended in what would have been a small waterfall, if there had been any water in the stream. As they looked down, they couldn't believe they had spent so much time to get to the river. It looked like it may have fish, but only in pockets of deeper water.

Because of the width of the river, the forest canopy opened up and the sun was bright and warm on their faces. They could see downstream for a little ways, but because of a curve in the river, they couldn't see very far up river.

"Let's climb down and take a closer look," said Tymber, already starting down.

"Wait, Tymber," Pred said. "When I was here last, I remember looking up at this point from down there. I think if we move a little down river it slopes down and we won't have to climb."

"Be sure to mark the trees for our return," Tymber reminded Jait.

They climbed up a short rise and then headed downhill toward the river just as Pred had predicted.

The bank of the river was deep sand and the river bed was exposed in most places near the bank from the lack of water. Many animal tracks marked their way to and from the small amount of water that was in the middle of the river.

"At least it looks like this may be a good place to hunt," Tymber said, as she inspected all the different types of paw prints in the sand.

"As dry as the forest seems to be, it will be good hunting anywhere there is water," Jait said, looking farther down the river. "Where does this river go? It must end in a lake I would think."

"I'm not sure," answered Pred. "This is the farthest I have ever been in the forest. My father and I had never any reason to travel farther. Hunting and fishing were both always good here."

"Let's go see," said Tymber.

"We will have to wait till another time for that. It is late day already and we will never have time to get back to the cabin before dark. Let's throw the net in the water and see if we can take a couple of fish back with us when we go."

They walked across a sand dune toward a deep looking pocket of water. Jait took the throw net out of his backpack, opened it, wrapped the throw rope around his wrist and tossed it in the water.

"Wow," he shouted as started to pull the net back. "I've got some."

That was an understatement. When he got the net back to the bank there were five large fish and a couple of handfuls of small fish in the net.

"That's the largest one throw catch I have ever seen," said Pred, sorting through the catch.

"Looks like we have fish for supper," Jait said, gleaming with his toss of the net.

"That is more than we can eat at one meal," replied Pred. "Jait, empty your water pouch into Tymber's pouch and fill yours up with river water and the small fish. We will go by the fishpond on the way home and we can add these few small fish in as we pass. It's not much but it will be something."

"We can give Drel, I mean Keeper, a fish as we go by," said Tymber. "I'm sure since the village has a ban on fish he would enjoy it as much as we will."

Pred chuckled at Tymber's slip in calling Keeper by his name. Usually children were only permitted to call adults by their craft name.

"I'm sure Keeper would not mind for you to call him by Drel." Pred said. "You are only a few years younger than him and I'm sure with you coming into the forest, he would think of you as an adult."

"He became Keeper so young he seems much older," Tymber said.

"Tymber has a crush on Keeper, Tymber has a crush on Keeper," teased Jait.

And with that Tymber pushed Jait in the river.

Jait was nearly dry by the time they got back to Drel's cabin. Drel was at his table writing when they arrived. He asked them in, but they declined in that it was getting so late.

"Tymber wanted us to stop by and give you a fish that we caught today," said Jait, smiling at Tymber, who had a deep blush going.

"Thanks very much, Tymber," he said, as he took the fish from Jait. "I will cook this for supper tonight."

"You're welcome, Keeper," she said, looking away, completely embarrassed by what Jait had said. "We need to get going, Father. It is getting very late."

"Pred, are you going back in the forest again tomorrow?"

"No, I think we found what we were looking for. We need to work on our fishing and hunting gear starting tomorrow."

"Can you come over in the morning? Shortly after sunup would be good."

"Sure, I'll see you then."

"Goodbye all," said Drel. "Goodbye, Tymber, and thanks again for the fish."

They were about halfway to their cabin when they went by the fishpond. Jait opened the water pouch and emptied the small fish into the pond.

With that, Tymber pushed Jait into the fishpond.

"That's for embarrassing me in front of Keeper," she said.

She hurried over to her father in hopes of getting protection.

Jait went under the water, but when he surfaced, he was laughing. He took a breath of air and yelled to her, "It was worth it!"

Pred and Tymber got to the cabin before Jait. When they walked in the cabin, Sella greeted them.

"Where is Jait?" she asked.

"He will be right here," answered Pred.

"We caught some fish for supper," said Tymber, trying to change the subject. "Jait caught them with just one throw."

"The river is very low on water," Pred said. "I guess the forest has had less rain than we have."

Sella stood and looked at the two travelers and with nervous eyes asked if they had seen any predators. Well that changed the subject all right.

Just about that time, Jait walked in the cabin bare–naked.

Sella stood there in shock.

"Where are your clothes?" she asked.

"Soaked wet on the porch," he answered. Then he looked at her, held up his hand and said. "Don't ask."

Sella looked at both Pred and Tymber who just shrugged. Both of them were very glad that the subject changed from predators.

The next morning, Pred asked Jait if he wanted to go with him and Tymber to Keeper's cabin. He declined saying that he only had one pair of dry clothes left and could not afford to get Tymber mad again.

Pred knew that Jait had too much to do around the cabin. He could not afford to spend a morning at Drel's house. Tymber wanted to learn more about the star and the glowing rocks so asked to go.

They arrived at Drel's just before sunrise and found Drel on his porch in his rocker.

"Good morning, Pred, good morning, Tymber," he said, as he saw them approach.

"Morning Drel," said Pred.

"Morning Keeper," said Tymber.

"I thought you said you weren't going to have to get up so early now?" Pred said, sitting down in the rocker next to Drel.

"It looks like I'm going to have to watch the sun rise for a while yet. That is why I asked you to come this morning. I need to talk out some ideas I have and I want to see what you think about them."

"Sounds mysterious, but I was thinking that with the star gone, so was the mystery."

"Well that's part of what I wanted to talk to you about. I don't think the morning star is a star. I actually think it might be the Lost Moon."

In the dim light, Drel couldn't see Pred's face or his reaction. However, he did stay silent while he thought about it.

"Why do you think that?" he asked.

"Why don't we wait till the sun rises and I'll show you?"

They sat in silence for a while thinking about the Lost Moon.

"The fish was excellent last night, I want to thank you Tymber, for wanting to leave one here."

"Your welcome," Tymber said, glad it was too dark to see her blush. "Mother cooked our fish last night. We enjoyed it very much too.

"The Lost Moon is coming back," she asked quickly to change the subject. "I don't remember it very well the last time. Mother and Father made me stay inside while it was here. I do remember everyone afraid and talking about all the things it caused, including groundshakes."

"We don't know exactly what it caused," Pred said, trying to lessen the impact of the situation.

The sun was rising in the east, and Drel asked Pred and Tymber to come inside the cabin. They were a little confused about going inside but Drel quickly explained.

"I'm going to show you why I think the star is not really a star and is more likely a moon, and very well could be the Lost Moon," Drel said, as he set up his sun viewer on the table.

"What I've made is a viewer so we can see the sun without looking at it. I line up the sheet with the pin hole in it towards the window. The sun will shine threw the hole and on this other sheet. When the sun gets up just a little higher I'll show you.

"While we wait I'll make some root tea. I haven't had any this morning and I'm sure you two would like some also."

The two visitors nodded their heads.

Tymber thought that it would be a good time to see if she could call Keeper by his first name. All he would do is look at her funny and wonder why she did that. It was not like she would get in trouble or anything. Her father said that he probably wouldn't mind and after all, she was adult enough to go into the forest.

"I would love to have some tea, Keeper," Tymber said, chickening out.

"It looks like it is finally warming up," Pred said, while they were waiting for the root tea. "This is the first warm morning we've had since last summer."

"I just hope we get rain soon," answered Drel. "All the crops in the village could use a good drink of water."

Tymber was at the table watching the sheet waiting for the sun to appear. "There's a yellow circle on the sheet now,"

"That's the sun."

Drel brought the cups for the tea to the table and Pred and he sat down with Tymber.

Drel showed them how the trees brightened by the sun also showed up on the sheet.

"Keep in mind that everything you see on the sheet is backwards from how you see it looking out the window. It is like looking outside in a mirror. See how the clouds appear to be moving across in the opposite direction?"

They were impressed by how Drel was able to make the sun viewer.

Drel began his explanation of why he thought that the morning star was a moon and perhaps the Lost Moon and that it was on its way back.

"If the star went behind the sun like we thought yesterday, we would not be able to see it of course."

Pred and Tymber nodded their heads.

"If the star really was a star and went in front of the sun, we wouldn't be able to see it because it too would be shining.

"Look at the sun more closely. Can you see the black dot near the right edge?"

"Yes," they both said.

"Well that is what I believe to be the morning star that we have been seeing and the Lost Moon. Of course, the Lost Moon is farther away and appears smaller."

"So this time," Tymber stumbled over how she wanted to ask this, "the Lost Moon is going to be small at a greater distance?"

"Good question, Tymber, and I really don't know the answer," Drel replied, as he went to retrieve the freshly brewed root tea. "I'm hoping that we can think this out and try to guess at what will happen. I know that the leaders will be seeking me out to see if the Lost Moon will be showing up. I don't think that I know enough about what is happening to talk to them. I'm not sure I'm prepared to show them this."

"Well I can't blame you for that," Pred said, as he continued to look at the sun on the sheet. "What do you think is going to happen?"

"I think the Lost Moon will be moving this way and growing in size. I think that is what happened last time. Nobody saw the moon when the sun outshone it and it took half a season to approach and grow large enough to be seen.

"The first day we saw the Lost Moon five years ago, it was partially blocking the sun. It grew in size as it came closer and shrunk as it left. We never knew that we saw it this small."

The sun rose further and its image sunk and left the sheet of paper.

Pred continued to stare at the sheet as if the sun was still visible.

"The morning star, or now you're saying the Lost Moon, is not really doing like it did last time. It was visible for around eight days and this time it was visible for only three."

"For some reason it is moving different this time," answered Drel. "Also, remember, I think Adentta is somewhat farther from the sun than it was then too."

"So the Lost Moon is moving with the sun as it goes across the sky?" asked Tymber, trying to understand what was being said.

"Well Tymber, we generally think that the sun pretty much stays still and Adentta spins and moves around it."

"Oh, yes, I remember that from lessons now," she said, a little embarrassed by not remembering. "That complicates things even more, doesn't it?"

Drel smiled and shrugged.

"I am having trouble seeing how all that works," Pred admitted.

Drel brought a muskmelon to the table.

"Imagine this is the sun, and this grape is the Lost Moon. This apple will be Adentta.

He arranged the fruit to suit his situation.

"In this position, if you are sitting on the apple looking in the sky, you would see the Lost Moon to the side of the sun. As Adentta moves to the side circling the sun, you no longer can see the Lost Moon because of the shine of the sun even though the Lost Moon is in front of it."

"True," answered Pred, "but the moon was not just at the side of the sun. It was also above the sun. That is why we saw it before the sun came up."

"Exactly," Drel said, as he put the grape in the approximate position it would have been.

Drel continued, "So Adentta is moving this way and the Lost Moon is moving this way. Like this it would appear like it does now, if you remember that the view of the sun on the sheet is backwards."

"Now I see why you don't want to talk to the leaders about this," Pred said. "It gets very complicated. I think I am following you though. You are suggesting that both Adentta and the Lost Moon are moving to get in the position they are now."

"What I noticed the most," said Tymber trying to follow the movements, "is that when you moved the grape you moved it towards the apple."

"And I am thinking that is what is happening."

They all three sat silent and thought about movements of moons and suns sipping their hot root tea wondering what to expect.

"Where was the black dot on the sun yesterday?"

"About the same place," Drel answered.

"You had it move from up here," Pred said, as he held the grape up above the muskmelon, "to down here in three days and then today it was in about the same place as yesterday. That doesn't make sense that the object would move and then just stop."

They sat for awhile in silence again, when Tymber answered. "It would appear not to move if it were moving directly towards us."

Drel and Pred looked at each other and then both looked at Tymber in surprise.

"That would explain why the moon did not appear to move but, I'm not sure I like that," said Pred.

"The black dot should get larger with time if that is true," Drel said, moving the grape towards the apple. "It's good that the dot is not moving now and it seems to be heading towards us."

Pred and Tymber looked at him like he was crazy.

"No, look at this," he said, "Let's say the moon is moving directly towards us. But, remember, Adentta is moving around the sun. So, if it is moving directly towards Adentta now, it won't be by the time it gets here because Adentta will have moved."

"So you're saying that at least it won't hit us?" Pred asked, in a thankful voice.

"Hit us," Tymber said. "Thanks I had not thought of that."

"Tymber and Pred," Drel started, "we need to keep this information to ourselves right now so we don't start any kind of panic in the village. All we know, or think we know, are just guesses and we need to know more truths before we share this with anybody.

"Most of all, we don't know what the moon will cause if it does come close. For that matter, we don't really know that it caused anything the last time.

"My guess is that it did cause some of the things to happen," said Drel, as he played with the fruit on the table. "Somehow the

Lost Moon had some kind of influence on Adentta as it went by. I just don't have a clue what that was. I do know that it's not a curse like Slippers was saying. Somehow, the effects on Adentta can be explained."

"I was young and my mother and father didn't tell me everything," Tymber said, glancing at her father, "but what exactly did the moon do or was blamed for doing?"

Pred and Drel looked at each other and Pred sat back in his chair as a signal for Drel to go ahead and tell her.

"Well Tymber," Drel began, "There are a lot of things that happened and a lot of things that I suspect were imagined.

"The summer that year was very cool and the crops did not grow well. We had to use much of our reserve of grain and meat to make it through the following winter. That's the reason I've been visited by the farmers. They want me to predict if the summer will be cool again since the morning star is back.

"The overflow of the fish pond is one I still don't understand. It was during a dry spell and the water in the pond simply overflowed its banks. We lost a lot of fish that year from the loss of water when it returned to normal. That's one thing I would have to say for sure was caused from that moon."

"How is that possible?" asked Tymber, looking rather stumped.

"I don't know how that happened. Like your father said, the moon had some kind of influence on us.

"We know that Adentta's moon has an influence on the rise and fall of water, I guess with both moons, it caused the pond to overflow.

"And of course you know about the groundshakes we had."

"Yes, I was at home when they happened. Mother held us kids as tight as she could during the shakes. They seemed to last for a long time, but they didn't."

"All the birds and other animals seemed to act strange while the moon was here. It seemed to confuse them as much as it did us. And of course what I've been measuring ever since then, the years are getting longer."

"The years are getting longer?" she asked.

"I think so."

"How could the moon cause that?"

"I don't know. It all started five years ago when the sun was not where it should be at Plant, or any other time of the year for that matter."

As Drel was explaining the length of the year, a storm came overhead. In an instant it was raining hard with lightning and thunder. The wind kicked up and the trees outside bent to their limit.

"Drel, I remember something else that happened during the Lost Moon's visit," Pred said, as he stood by the window looking out. "Sudden and violent storms."

TEN

The next several days were trying for Drel. The farmers came by on a daily basis for information.

Drel had to explain what he thought was going to happen many times and then tell them it was only a guess. The more days that passed, however, it became less of a guess.

Looking at his sun viewer, the dot was getting larger and larger and to his dismay it wasn't moving very much. He took to heart what Tymber said as to why it wasn't moving, because it was heading straight for Adentta.

It seemed to Drel, that he could almost see the dot on the sun while outside. The closer it came the more he thought that it could get close enough to completely block the sun.

When Drel was by himself, he continued to play with the fruit on his table. He moved them this way and that way trying to imitate what he was seeing in his viewer. He decided that for Adentta to go around the sun, it of course had to be moving. He placed a large circle on his table, divided into 320 lines radiating from the center outwards. The number of lines was what he now estimated was the number of days in a year.

He moved the apple, his pretend Adentta, around the table one line each day, with the muskmelon in the middle. He would look at the dot on his viewer and move the grape to indicate its growth and lack of movement.

He did notice something. To make the grape appear not to move to the apple, he had to move the grape around the muskmelon too. The moon must also be moving around the sun. He hadn't thought about that before. Does that mean that Adentta is attracting the moon? That Adentta is actually pulling the moon towards itself? Or is it simply the motion of the moon around the sun similar to what Adentta does.

Over time, Pred, Jait, and Tymber made a few trips into the forest and river. They decided to fix up the stone cabin and use that as their base while in the forest, much to the dismay of Sella, but it gave them over a half of day longer at the river.

One of the places Pred wanted to go was on the other side of the stream. He wanted to see what that circular object was on the Stone Cabin's map. He hoped it was a small lake and that it had an abundance of fish.

They spent the previous night in the stone cabin making sure their fishing equipment was in good shape. Pred was once again studying the map he had copied.

"If the distances on the map are the same," he said, "it looks like the stream will be about halfway to that pond. So we should get there just about lunchtime."

They left after breakfast the next morning.

The tree canopy was dense on the other side of the stream with wide leafed lowland trees. Even though it was midmorning and they were traveling east, the sun was only seen rarely peeking through the leaves. If they would take the time, this would be a great place to hunt for mushrooms.

As they walked, the land rose from the stream flood valley and the kind of trees changed to a mixture of cone woods. The farther they walked the higher the land got and soon they were climbing up a high hill. There were rock outcrops in the side of the hill the same color of the rock in the cavern.

"It looks like the circle on the map meant hill and not pond," Pred said, in a disappointed manner.

Tymber was in the lead and stopped and pointed ahead.

"It looks like the forest breaks up there," she said.

They walked up to the edge of a meadow.

"Looks like the meadow is the object on the map," Jait said, when they stopped.

Jait ducked down and Tymber and Pred followed.

"What is it?" she whispered.

"Look about halfway through the meadow over to the forest edge on the right."

"It's an antelope!" Tymber whispered excitedly. "She has a youngling with her."

They sat and watched the animals for a while.

"I haven't seen an antelope since I was a young child and they came up to the field by the cabin and feasted on Crops' grain."

"It looks like this meadow is well-grazed," said Jait. "There must be a herd of antelope up here."

When he said that, the mother antelope held her head up high and looked toward them. They knew if they didn't move she would probably not see them.

"This will be a great hunting place this autumn," whispered Jait. "We could hunt here and get enough meat for the village to last a season."

Tymber had a little trouble thinking like a hunter while looking at an antelope with her youngling.

"We are up wind from them so they will not stay around long," Pred said, looking at which way the leaves were blowing.

Just as he said that, the antelopes got a little spooked and moved off into the forest.

The Trelops sat down in the shade of the forest's edge and ate lunch.

"Well it isn't a fishing spot, but it wasn't a waste of time either," Pred said, taking a sip from his water bag. "Finding a good hunting spot may prove to be more important than a good fishing place."

"If we keep going in this direction, will we reach the river?" Tymber asked, pointing to the east.

Pred really didn't know that answer. The map didn't really show the river this far north.

"I'm sure we would if we went far enough east, but there really is no way of knowing how far it would be."

"I think we should find out," Tymber said, with a smile. "We may need to know how far it is during the autumn hunt."

Pred looked out onto the meadow. It appeared that they were on a point. Both to the right and left the ground sloped down, but across the meadow it rose slightly.

"I think I can see the tree line on the other side," he said. "We can go that far at least and see if we can get a feeling for how far the river is."

When they were finished eating, they headed out into the meadow. They saw many signs where the antelope had scraped the ground or nibbled the grass down to a stub. It appeared that the meadow was like a cap on top of a small hill. Everywhere the meadow ended, the land started downward. It looked like whether by accident or by design, the antelope kept the meadow in grass by eating the leaves of any small trees that started growing.

They could hear rushing water when they neared the tree line on the east end of the meadow. The edge of the meadow dropped off into a deep valley with the river below.

"Well we didn't have to go far," said Tymber, peeking over the edge at the river below.

The side of the cliff at the meadow had unstable ground from erosion so they could not get a good look at what was over the edge. The river was narrow there and they could just barely see the other bank. The valley on the other side of the river extended east as far as they could see. They stood on the cliff and were about as high as the large trees on the other side of the river. Taking in the view, they did not see everything that was there to be seen. But something on the opposite bank was noticing them. Far below on the other side of the river, a large dark gray animal lifted its head from drinking from the river. It noticed their scent first, then heard their voices, and then saw them leaning over the edge of the cliff. The predator was familiar with that scent, the scent of the three humans. The predator knew that the humans would not see her, so she took a few more licks at the water, and slipped into the bushes and out of sight.

"We need to head back to the stone cabin if we're going to get there before dark," said Pred.

All three had trouble turning around and leaving the beautiful view of the valley to the east. They decided that during hunt, they would make camp and spend at least one night where they stood so they could watch the sunrise over the valley.

They left the way they came, pointing out places they could hide while hunting, depending on wind direction. Mostly they considered the edge of the meadow where the tree line began, the best place to hide.

Back at the stone cabin, Jait and Pred collected firewood for the wood stove in the kitchen. Tymber decided to cook supper, well at least try. Her mother had always asked her to watch and learn as she cooked, but Tymber seldom did. She was usually helping her father with his chores. They had left hens eggs there that morning. Jait said they were lucky that she was just cooking hen's eggs and fried bread and nothing more complicated. As they ate, he did have to admit that the eggs did taste good, particularly with the buttered fried bread.

After supper they talked about their day and then added the river to their maps.

Tymber was looking at her map trying to decide how to draw the river.

"Father, do you think we need to continue the drawing of the river south down to where the stream and the river meet? We really don't know how it runs except that it goes on the east side of High Meadow."

"Leave it to Tymber to give the meadow a name," Jait said, smiling at her. "I bet she has all ten of her fingers named."

"I am going to connect the two points," Pred said, after thinking about it for awhile. "It can always be changed if it becomes known not to be true."

The Trelops decided to use the sofas in the main living area to sleep on. That way they could build a small fire in the fireplace to warm the night air. At times, Tymber would look up as she tried to sleep and see the flashes of light and shadows from the fireplace on

the head of the predator. It seemed to be more ferocious looking in
the dim light and shadows.

The next few days they continued going down the dry stream to the
river.

Fishing in the river had declined and they were thinking they
may need to move down river. Tymber, of course, had always wanted
to keep moving downriver. She wanted to see where the water in
the river went. Pred had said that the river may end a very long way
from there.

Jait had caught only a couple of fish the last couple days, just
enough to feed them, so Pred agreed to move down river. It will
be the first time they camped in the open since they entered the
forest.

The river water level was still low so the quickest way down
stream was to walk the sandy river bottom next to the banks.
Tymber had no desire to even check to see if there were fish as they
progressed. She was simply intent on exploring. Pred and Jait understood that and simply let her go and investigate while they stopped
and fished.

Still the only fish they found were enough to eat for meals.
Tymber, on occasion, found berries and nuts to supplement the fish.
Jait called it dessert.

"Tymber, pick a good sandbar, the sun is getting low and I'm
getting tired," Pred said, as he threw the net in the river for what
seemed to be the hundredth time.

Tymber picked the camp site and set up the small tent. Jait
climbed the bank and gathered firewood.

The sun was getting low and Tymber was in the tent when she yelled for her father to come quick.

He ran over and into the tent to see Tymber sitting on the ground smiling.

"I thought you were in trouble," Pred said, as he looked at her in surprise.

"You see that small hole in the tent?" Tymber said, pointing to the side of the tent,

Pred nodded his head.

"Well that bright dot on the other side of the tent is the sun."

Pred looked at the sun image and then to Tymber. "Are you sure?"

"Yes."

Pred leaned over and got a better look at the sun. "I can see the dark circle of the Lost Moon. It has gotten a lot larger."

"And has moved only slightly," Tymber added.

"It looks like it is nearly blocking one–fourth of the sun."

"It looks like a black ball in front."

"The sun is still too bright behind it to get a good look."

Pred stuck his head out of the tent and called for Jait. Jait entered the tent complaining because he just about had the fire going.

"Look on the tent wall," Pred said. "That's an image of the sun. Like the image I was telling you Tymber and I saw at Drel's cabin.

They spent the whole time the image was on the tent wall explaining to Jait what he was looking at.

Tymber showed Jait how much smaller the dark circle was when they first saw it as compared to its size now.

Jait didn't seem to be as interested as Pred and Tymber in the Lost Moon. His attitude was mostly: *what happens, happens.*

When Pred and Tymber were done talking about the moon they realized that Jait left and had the fire blazing and the fish frying.

Pred remembered Jait during the last visit of the Lost Moon. He was around the age of fourteen and it seemed to be very disturbing to him. He wouldn't go outside at night when it was visible. During the groundshakes he would hide under the table and not come out for a long time after they were over.

Jait was older now and not as afraid of things, but Pred was sure that Jait remembered how he felt during those days. He may even be a little embarrassed about how he had acted.

However, he was not the only one that was terrified of the groundshakes five years ago. Most adults feared the uncertainty of the ground moving under their feet and the lack of control when it happened.

Pred decided to be more careful talking about the Lost Moon around Jait. He was glad that he remembered about Jait during that time.

Pred and Tymber sat on logs around the campfire. All three talked about what they were going to do tomorrow. They decided to go as far as they could downriver till midday and then return. Tymber was hoping that would be long enough to get to the end of the river.

The sketch from the stone cabin had the river just end at a curved line at the end of the sheet. She wanted to know what that line was. Probably a lake like her father had suggested.

As they sat around the fire, the sun set and it became completely dark except for the light of the campfire. The sounds of the forest seemed to grow with the increased darkness. Some nocturnal animals, insects, and birds seemed to come to life.

A couple of times they watched eyes that shone from the camp-fire, go down to the water's edge for a drink. One of the animals looked like it had caught a small fish from the water as it sat there. It looked at the firelight and headed back into the forest to eat it.

In the distance they could hear the sound of thunder. The wind shifted and they could smell rain in the air. The forest became quieter as the animals took cover. The stars in the sky quickly disappeared as the clouds rolled in.

"If we get a heavy rain we will have to pack up and go uphill," Pred announced, standing up to go into the tent. "I don't know how much rain will cause the river to rise.

"Put the rest of the wood on the fire and we will see how long it lasts."

Pred went into the tent as Tymber and Jait added the rest of the wood to the fire. Jait then went into the tent but Tymber stayed and sat on the log and watched the storm brewing. Storms always were somewhat exciting to her and she loved to watch them in the distance. She could see lightning flashing that lighted up the edge of the clouds that gave them the appearance of great mountains and canyons.

As she sat there, the wind got stronger, but it appeared that the storm was going to go upstream from them. She wondered if the storm was going over High Meadow. She sat and enjoyed the flashes of lightning and the distant sound of the rumbling thunder.

After one clap of thunder, she thought she heard it answered by a roar in the distance. Well, it wasn't exactly a roar or even a growl, but more of a yawn of a large animal.

She instinctively felt for her knife strapped to her leg and found it just where it should be. Tymber took comfort in that fact. She glanced over and saw her bow and quiver of arrows lying by the side of the tent. In and instant, she could grab her bow and have it ready if needed.

She felt a fine mist in her face and for some reason it felt good. She wished she knew more about how the weather worked, why it rained, and what lightning and thunder were.

The wind started to subside and the storm passed. She knew morning would come too soon, so she, too, headed into the tent to get rest.

The next morning Tymber woke with the sound of Jait's voice outside the tent. He was talking to Pred about the storm last night. She didn't want to get up. Her muscles and bones were sore for the exercise, so she just laid there. Then she remembered she wanted to get going this morning to have time to see what was downstream.

She jumped up and went out to see Jait and her father sitting by the fire.

"Here's breakfast," Jait told her, as he handed her the last of the packed food they had brought with them. "From now on its hunt, fish, or starve."

"I can't believe I slept so late," she said, sitting down by the fire. "I'm so hungry I could eat a beast."

"We let you sleep," Jait said, with a smile in his eyes. "We know how girls need more sleep than men after a day of work."

"You must want to go swimming this morning," she said, without skipping a beat.

They both smiled at each other and secretly plotted a scheme of revenge.

After they finished breakfast, they packed up their supplies and started their journey.

The way downriver was troublesome. The banks of the river rose sharply and the trio had to move away from the river to travel. The forest underbrush grew closer together the farther they ventured. They found themselves chopping their way to higher ground where it was much less dense.

It wasn't until they were clear of the underbrush when they realized how much higher they were. As they looked over the tree tops, they could see the river winding below until it bent and disappeared behind the hill they were on.

"This is the highest I have ever been," Tymber said, smiling as she looked out as far as she could.

All three of them sat down on the side of the hill, tired from all their chopping.

"It is so beautiful up here," she said, looking at Jait for his response.

He was looking up the hill at what the coming journey was going to be like.

"Father," he said after a while, "see how the river bends around this hill? I think if we went around the hill in the other direction, we will save many steps to get back to where the river runs."

"Sounds like a good plan to me," he said. "We may be able to get where we're going faster, wherever that is." He and Jait looked at Tymber and smiled. They knew that the reason they were there was because of her curiosity.

As they sat there, they noticed a somewhat pleasant scent. They had no idea what it was, but enjoyed it nonetheless.

They got up and decided to try Jait's plan and go around the hill in the other direction, staying high enough to be out of the underbrush.

The hill was larger than they expected and took more time to go around than they thought it would. But they were still sure it was faster than going around the other way.

When they got to the other side of the hill, they stopped and stared in amazement. They looked down onto the valley that lay out in front of them. The river split the valley in two as it ran east along the valley floor. North and south, at the ends of the valley, stood two mountains which appeared to be guarding the valley. At the end of the valley between the mountains where the river ran, they could see where the river ended. A lake. A lake so large they could not see across to the other side.

The breeze from the lake was directly in their face as they looked out into the distance. The scent that they had noticed was now strong and it came from the lake. It was a salty smell.

"Father, build a cabin here for me," Tymber said, only slightly in jest.

"Well Tymber," Jait began, "This view has been worth our trip. Thank you for insisting on coming." He too could not take his eyes off the marvelous view.

"Let's call this View Hill," Tymber said.

"View Hill, it is," Jait proclaimed.

This is like a different world," said Pred. "I take it back about not wanting to live anywhere but the village. Next to this, the village could seem pretty boring."

"We could build cabins here and go back to the village for boots and things we don't have," said Jait. "In fact, if everyone in the village saw this, they would want to move here too."

"The question is what to do now," said Pred, picking up his water bag for a drink. "We can easily see the end of the river."

"We have to go on," Jait and Tymber both said.

"That's still a long way off, it will be nearly dark by the time we get to that lake."

"That just means that we need to hurry," Jait said, picking up his backpack and heading down the hill.

"You know this is going to take at least another day," Pred shouted to the backs of his children as they hurried down the hill. "Your mother is expecting us back in three days."

Tymber was enjoying the fact that Jait now wanted to continue. She knew wanting to go to the rivers end was something that she wanted to do and they didn't, but they agreed out of their own curiosity.

In no time, they reached the river's bank and found that it again was easy walking. It looked like the river flooded in the valley on occasion, which made the banks free from underbrush.

While they were walking near the river's edge, Jait spotted a small boar hog drinking from the river. It was standing on one of the very few sand bars that were on the river this far down. It seemed unaware of the Trelops.

"Well what do you think," Jait whispered, not wanting to spook the hog. "I'm getting a little tired of fish."

Tymber already had her bow strung with an arrow. Pred wasn't far behind.

"I take that as being a yes."

They each took aim hoping to down the animal quickly. With all three shooting, it increased the odds tremendously.

"On the count of three," Pred said.

They all three shot and the pig went down in just a few steps.

"Lunch!" He proclaimed, while approaching the downed hog.

Pred and Tymber waded through a little river water to get to the sand bar and began skinning and carving the hog. Jait began gathering the firewood on the bank. He decided to build the fire on the sandbar so carried the wood out to where his father and Tymber were.

As a passing thought, Pred considered that this may be a good place to fish, but he knew that neither of his children would want to stop now. It was just something he would have to keep in mind if they didn't find a better place.

When they were finished eating, they carved up the rest of the hog. They knew that there was plenty for supper and maybe breakfast in the morning if they could find a nice cool place for the carvings. If they happened to find a salt deposit, they could cure the meat well enough to take leftovers with them on their return.

Before anyone else was ready to leave, Tymber was standing on the bank looking ahead, anxious to get on the way.

They walked swiftly from then on, hoping to make the lake before sunset. At times the forest broke and they could see the mountain on the far side of the river. Tymber thought that it must be the tallest thing on Adentta. Toward the top was white and void of any trees and the very top was shielded by smoke looking clouds. It made her somewhat dizzy just looking at its height.

She looked ahead and could see the end of the forest and was sure it was the lake. The wind was getting stronger in her face and her step quickened. She could hear the sounds of the lake coming from between the foothills of the two Guard Mountains. It looked like foothills were hands that were reached out to hold the mountains back to allow the river to flow through.

The landscape unexpectedly fell downwards to the lake. The river water began to tumble and churn with its increased speed over the rocks that rose up within it. The sound of the rapid water made it hard for the three to hear what each other was saying.

Jait and Tymber took off running, trying to be the first with their feet in the water of the lake. The sand was very deep on the banks of the river and they both fell a number of times before getting to the water's edge. Jait won the race but waited till his sister was there so they could enter together. They took off their boots and stepped in. The water was much warmer than they expected and they proceeded to walk out till they were up to their knees.

"Not too far you two," their father shouted. "We don't know what lives in there."

Tymber could hardly take her eyes off of the horizon. They had never seen a lake so large that you couldn't see the other side.

Up and down the bank of the lake were many types of birds attacking the water, feeding on the fish. Birds with long legs stood in the shallows and simply reached their head down and picked up fish. The air was now mixed with the scent of salt and of a slight smell of fish.

In a little while, Pred got to the water's edge carrying all the things his children dropped as they raced to the water.

"Come in," Tymber shouted, over the crashing of the large waves. "The water is so warm."

When Tymber turned around to talk to her father, a wave nearly knocked her down. She was very surprised by the wave's power.

Pred, of course, joined them in the lake.

"Have you ever seen anything so wonderful?" Tymber exclaimed, as she looked from the water to the mountains. "I take back what I said earlier. This is where I want you to build my cabin."

"That, young lady, will be a task for your husband to endure," he said, with a smile in his eyes.

"Do you two remember the stories about the great sea? How you could row in a boat for your whole life and never get to the other side? Well this, I believe, is the sea."

Both Tymber and Jait looked out onto the horizon, wondering if the stories were indeed true.

"At least part of the story is true," he continued. "There is a sea."

"The sun is setting, and it will get dark soon. Tymber, pitch the tent, and Jait, get the fire going. I'm going to go back up the river and fill up our water bags."

Tymber and Jait looked at each other and then at the water they were standing in.

"This sea is salt water and not good to drink."

They both reached down and tasted the water and spit it out. Their father was right about it being salty.

"I'm surprised any fish can live in such waters," Jait said, leaving the water on his way to get firewood.

"Animals can adapt to nearly any situation," Pred replied.

It was after sunset before they started cooking their hog carvings. It was a beautiful night according to Tymber. Adentta's moon was just above the eastern horizon leaving a gold and silver shimmer on the waves in the sea.

They cooked and ate their meal in mostly silence looking at the surroundings in the moonlight. As they faced the sea, to their left were sand dune banks about head high with tall grass growing on them, but to the right the sand shore turned into rock cliffs not far from the water's edge. Of course, Tymber was hoping to have time to investigate the cliffs in the morning.

Jait, in a teasing tone, broke the silence.

"Which one of us is going to tell mother that she has to leave the village and come live by the sea?"

Of course, nobody volunteered.

After some thought, Pred decided that she would love it there. She would want a cabin built first, a garden growing, and neighbors living there before she would move.

As Pred sat and watched the waves break on the shore, he thought about his father. Why hadn't he ever come here to the sea? If he had, he never spoke of it. His job though was to hunt for the village. This was much too far for a hunt. Without curing, the catch would spoil before it got home.

His children were too quiet and he realized they were both sound asleep where they sat. The wind had lessened and the waves on the sea had shrunk to large ripples.

He watched them for awhile as they slept. He knew he had remarkable children. Not many would venture into the unknown forest that was forbidden to enter for so long, much less sleep on the banks of an endless sea. The warm breeze of the sea was refreshing and peaceful. It was one of those moments that he didn't want to end, but he knew he should get some rest.

"Well, I'm ready for bed," Pred said, getting up and stretching from being so relaxed. He had said it loud enough to wake his children. "We will decide what to do tomorrow, tomorrow."

Both Jait and Tymber got up pretending that they weren't asleep and agreed that it was time to get some rest.

"Father, I am going to get my quilt and sleep here by the fire under the moon and stars," Tymber said, as she too stretched.

"Okay, goodnight, but keep the fire burning bright."

As Tymber lay down she thought she saw a small animal move from the light into the moon's shadow. Maybe that will be breakfast in the morning she thought as she once again fell sound asleep.

Later that night, Tymber woke up startled. She wasn't sure at first what woke her, until she realized her feet were wet. She gasped as she saw that the sea had risen to where she was sleeping. They had made the campfire a good thirty feet from the water and now that spot was underwater.

She looked at the tent and it was still another twenty feet away but didn't know if that was safe or not.

The moon had gone some distance in the sky but she felt like it was some time yet till dawn. She moved her quilt up to the tent. The sea had put the fire out so it wasn't a good idea to just lie out in the open. She went in the tent and woke her father.

"Father, the sea is rising and put the fire out. It got to my feet before I awoke."

"Are you all right?" he asked, in an almost frightened manner.

"Oh yes, Father, I am fine. I don't know if the sea is still rising but I thought I better tell you."

"Of course," he said.

He jumped up and stood at the door of the tent and watched the sea for a while. Tymber stood next to him. The waves of the sea were calm but it looked like, from what they could see in the moon-light, the water was still creeping up the shore.

"It has risen quite a bit in a short time," he finally said. "We need to move our tent uphill. Wake your brother."

They moved the tent to the top of a small rise near the bank of the river. That wasn't the best place but it was high enough and all they could see to do in the moonlight. They started another small fire for light and protection.

"Maybe I don't want my cabin quite so close to the sea," Tymber said. "Right here will be fine."

They could still see the sea from where they set up the tent, but it was fading as the moon moved behind them. Just the light from a thousand stars was all the light that was now on the sea.

None of them wanted to sleep anymore that night. They just sat and watched the fire and the sea beyond. Pred noticed that Tymber was turned away from the fire and looking up at the cliff face. After a while, Pred had to ask her what she was looking at.

"Turn your back to the fire so your eyes will adjust to the dark," she said, "and then look about a third of the way up the cliff to where that dark area is."

In a little while after his eyes adjusted he looked up the cliff face. "I don't see what you see, Tymber."

"Look closer."

She had not realized it but Jait was also adjusting his eyes to the dark. "It's a cave," Jait said, "with glow rocks."

Tymber looked over at Jait smiling.

"That's what I'm thinking too."

Pred never could see the faint glow of the glow rocks from the cave; however, he did have to admit that the dark area looked like a cave.

"So now we know what we are going to do tomorrow," she said, lying back down to rest.

"There goes another day," Pred said, shaking his head. "Sella will not be happy."

ELEVEN

Pred woke up just before dawn. He wanted to make sure he could use Tymber's trick of using the small hole in the tent to view the sun. He was very careful to be quiet not to wake his children, so it surprised him when he heard talking outside the tent. He jumped outside to find Jait and Tymber sitting by the fire preparing breakfast.

"I thought you two were still asleep. I was trying to be quiet."

"Us too," said Jait, with a smile.

Pred looked at the water line and it was up all the way to the base of the small hill they were on.

"I'm glad we moved this far uphill," he said, while judging about where the tent was set up at first.

"We would have woke up drowned," added Tymber.

"Father, why did the sea raise so much through the night?" she asked.

"Well that's a question for Drel; however, I don't know if he would have the answer to it either. We know that the water rises in Simpton Lake on a regular basis and then goes back down because of Adentta's moon. I am guessing this is the same reason on a larger scale. I think that moon's attract water somehow and pull it towards them."

"It must be powerful," Jait said, motioning with his hands the rising of so much water. "It would seem like the moons could pull us up if it could pull so much water up this high."

"That is too hard of a question for so early in the morning," Pred said, with a grin.

"I've been thinking about it all night," said Jait.

"I've been thinking about that cave all night," said Tymber. "I can still see the glow in the mouth of the cave. I'm not sure I can wait till dawn."

Tymber smiled at her father, but was unsure if he saw her in the dim firelight.

"I think I saw an easy way up to it if there aren't too many obstacles along the way."

"Tymber, you would think scaling the cliff face was an easy way to get up there, if that's what it took to get into that cave," Jait commented.

The sun started to rise over the sea. It was bright orange while near the horizon. Pred went to the tent to look at the sun through the hole in the tent, but stopped in his tracks.

"No need to look at it that way. I can see the Lost Moon at the edge of the sun directly. It appears to be getting very close judging from how large it looks."

Jait glanced up at the sun that was partially blocked by the moon.

"I'm ready for that thing to shoot by us and let us go back to normal life," he said to himself.

Tymber finished eating before the guys ever started. As soon as it was light enough, she headed toward the cliff face. The cave opening was about twenty–five feet above the beach. She could see a ledge in front of the cave that slanted somewhat downward and in the direction of View Hill.

She wandered too far ahead for Pred's liking and he asked her to wait for them. She stood there rather impatiently as the guys loaded up the rest of the supplies.

"Father, we can leave the supplies here with you while Jait and I go look for an easier way to that ledge. When we get up there, we will throw you a rope and lift them up."

The closest to the ground the ledge fell was about ten feet, so Jait and Tymber had to climb to that height. In no time, Jait and Tymber were lifting the supplies up to the ledge.

The cave opening was about ten feet high by ten feet wide. It didn't look that large from down below. They entered the cave and the floor sloped downhill sharply. They didn't need any torches because the glow rocks came nearly to the mouth of the cave.

"The sea air must agree with the glow rocks," Pred said. "They grow thicker here than in Stone Cabin Cave."

The cave floor leveled out and they had to bend down to progress as the chamber narrowed and the ceiling lowered. The number of glow rocks was declining as if the glow plants did not like to grow in the narrow chamber. There was a steady sound of dripping water, and in the dimmer light, it gave their progress an eerie feeling.

It was starting to get pretty dark when they could see more glowing ahead. They continued to walk toward the light. As far as Pred could tell they were heading under the foothills of South Guard Mountain.

The air in the cave smelled fresh and they could feel air movement of both cool and warm air. They traveled for a distance bent over before the chamber ceiling began to rise again and the faint glow of the rocks returned. Strangely, the air seemed to get warmer as they progressed. Just the opposite of what they would have expected.

Their feet started to get wet with running water as the passage-way became a small shallow stream but then soon opened up into a large tall chamber.

They stepped up out of the small stream onto the chamber floor. The floor was made of mostly dark, almost black, sandy soil. In places there were patches of grass growing.

The walls of the cavern were mostly dark brown with veins of black rock running through it. At times, there were patches of light gray rock that stuck out from the rest of the wall.

Columns of rock reached up to the high chamber ceiling. They looked like stone drippings from the ceiling that piled up into a pillar of stone, wide at the ceiling and the floor, and narrower in the middle.

A larger stream that ran through the chamber entered through what would be best described as an archway and exited in much the same way. The water flowed steady but not as swift as the stream in the other cavern.

As they approached the other side of the chamber, they could see that there were actually a series of chambers separated only by low areas of the ceiling.

They were in more awe over this cave as they were in the first, simply its larger size made this cave more impressive. Tymber bent over the larger stream and sipped the water. She expected it to be salty, but it was not. In fact it was pleasant tasting and was warmer than expected.

The only way into the next chamber, without getting wet, was a small walkway just wide enough for one person to fit through at a time.

Each chamber that they visited was warmer than the last, with less sand and more dirt.

"It would appear that the glow hairs, or whatever they're called, like growing and glowing in the warmer temperature," Jait said, in passing.

"I was thinking about that too," Pred said, stopping to examine some rocks. "The hairs are easy to see on these."

"Did you hear that?" asked Tymber. "I heard something that sounded like water gushing."

As they passed through the next few chambers, gushing sound became louder. They quickened their pace to see what it was. The passageway to the next chamber sloped down and steam was rising from the entrance.

When they entered, they saw a medium–sized chamber with a pool of water. One side of the pool was open and water flowed from it. Where the water came into the pool, was not obvious. They heard a rumble and out through the center of the pool shot a gush of water twenty feet into the air.

Steam sprayed in all directions. The splash of the spray was hot and they had to back away. The spray lasted for just a little while and then stopped.

"Now I have seen everything," Pred said, looking around the chamber.

The water–gush happened three more times before they gave up watching. It seemed to happen at regular intervals. They were wet from spray and heat in the room. The ceiling dripped with condensation.

"I'm getting hungry, lets leave," said Jait, walking back the way they came.

At the entrance to the chamber, Tymber turned to watch for the gush of water. She hoped to see the spray of water again before she left.

In a moment or two she heard the rumbling sound again and saw the gush of water.

Simply amazing, she thought.

They walked back to the large chamber they first entered and talked about all the places yet to explore. Pred, however, decided it was time to make their way back to their cabin. Nobody wanted to leave the wonderland they had discovered but each knew it was time to return. They would already be nearly a day late if they hurried.

"Let's try to make View Hill by dark," Pred said, while walking back up the passageway to the cave opening.

When they exited the cave it was much later than they expected. They did make it to View Hill before dark though.

Feeling tired, they all went to sleep early.

During the night, Tymber woke from noises she heard. It was a low humming and a gurgle sound. When she raised her head, she didn't hear it anymore. She was somewhat confused and when she laid her head back down she would hear it again. It was coming from the ground.

"Where could they be?" she asked, to nobody. Her two youngest daughters were walking next to her but they certainly didn't know the answer to the question.

"Mother, they are going to be all right," Ispis said, convincingly.

"I know. But they said they would be home last night."

Sella didn't know what else to do. She paced the floor all night waiting for Pred, Jait, and Tymber to return like they promised. At first light, she had Ispis and Janna up, dressed, fed, and heading out the door.

She thought if anybody would know what to do it would be Drel. She could ask Slippers to watch the kids and she could go into the forest and look for them.

"I should have brought a knife," she whispered, but the girls heard her anyway.

"Keeper needs a knife?" Janna asked, looking up at her mother as she ran next to her. Janna being only six years old was holding her mother's hand but was having trouble keeping up to her mother's hasty–paced walk. She had never seen her mother in such a hurry.

Ispis, an eight–year–old, was having almost as much trouble keeping up to her mother as Janna. Her light brown hair was wagging behind as she ran along side. She had to stop quickly to retrieve her green bow that had fallen from her hair. Her mother stopped, too, so she could pull Ispis' hair back and tie the bow.

They passed by Slipper's cabin and they were grateful she wasn't outside and didn't notice them going by. She didn't have time to socialize.

As she entered the field just past Slipper's cabin, she realized that she had never been past her cabin before and wasn't really sure how much farther Drel's cabin was.

"What on earth is Drel going to think when I show up at his door with two children?" Sella didn't usually talk to herself, but she did find it comforting this morning.

"Have I ever met Keeper, Mother?" asked Janna.

"I'm sure you have," said Sella. "It's been a long time since we had Drel over and you may have been too young to remember him."

She came to the last cabin, so she knew it must be Drel's.

She stood on the porch for a second before knocking on the door.

What if he isn't awake yet? It would be rude to wake him up without a good reason. For a moment she regretted coming, and then she knocked on the door.

Drel came to the door within just a moment. It had become common place for him to be surprised at who was at the door. This morning didn't seem to be any different.

"Sella?" he said after a moment of shock. "Good morning. What can I do for you? Oh please excuse me. Come in, come in and sit down."

Sella shook her head and Drel thought that she might start to tear.

"Pred said he would be back by last night," she said. "They have not yet returned. I am trying not to get too excited because I know they went to explore, but I just don't know what to do. What if something has happened to them?"

"Calm down, Sella," he said. "I am sure there is nothing wrong. Pred wanted to go to the river and explore and Tymber said she wanted to go all the way to the end of the river. It probably was much further than they expected and took longer."

Sella decided she would sit down at the table. The two girls looked up at Keeper, as to get permission to sit. Drel nodded to let them know that it was all right.

"Thank you, Keeper," Ispis said, smiling as they sat down. Ispis reminded Drel of Tymber when she smiled.

When he thought about Tymber he had a twinge of worry, as well. She was too young to be off in the woods. What was Pred thinking taking her with him?

Now he was thinking silly. If anybody could take care of themselves it was Pred, Jait, and Tymber.

While Drel was trying to calm Sella down, they heard a rumble that sounded like thunder. Then came a second rumble, then came a vibration, and then came a shake.

"Groundshake!" Sella screamed.

She grabbed the two girls and headed out the door.

The shake didn't last long and by the time Sella got outside it had stopped.

Drel joined her outside just to settle her down a little.

"It seems to be over now," Drel said, as he walked over to them making sure they were unhurt.

The girls were holding on to their mother tightly not understanding what had just happened. The fear was plain in their eyes.

"Drel it's that moon that is causing all this trouble isn't it? It has a curse on us."

He glanced up at the sun that was still rising in the east. The top right quarter was clearly being blocked by the Lost Moon.

"I'm not sure I know what to believe Sella. I would like to believe that it isn't a curse, but a science we don't understand. But I may be the one that is fooled."

Drel didn't want to cause Sella any further alarm, but he noticed that the birds squawked and chirped and seemed confused as they fluttered about.

Sella held the kids close. She tried not to show how upset she was to her children, but it was her children that comforted her.

"Its okay, Mother," said Ispis, "it's over now."

The moonlight was bright enough that they could hurry on their way. Pred knew Sella would be a nervous wreck and didn't want her to suffer. He was hoping to get home before she woke up.

The stone cabin was very comfortable last night and they had gotten a good rest. He knew it was perhaps foolish to start the trip home in the dark but it would not be long till dawn.

The sun had come up during their travel and a short rest was needed, so they stopped for a moment. They were talking about the cave at the sea when all the birds at once took flight. It seemed like something had scared them. The trio stood and pulled their bows as they looked around. They didn't see anything. That's when they felt the groundshake. Every animal squawked in surprise by the event, including Pred, Jait, and Tymber.

It didn't last long, but the feeling that the groundshake was just the beginning of troubling times filled their souls. They couldn't see the sun through the trees, but they knew the Lost Moon was there too.

They grabbed their gear and picked up the pace of getting back to their cabin.

When they got back to Drel's cabin, they saw Sella standing outside holding the two girls.

Sella saw them and smiled with a couple of tears. She set the two girls down who ran to their father.

Pred quickly scooped up his two youngest girls and continued to walk to Sella.

"I've been so worried, Pred," Sella said when the lump in her throat went away.

Pred looked up and was able to see the sun for the first time that day. He shook his head, put the girls down, and held Sella in his arms.

"Everything is going to be fine now. We are back."

Drel invited them all inside and made hot root tea, hen's eggs, steer meat, and sliced apples. Well he tried to do the cooking, but Sella insisted on doing most of the work, including adding biscuits to the menu.

The travelers couldn't remember when they had a nicer meal. They sat around the table and talked of the mountains and finding the sea and another cave and all the wonders inside the cave by the sea.

Pred apologized countless times for being gone six days instead of five. He explained that while they were there they had to explore. In fact, they could have stayed there for days longer and not have seen everything.

His younger girls sat in awe as he told them of the things that they had seen. He described how beautiful the sea was at night and the mountains that reached to the clouds. He told them of the large chambers in the cave and how the stream flowed down deeper into the cave and how hot water sprayed out and warmed the cave.

Pred promised them that when they got older he would bring them to the sea cavern to see all the beautiful sites. Sella looked at him in dismay, but then smiled knowing that they would enjoy a trip with their father when they were older. Secretly though she hoped that by that time, they would have forgotten about the cavern by the sea.

"If we choose to go to the sea cavern often," Tymber said, "maybe we could build a cabin or two along the way as stopovers, to make the travel there easier."

Pred looked at his oldest daughter and wondered how many cabins she has asked to be built in the last few days.

Drel was about to tell Tymber that he too would like to go to the sea cavern, when there was a knock at the door. After the ground-shake, he was not surprised to have visitors.

When he opened the door, a small boy panting for air stood there.,

"Keeper, I am a runner for Messenger, I have been told to ask you to please come to a leader meeting at midday today."

He seemed quite proud to have gotten the entire message out in a single breath.

"I have been to Hunter's and there is no one there. I have been told that you may know where he is so I may tell him of the meeting."

"Yes I do, please come in."

The runner was so happy to see that Hunter was close by.

"Hunter, I am a runner for Messenger, I have been told to ask you to please come to a leader meeting at midday today."

"Runner, please tell Messenger that we will be coming to the meeting," said Hunter.

"Thank you very much," Runner said, as he was leaving.

TWELVE

Pred and Drel were surprised as they entered the Hall that nobody was in the large meeting room. The runner that was at Drel's cabin came from the back of the Hall and motioned them to go to the small meeting room. The door was closed so they knocked and were let in by Leader.

"Come in come in," he said, as he showed them where to sit. Also in the room were Farmer, Builder, Crafter, and Crops.

They didn't seem to be in the mood to be social. A glance up from their thoughts and a quick smile was all they offered.

Pred had a quick thought about the Lost Moon causing people to change, too. These men sitting around the table in the past could talk for hours about practically nothing. Their silence was somewhat ominous.

"I'm sure you know why we have asked you two here," Leader started. "With the return of the Lost Moon, we are experiencing the same things as during its last visit. The people are scared and that groundshake this morning didn't help. Every time we walk outside and see the sun, we are reminded of its presence.

"I've called for you to help explain what has happened and to try and anticipate what is going to happen.

"Keeper, you tried to tell us that things were not right at Plant. You obviously have the best ideas about the outer objects. Do you have any ideas on what is happening and what will happen next?"

Drel was not looking forward to explaining his theories of the outer objects and their motions. He was not sure what the men at the table knew about outer object motion during normal times.

"Remember, everything I say is just my theory," he started. "I have little or no proof of what I say. To be brief, I believe that the Lost Moon is moving towards Adentta. Each day it appears larger because of its movement toward us. It is blocking more than a quarter of the sun now and at some point, it may block the sun completely."

The room became extremely quiet. Even Pred had not heard Drel say that the moon may completely block the sun.

"Could that moon crash into Adentta?" asked Leader, looking at Drel.

Drel didn't know how to answer that question. He looked at Leader and then to everyone seated at the table.

"I don't know. I have tried to imitate what I think are the movements of Adentta and the moon and I just don't know that answer. I'm thinking that if the moon appears to move off from covering the sun as it grows larger, we have a better chance of it missing us."

Pred felt very uneasy. He had not thought much about the Lost Moon blocking the sun completely, or of it hitting Adentta.

"Of course, those things are the worst things that can happen," Drel continued. "More likely, is that it will go by us like it did five years ago."

Farmer sat up in his chair to speak, but looked like he was searching for appropriate words.

"The crops and herds have been slow to grow. You are telling me that there are worse days ahead for growing the food for the village.

Storer has told me that we have enough grain to last till harvest, but we need to have an excellent harvest to last for a complete year. We will have no reserves this year. If the Lost Moon is going to block the sun but move past Adentta, how long will it interrupt growing?"

"Those are things that I can not guess at," said Keeper. "It may just last a day or so and then move away so the sun will begin to shine again."

"I think everyone is missing the point," Crops yelled, as he jumped into the conversation. "The Lost Moon, if it is the same moon as five years ago, is not acting like it did last time. It was never very close to the sun, and it was visible only at night. I think that it is a different moon and we don't have a clue what is going to happen, including hitting Adentta and killing us all."

"Crops..." Drel began.

"Crops," Leader said, "we know that what we are saying are guesses as to what will happen and the very worst, may happen. But our jobs as leaders in the village are to plan for the worst, and the best. We have planted all the fields we can, we will harvest as much crops as we can, then we have done our best, regardless of what happens."

Crops looked down at the table and turned somewhat red knowing that he should not have had an outburst as he did. His age was in his eyes and the stress of this planting season was obvious. He had done an excellent job getting all the fields planted and most of the crops were doing well. The crops were maturing, but at a slightly smaller size than normal. Crops took that as being a bad reflection on him, when actually, it had nothing to do with how he farmed.

"The herds are growing slowly," said Farmer, "because they have to graze the grass in the small fields that we did not use for crops."

Farmer wanted to make sure that everyone understood that the grains were a priority over meat. He added that the vegetables were growing good, but ripening slowly. The fruit and nut trees seem to be the furthest ahead in development.

Leader got up and looked over the group. "I think we need to make a plan in case the moon blocks the sun for days at a time. We should plan on being in the dark.

"Crafter, I need you to find help in making additional sapburn for the lanterns and wax for candles to add to Storer's supply."

"Without the sun, the crops will not grow," Crops said, with a shake of his head. "We will not be ready for harvest before winter."

"Hunter," Leader said, with resolve, "speed up with the fishing. We need to supplement our reserves immediately."

"Very well," Pred responded.

"The winter was longer this year and I believe that the summer will be longer as well," Keeper added, reluctantly. "That should give the crops and herds a little extra time to mature."

"Hunter," Leader said, "in your exploring I have heard that you have found rocks that glow in the dark. If the moon blocks the sun we could use those rocks in our cabins. Bring some people with you and…"

"Leader, I would be glad to get the rocks you ask for, but we found that they don't last but a few days outside of the caves. As you know, it is not the rocks that glow but the hair–like plants that grow on the rock. I think that those plants need the moist air in the caves to live. It looks like they are just living on the rock and probably gets water from the air, similar to the moss we find growing on rocks."

A boom of thunder was heard in the distance. It made every-one a little nervous. It sounded too much like the rumble of the groundshake. The rain started moments later and everyone was glad to know that it was indeed thunder.

The wind started howling and the rain was blowing hard against the walls and windows. Inside the nearly empty Fendal Betalum Community Hall the sound seemed to echo.

Just as quickly as the storm had started, it ended.

There was a knock on the door. After receiving permission, a runner came in.

"Farmer," he said. "Fisher told me to come and tell you that the fish pond has gone over its banks."

"Thank you, Runner, please tell him I will come and help," Farmer replied. "It is happening just as it did five years ago. I must leave and try to save or harvest any fish that has been pushed from the pond. There is no need to waste any."

Farmer got up and rushed from the room.

"Please everyone think of things we can do during this troubled time," pleaded Leader. "We have to show the village that we have confidence that everything will turn out well and that we have plans that will get us through these difficulties."

Everyone left except for Pred and Drel.

"Completely block the sun?" said Pred. "Crash into us? You haven't talked much about those things happening. I was thinking it would pass and everything would go back to normal."

"Those are just the worst things, Pred. I'm not saying that they won't happen, but not likely."

"That's good to hear."

"Honestly the biggest worry I have is that the Lost Moon will get closer to us this time. I'm not sure what that will do to our year."

"How much longer do you expect this year to be?" asked Pred, tapping his fingers on the table as he sat thinking.

"I guessed eighteen days at the beginning of Plant, but now I think even longer. When I checked the shadow dials the last time, they showed that the sun had just got to longest day. That means fifteen days longer between shortest day and longest day compared to six years ago, or thirty days longer for the whole year."

"That's a long time, but it doesn't mean that just the winters are longer but the summers too."

"That's right, I think," Keeper said, knowing it was just another guess.

"Why were the days of the year continuing to get longer if the Lost Moon went by five years ago?" Pred asked.

"That's a real good question, Pred. I wish I had some true answers for you, but as far as I can tell when the Lost Moon went by five years ago, it left a significant and lasting effect on us. The best way to explain it, I think, is to look at Simpton Lake. You know as well as anybody that the lake rises and falls with the movement of our moon. Well I think that the Lost Moon has an effect, or attraction, or a force on Adentta in much the same manner.

"I think the way that Adentta went around the sun was circular and took the same time each year, but now it is more of a slow spiral outward getting farther from the sun each year."

"That doesn't sound good."

"What's your plans now, Pred?" Drel asked, wanting to change the subject.

"I'm really not sure. I may be building Tymber some cabins."
They both chuckled over that.

"It looks like we will need even more fish with the pond going over the banks. I will pack fish curing salts and head to the sea. I think there may be very large fish there. We can catch and cure them for travel back to the village. I should think that Jait, Tymber, and I should be able to pack a large load, if we catch them."

"That might be worth having other men go with you and pack larger amounts back."

"I think the three of us should go to see what's in the sea first. What we catch may not even be edible."

"How will you catch the fish in the sea?"

"I think we'll throw the net to catch small fish and then use them as bait on hooks for the larger fish. I will ask Smith if larger hooks could be made before we go, just in case we get into some very large fish.

They left the meeting hall and Pred went by Smith's metal craftery. He told Smith of what he needed, and to Pred's surprise it didn't take that long for him to craft five large hooks. As he explained to Pred, he had the materials on hand to make hooks; he just had to make them larger.

He then went to Storer and got thin strong twine and some curing salt. Of course Storer had to talk about everything that had been happening. That took longer than it did to make five large hooks.

That evening he told Jait and Tymber to make ready to go back to the sea the next morning.

"What if there are more groundshakes?" Sella asked Pred, as he was preparing to leave. "I have never seen the girls as frightened as when the ground shook."

"I can't keep the ground from shaking Sella. I can however help the village eat. We may be in more trouble feeding the village than we originally thought."

"I'll be back in a little while," Tymber said, as she went through the room like a whirlwind.

"She must have thought of supplies we need," said Pred, trying to change the subject if possible.

"Don't change the subject," Sella said.

Pred looked up at her and shook his head.

"Sella, the best thing to do in a groundshake is either go outside if you have time, or get under the table to keep things from falling on you and the girls. If I was here in the village, I would be gone most of the time anyway."

"I know—at night I will worry about the shakes the most."

"We don't even know if there will be any more shakes. The village needs help and I'm the one they chose. I have to go and do my job."

"I know Pred. I just hate it."

"I'm going to send Drel here to spend the nights with you and the girls."

"He's not going to do that."

"He's already agreed."

"I don't want to cause trouble, Pred."

"You're not. He said he would be glad to. In fact, he insisted. That will ease everyone's mind."

Pred did a few more things around the cabin and then left for a while. He had to go ask Drel if he would come and stay with Sella and the girls. He knows that he will agree to help.

Pred almost passed up Drel's dial field. He didn't recognize it planted in crops. Drel was in the field standing over his dial looking intently at it and didn't notice Pred approaching.

"You look serious," Pred said, as he approached close enough for Drel to hear.

Drel looked a little startled.

"Well I'm getting more confused by the day."

"You looking at the dials and confused doesn't sound good."

"You see this line on the dial?" Drel pointed to the smallest circle on the dial. "Well the sun has never been closer to the center of the dial than that line. That line indicates that it's the longest day of the year."

"The shadow is past that line," Pred said, as he looked closely at the dial.

Drel looked up at Pred.

"Yes, and I don't have a clue what it means."

They stood in silence for a while looking at the dial.

"It's such a dim shadow with the Lost Moon blocking part of the sun," Drel said as he marked where the shadow is on the dial. "It's sometimes hard to see."

The two started walking towards Drel's cabin.

"So what can I do for you today, Pred?"

"I have a big favor to ask," Pred began, in a hesitating manner. He was never fond of asking people for help. "In the morning, Jait, Tymber, and I are heading back to the sea to fish. We will be gone for days. Sella and the girls are worried about more groundshakes. And, I was wondering if you would stay at our cabin during the nights while we're gone."

Pred looked over at Drel for a reaction but got none.

"I think that's an excellent idea," he replied. "Sella and the girls will certainly be scared at night with the possibility of more groundshakes. And besides, they would probably show up at my door anyway."

Drel smiled but it was unnoticed by Pred.

"I'm so glad you will do this." He looked at Drel and added, "And Sella thinks that you have already insisted on staying there."

"If it makes you feel better, I insisted to do it yesterday."

Drel and Pred walked to Drel's cabin mostly in silence.

They sat down on the porch and started rocking.

"It has to mean that Adentta is not going around the sun like it used to," Drel said, breaking the silence.

"All I know is that we need to do whatever we can and hope for the best."

The next morning Pred, Jait, and Tymber headed back to the forest. They told Sella they would be back in no longer than seven days.

They stopped at the stone cabin to rest for a few moments. It was starting to feel like their second home. From the stone cabin it is nearly two days travel to the sea, but they had to hurry to get there that quick.

They ate a quick lunch from their backpacks.

"Something about the river has been bothering me," Pred said, out of the blue. "The river at the sea had more water in it than it did up river."

Jait and Tymber sat and thought about it.

"A lot more water." Jait said. "I never really thought about it."

"I think we missed a stream running into the river when we detoured over View Hill. There could be a deep hole with fish in it where the two join."

Pred looked at Jait and Tymber for a reaction. He knew that Tymber was in a hurry to get back to the cavern by the sea. Normally, she would be all set for exploring new territory but didn't really want to delay.

"I think we need to follow the river all the way to the sea," said Jait, getting his backpack on. "I'm ready."

Tymber was more reluctant than Jait about the need to follow the river, but agreed that they needed to do that first. Tymber was afraid that if they found a good fishing place, they wouldn't be going to the cavern and fish in the sea.

"So it's agreed that we follow the river all the way to the sea to find the other water source?"

Both his children nodded.

"Well let's go."

They traveled as fast as they could and rested only briefly. Going down the river to the sea was going to take longer and they wanted to try to make up the time.

It took them till dusk to get to the furthest they had been down river. They decided to camp the night there and hopefully they will either find a good fishing spot or be at the sea by nightfall the next day.

That night was uneventful except for a ground vibration that all three felt when they laid down. It wasn't a groundshake just a vibration, but it lasted most of the night. They didn't think that anybody not lying on the ground would even know it was vibrating.

The next morning they headed down river. They remembered why they had left the river the first time. It was very difficult travel. The banks were high and with heavy underbrush.

The travel was slow until midmorning when the banks of the river widened out and the underbrush lessened. Ahead they could see what appeared to be where the river took the wide bend to the right, the bend that wrapped around View Hill and aimed the river at the sea.

"At the bend in the river, let's break for lunch," Pred said, as he stopped to wipe the sweat off his face.

"I was hoping you were going to say that, Father," Tymber answered. "I hope the rest of the travel is easier than this has been."

At the bend in the river, they stopped and ate from the food that Sella had packed.

"Do you hear running water?" Jait said, standing up.

The other two stopped chewing and sat and listened to it too.

"That's probably the stream we've been looking for," Pred said, continuing to eat.

Tymber finished eating first and got up and walked around look-ing at all the animal tracks in the sand. She found what she thought were probably wolf tracks, but she was not sure. For some reason, she thought it best not to show them to her father. She walked down river waiting for the others to finish. The farther she walked the louder the running water became. She could tell by the sound of the water they would be spending at least the rest of the day there.

"I think Tymber is trying to tell us to hurry," said Jait, setting down his empty plate. "She thinks that we will hurry to catch up to her."

All of a sudden they heard Tymber scream.

"Father! Jait! Come quick!"

They grabbed their bows and quivers and ran over to her. She was running back towards them looking like she had just seen a ghost.

"Tracks ... up there, tracks," was all she could say.

"Calm down, Tymber. What did you see?" Pred was trying to get her to take deep breaths so she could explain.

"What kind of tracks did you see?" asked Jait. He understood what she had said.

"People!"

THIRTEEN

Pred and Jait ran with Tymber over to where she saw the tracks. The tracks were all over the place, definitely the tracks of people. There were many people that had been there and not long ago. The tracks showed where they had walked up river and then back down.

The trio followed the tracks back down river and came to the source of the sound. The sound was the rapids of a stream flowing into the river. The stream had more water flowing from it than the whole river had before the stream.

"So it's true about the stories of other people far from our village," said Jait. "Of course, we knew it was possible ever since we found the stone cabin."

"They wear a different type of boot," said Pred, as he examined one of the tracks. "It looks more like a slipper than a boot."

"It looks like you were right about the deep hole where the two streams run together," Jait said, looking out on an area that could almost be considered to be a small lake.

"Those people come here to fish I'm sure," Pred said, sounding rather disappointed. "I sure don't want to fish at someone else's place of fishing."

"We need to go meet these people," said Tymber. "We need to let them know we are here, we are friendly, and we won't fish or hunt in their areas."

"I agree, Tymber," he said. "We have never met anybody from somewhere else before and we need to make sure that they know we mean them no harm."

"It looks like they have a trail going away from the river, past the rapids, and up that stream," Tymber said, pointing in the direction of the trail she found.

They stood looking at the trail leading upstream, and then down at the tracks in the sand. They thought about just going to the sea, but when they were ready to go, they all moved to the trail leading upstream to meet the new people.

While walking down the trail they could tell that it followed the stream and at times there were forks in the trail that led down to the stream. The trio chose to follow what appeared to be the main trail.

The tree canopy was closed for the most part so the walk down the trail was in the shade. The forest floor was scattered with little yellow wild flowers, which they decided was the source of a very pleasant sweet fragrance.

The trees were larger than any they had seen on their trips so far. Both Jait and Tymber could hold hands and not reach around some of them. They didn't seem to have ever harvested any of the trees in the area. There were many small forest animals that ran through the very high treetops and there were sections of the forest that looked like the sun never reached the forest floor.

"We have found that a lot of the stories we have heard for years are based on truth," said Pred, thinking about the stories he had heard of giant trees in areas of the forest.

"Do you think these are the people that built the stone cabin?" asked Tymber, not really expecting an answer.

"We will just have to ask them," Jait replied.

They continued until they came to the first fork in the trail that went away from the stream.

"Any guesses as to which way we should go?" Pred asked, as they all looked down each way.

"I think that would depend on if you want to meet a few people or a lot at once," answered Tymber. "I think that fork probably goes to just a cabin or two. The other way goes to more people, judging by how traveled the trails appear."

"Let's go to where we think there are more people," Pred answered.

They continued on the trail of most traveled and it wasn't long when the trail bent away from the stream and they walked out into an open field.

"This field had been planted this spring but died," Pred commented, as they looked around at the dead sprigs of wheat. "I wonder why it had never been replanted."

Ahead they could see a couple of stone cabins. The trail centered between them.

"I see their cabins are made of stone," said Jait.

The cabins looked very similar to the stone cabin that they had found. They were constructed of large stone of many colors. They had wood porches with a wood roof, but that was all the wood that was visible. Their age was not easy to tell. Stone did not age like wood did.

They had gardens behind their cabins along with a cow or two and a chicken hut, much like they had in their own village.

"Do we stop at those cabins, Father?" asked Tymber.

"I think we should, but I hate to just knock on their door."

They didn't have to knock on any door. Out of one cabin came a lady and out of the other came an elderly man. The two people talked to each other pointing and looking at the trio as they approached. They seemed to disagree as to what to do.

Out of the cabin with the lady, a child came out and ran farther down the trail obviously he was going to get someone.

"Just don't look aggressive," said Pred. They continued to approach the cabins.

The lady looked like she was getting a little nervous and stood in the doorway half in and half out of the cabin staring at the visitors.

Pred stopped so Jait and Tymber followed his lead.

"They don't look like they are about to attack us or anything," he said. "Of course they probably don't get many strangers coming up to their door, so they may not be prepared."

"Father," said Tymber, "I am going to lay down my backpack and bow and approach them while you two stay behind. I think that would be a sign of friendship."

"I can ready my bow in a flash if you need me to, Sis," said Jait.

Before Pred could object, Tymber was on her way to talk to the lady at the cabin. She stopped on the trail just before the walk up to the cabin. She held out her hands palm up.

"Hello, my name is Tymber. We are from another village."

"Greetings," was the lady's reply, as she looked at Pred and Jait, then in the other direction further down the trail, hoping somebody was coming. She looked to the old man rocking in his chair on his porch across the trail, and then back to Tymber.

The old man across the trail stopped rocking for a second and hollered to the lady.

"I told you they would come! It was just a matter of time." He then continued to rock.

The lady saw Tymber smiling and smiled back.

"We are from up the river. We live in a village with other people.

"What is your name?" Tymber asked the lady trying to be friendly.

"I am Goshenta," was her response. She looked back at Pred and Jait.

To Tymber, Goshenta seemed to be about the same age as her mother with slightly graying hair. She did not seem friendly and she was very nervous. Her smile, however, was bright as if it was well used.

"That is my father, Pred, and my brother, Jait."

Tymber looked at them and motioned them to approach.

Pred and Jait picked up Tymber's gear and slowly approached to where Tymber was standing.

The lady quickly went in the cabin and shut the door. Pred stood by Tymber and waited for her to open the door again, which she did.

"Father, Jait, this is Goshenta."

"Hello," they both said.

"Greetings," Goshenta said again, nervously glancing down the trail.

"I told you they would come," said the old man, again continuing his rocking.

"That is Ger," said Goshenta, looking and pointing to the old man. "He is my father, but don't pay any attention to what he says. He is very old and thinks and says crazy things."

"My father does that too," said Tymber, pointing to Pred trying to get Goshenta to laugh.

But Goshenta's thoughts were towards the people coming up the trail and didn't hear Tymber.

At least twenty people were coming up the trail towards them. They all carried shovels, rakes, and hoes. Jait gripped his bow tighter and looked to his father to see what to do next.

Pred walked to the middle of the trail and laid down all that he carried. Tymber did the same. Jait stayed where he was and held on to his bow.

The group of people approached closer and saw Pred and Tymber standing with their belongings on the ground. The leader of the group held back his arms as to keep them from approaching closer.

The group did stop. The leader laid down his shovel. He turned around and spoke to his friends. In a moment or two, another person laid down a hoe. The leader then turned back towards Pred and the two approached, the others nervously talking behind them.

"Smile, Father," Tymber whispered. "to them you look pretty scary."

Pred, of course, had to smile after his daughter told him he looked scary.

When the leader got close enough to speak, they stopped.

"Greetings," said the leader. "If you come in peace, welcome."

Pred nodded slightly.

"We indeed have come in peace and we look forward to meeting our new friends." He gestured to indicate the people that stayed behind.

The leader looked down at the two bows and arrows on the ground and then to Jait who still had a grip on his bow.

"We are hunters of our village." Pred said, worried about the appearance of the bows. "We use the bows for hunting and for protection when we are in the forest. We come from upriver and didn't know anyone was here until we saw your tracks by the river."

"Why does he still hold his bow?" the leader pointed at Jait.

"Why do they still hold their tools?" Pred pointed to the group of men.

The leader gave Pred a slight smile.

"My name is Midton, leader of Hantfel. This is Trent, my son." He pointed to the person standing next to him.

"I am Pred, Hunter of our village and this is Tymber, my daughter, and that is Jait, my son."

"Goshenta, please go and juice a drink for our new friends."

She disappeared into the stone cabin and Midton invited them to sit on her porch while she made the drinks. Pred, Jait, and Tymber sat down and Midton and Trent joined them. The group of people kept their distance and didn't seem to want to approach further.

"I told you it was close enough for them to just jump over and kill us all," the old man shouted.

"How far away do you live," Midton asked, trying his best to ignore the old man.

"We have traveled nearly two days," said Pred, looking up at the sun which was nearly setting.

"What do you think of our visitor?" asked Midton, also looking at the sun and the Lost Moon.

"I think that it will cause us a lot of trouble before it leaves," Pred answered, perhaps too honestly.

"We have had ground rumbles that have caused us great concern, and overflowing of our streams and lakes. We believe them to be caused by the Visiting Moon."

"All those things have happened in our village as well."

Goshenta came out with the juiced drinks. The travelers were anxious to see what it was that they were going to be drinking.

They took a sip and realized they had never tasted anything like it before and it was delicious.

"You must show us how to make such a delicious drink," said Tymber, to Goshenta. "We have never had this before. It must be made from a fruit we do not have."

When Tymber said that, she remembered the orchard that they found of fruit trees they did not recognize. She hoped that the fruit was the same as this drink.

"It is just made with water, lemon, and honey."

"I have never heard of lemon before," Tymber answered.

They sat for a little while drinking the lemon drink.

"We need to move on," said Pred, setting down his empty glass. "We are on our way to the sea."

"I have been to the sea a few times in my life. You will never make it there by dark. Please stay with us for the night. We have an empty cabin just over the rise."

Pred looked at Tymber and Jait who nodded in agreement, and Pred accepted the invitation.

Midton led them to a small stone cabin not far from where they were. He told them that he would return after they had time to rest.

In a little while, they were greeted by a young lady carrying a pot of food. She introduced herself as Aliptis. Tymber introduced herself and then her father and Jait. She smiled and told them all greetings.

Aliptis apologized for only having one pot that she could share. She explained that the crops have been bad and that vegetables were in short supply.

Tymber told her that it was the same at her village and that everyone is blaming the Lost Moon. Aliptis looked confused when Tymber said Lost Moon.

"Oh, the Visiting Moon," she responded. "That is what we call it."

Aliptis laid the pot of food on the table, found bowls in a cabinet and dished up a very delicious smelling vegetable stew. She took a loaf of fresh bread from the bag she carried and laid it in the center of the table.

Tymber noticed that she was looking at Jait often and smiling. Her brother, however, seemed to be more interested in the food.

Tymber asked Aliptis to sit and eat with them but she declined any food; she did sit down with them at the table.

Aliptis had the darkest hair that Tymber had ever seen. It was as close to black as Tymber guessed was possible. She wore it straight down to her waist. Her dark eyes showed of someone that was happy most of the time and enjoyed talking with people. She wasn't much taller standing up as Jait was sitting down in the kitchen chair.

She told of how she was learning the craft of clothier and that she had started making much of the clothes for the village.

That surprised Tymber. She didn't seem much older than her. Maybe the same age as Jait and already was good enough in her craft to make the village clothes.

Goshenta knocked on the door and then came in with lemon drinks. She also sat at the table and talked while the Trelops ate. They told of their life, which did not seem too different than Tymber's life. They did question why a girl was hunting in the forest. Tymber could only answer with the truth: Because she wanted to.

After the delicious meal, they continued to sit and talk and tell stories of each others lives. They realized the confusion with the word village. This village simply called it Hantfel, named after the person in their history who started the village.

Pred wondered if that was one of the words he did not know in the writings or on the forest sketch.

Goshenta told them that there had not been much fish caught in the stream or the lake these days. They worried about feeding Hantfel. Many of the people did not think they would have enough food to last through next winter, with many of their crops dying with the late frosts.

Tymber told her that was why they were fishing and hunting. They were trying to add to their foods.

Midton returned as he said he would. A man named Batton came with him. He was introduced as Teacher of Hantfel.

When they came, Goshenta and Aliptis said their farewells, and left. They knew that their leader was going to want to talk to them in private.

Tymber walked with them to the door and thanked them for such a lovely meal.

"I hope you will be coming back to Hantfel soon," Aliptis said.

"I hope so too," answered Tymber. "Now that we know we have friends outside our village, I am sure that we will."

Midton and Batton wanted to know more about Pred's ideas as to the Visiting Moon. They sat and talked for hours on the subject. Pred told him what has happened and what he thought would happen.

It seemed that Batton had similar ideas as to what was happening, but clearly Keeper had a better guess of what will happen than what Batton did. Batton did think what Pred said helped explain things.

Midton didn't seem any happier about what Pred said than Leader did when Keeper told him his theories.

"Midton, do you have hunters in the forest as we do?" Tymber asked, not knowing if she should ask their Leader that or not.

"Tymber, we have discussed that but we do not right now. Our herds are holding up good, so far. It is the grains and vegetables that we are very worried about. Much of our crops failed this spring because of the late frosts and freezes. We had to replant and didn't have enough seed to replant all the fields.

"We did have fishers but they have since turned to herders. The fishing is very bad. I have not had a meal of fish all season.

"Teacher, you and I need to leave so they can rest for their journey in the morning."

"Midton, on our way here," said Jait, "nearly a day and half in travel, we passed a deserted stone cabin. It is built as these are built here. Do you know of that stone cabin? It is upriver and then up a stream from here?"

"I'm sorry Jait I don't know anyone outside the area of Hantfel. We have stories of other people, but you three are the first I have met."

Pred got up and went to Tymber's backpack and pulled out the copy of the sketch he found at the stone cabin.

"I found this sketch at the stone cabin that Jait talked about. We think we know what some of these symbols are, and of course we recognize more on the sketch than we did when we started.

"I would like you to look at it and see if you recognize some of the symbols or writing. Some of what is on the map and in the writings are not written the way we do."

Midton took the sketch from Pred and laid it on the table.

"This is how we traveled to here."

Pred ran his finger along the trail they traveled from the stone cabin to Hantfel.

Leader asked Teacher if he understood the writing that is at the top and bottom of the sketch.

To the surprise of Pred, Jait, and Tymber, he did not know those words. In fact, like Drel and Pred, he was not sure that they were words.

Somewhat disappointed Pred put the sketch back into Tymber's backpack. He was hoping that the maker of the stone cabin had come from this area and that Leader or Teacher could help them with those words.

"The people of that stone cabin must have come from somewhere else," Pred said, disappointedly and somewhat surprised.

"That cabin is still a mystery then," said Jait.

"In our history, we are told that at one time Hantfel was not located here. It says that we lived at the base of a great mountain far to the north."

"Why did your village move?" Tymber asked.

"Well, Tymber," Teacher began, "it is not well written as to the exact reason, but in the writings it is said that two great men lived in the village, each desiring to be leader. They had a contest to see which man would stay and lead their people and which one would leave.

"The two men were named Vallend and Hantfel. The loser and anyone that followed him would leave never to return. A man by the name of Hantfel moved here with his people."

They all smiled knowing that Hantfel had lost the contest and they are descendants of the people that followed him.

"I have not been many places," said Pred. "I do not know of a mountain to the north. Does it have a name?"

Midton looked at Teacher to see if he remembered the name of the mountain.

"The name is Pointer Mountain," he said.

"One last thing before you go," said Pred. "One day you must teach me how you make the mud you use to lay these stones of the cabin together. We have a mud mixture, but yours looks like it would last forever."

"I will do that my friend," said Midton, as he got up. "Now we must go."

"We will leave before the sun is up," said Pred. "Thank you very much for the use of this cabin, and I hope to see you again soon."

They shook hands and Midton and Batton left.

"Get out your maps and let's mark this village and their stream on our maps," said Pred. "It seemed like from the river we moved mostly north and a little east to get here. This is about where I think we are."

He pointed to his map and Tymber and Jait agreed that that would be close to where they were.

"We have had a long day and we have much to talk about," Pred said. "Let's start the talk in the morning on the way to the sea."

They nodded and lay down to sleep.

The sun was almost up when they woke. Upon leaving they found two water pouches on the porch, one with lemon juice and one with honey.

FOURTEEN

It was well after midday before they again reached the sea. They sat at almost the same place they were at the last time they were there and ate the last of the food that had been packed for them.

Tymber was anxious to get back into the cavern, but knew that she needed to help with the fishing first. There would be plenty of time in the cavern this trip, and in fact that's where she planned to sleep at nights.

Jait got the fishing nets out and Tymber was hacking down a few small saplings to use as poles. Pred was attaching a medium sized hook to the twine. At the end of the line he tied a small rock as a weight.

"Well let's see what kind of fish we can catch today," Jait said, throwing the net into the sea for the first time.

To Jait's surprise it took a few throws to net some bait fish. They did not recognize any of the fish he netted, and was very careful handling them. They didn't know if any of them had teeth but most of their fins were very sharp.

They each baited their hook with small net fish and threw their lines in the water.

"The last one to catch a fish cooks dinner," Tymber said, as she leaned her pole on a rock outcropping on the beach. She was sure she would be able to see the pole bend if she caught one.

Jait decided to hold on to his pole and backed up until the line was tight. Tymber and Pred was standing next to him talking when all of sudden Jait had a powerful jerk on his line. It jerked again and pulled the pole completely from Jait's grasp. They watched his pole go into the water and out to sea.

Jait stood there with his mouth open, Pred just looked at the sea in surprise, and Tymber was laughing so hard she was rolling on the ground. Then she realized she better get to her pole and hold on.

They caught enough fish for supper and some to cure for the village. Tymber had a good idea about blanching the cleaned fish in the hot water down low in the cavern and then cover them in the curing salts.

"I think that the hot water down low is actually water from the sea," said Tymber. "It has a smell of salt."

After they were blanched, they were brought back up into the cooler areas of the cavern, rubbed with curing salt, and wrapped in water bag material.

They made a fire to cook the fish for supper outside the cavern on the beach where they were fishing. The soft warm air blowing off the sea made the evening very comfortable. The light was getting dim but the moon was rising over the sea and the fire gave them enough light to eat by.

"Any idea of what kind of fish we're eating, Father," Tymber asked, as she took her first bite.

"No I don't. It has a different taste, but it's good."

Jait waited for the others to eat some of the fish before he did. He looked at them and then to the bite of fish he had, hesitating to eat the bite.

"The meat of this fish has a reddish color to it."

"Take a bite Jait," Tymber said, as she cut another piece.

Jait's hunger finally won out and he took a bite.

"It is pretty good."

They sat and ate almost the entire fish and it was a large fish.

"Tomorrow I'll go look for berries and nuts to go with our fish meals," Tymber said. She sat back against the log just as full as she could be. "I'll look for some new growth stantle vine, too, to give us something green and sweet to eat."

"Find some blue drop berries and make a blue stantle salad and we would really eat well while we're gone," Jait added.

He took a sip of lemon juice drink that Tymber had mixed.

"We really need to find some lemon trees too."

"I bet we walk right through an orchard of them on the way here," she said.

Pred stood up and looked in the direction of the rock cliff that had the entrance to the cavern.

"We should do some exploring of the cavern this evening," he said.

"The longer I'm in there, the bigger I find that it is," she said, standing up next to her father brushing the sand from her pants. "My biggest trouble is trying to understand where I am in the cavern compared to the outside."

"I don't think that is important," said Jait. "Just look at it as entering into a different world and just get to know and understand it by itself and not compare it to the outside."

"That makes sense. It doesn't really matter."

Tymber was exploring the cavern like she had a mission, and she did. She was looking for the ideal chamber. She brought grain and vegetable seeds to plant on this trip to see if they will grow in the silver shimmer of the glow rocks.

She wanted to find a chamber that was light, warm, humid, and had deep, moist, sandy soil.

It didn't take her long. Many of the chambers had some sort of water, either a small stream or a pool of water from drips. The chambers just below the entrance were fairly warm from vents of warm air that came up from below. The soil was sandy but appeared to have some mixture of soil in it as well. She tested the soil by poking a hole to see if the hole remained as it would in soil or collapse as it would in sand. It held its shape nicely. She only hoped that it was light enough for the plants to grow.

Tymber had not told her father or Jait about wanting to plant seeds in the cavern. She was afraid that they would think it was not going to work and would ask her not to waste the seed.

She spent a few hours planting. She planted grain, tomatoes, and a few seeds of potato eyes, squash, peppers, and muskmelon.

Leaving the chamber, she decided not to tell her father or brother about the planting until she found out whether they would grow or not.

She went back to what she started calling First Chamber, which was the first chamber after the entrance passageway. Jait saw her and yelled for her to follow him. She met up with him a couple of chambers in a direction she was not sure she had been before.

"Let me show you something," Jait said, still leading the way.

They went through a rather narrow walkway and came to a chamber that had, what best could be described as rain, falling from the ceiling.

It was a low ceiling, only about three times Jait's height, and in the entire chamber drops of water fell from the ceiling appearing like a shower of rain.

It was not a well–lit chamber, but they could see a passageway on the other side of the rain chamber that was lit with glow rocks.

"What would cause this chamber to rain?" asked Tymber, in a louder than normal voice so Jait could hear her over the rain.

"Well my theory is that this chamber is directly underneath the river. The chamber even looks like it is about as wide as the river."

The floor of the cavern was like a pond. At first it was not obvious where all the water that rained into the pond went, but as their eyes adjusted to the dimmer light, they could see that the water disappeared to the right of them over an edge close to the wall. The water never really was up against the wall that Jait guessed was towards the sea. They decided that they were looking at the top of a waterfall. Where the water went from there they had no clue.

Around the rim of the pond, was a raised narrow ledge about five feet lower than they were standing. It looked like it continued all the way around the chamber to the other side.

"Do you know how deep the water is?"

"No, I just found this chamber and went back to find you and Father."

"It looks like the cavern continues on the other side. Are you up for a look?"

"Sure, too early to lie down, I think. It's hard to tell when you can't see outside."

They climbed down onto the ledge on the left to walk around to the other side. As they walked, they got the feeling that the chamber pond was fairly deep. There were sections of the ledge that were getting rained on so the two got to the other side fairly wet.

They climbed up into the passageway, but didn't go too far from the rain chamber.

Ahead of them was a continuous series of chambers. Amazed at the extent that the caverns seemed never ending, they waded through a couple of streams to continue their adventure and then went back to find their father.

Tymber and Jait sat down on the deep sand in First Chamber waiting for Pred to come back. They talked about what could have caused such massive caverns.

Jait suggested that it was the streams that seemed to run underground everywhere that cut out the caverns.

"I bet the Stone Cabin Cavern is connected to this one by that underground stream," Tymber said, while they were stretching their imagination.

"I'm not sure anything would surprise me about these caverns, we have seen many amazing things."

Pred entered the First Chamber from the opposite direction that Jait and Tymber had been.

"Its getting late but I want to show the two of you something in the morning," he said, sitting down beside Tymber. "It's a rather long way and it involves some climbing, and I don't have the energy to do it again today."

"What did you find father?"

"Well I'm not real sure how to explain it. You will just have to see it."

They laid their bedding down on the deep sand in a darker section of the First Chamber and fell quickly asleep.

The next morning they walked out to the cavern entrance and made a fire to cook breakfast. They knew that building fires in the cavern would not be a good idea because of the smoke. Jait said that he was going hunting sometime during the day; he didn't seem to like fish for breakfast.

Pred asked Jait when they finished eating to bring his bow and arrows and led them to the place he wanted them to see. The way seemed to mostly lead downward. At one point, they had to scoot behind a waterfall of a stream.

"How did you find this place, Father?" Jait asked, going through areas that were not easily seen.

"By exploring."

They came to an end to the link of small lower chambers. Tymber and Jait looked at each other not quite understanding and wondering if their father had gone the wrong way.

As they moved to the opposite side of the chamber, they saw a rope tied off and leading down a shaft. They looked down the shaft and couldn't see anything because of the darkness.

"We're not really climbing down into that shaft are we?" Jait asked.

"Yes we are. I have tied knots every arm length so it will be easier to go up and down."

"You went down there by yourself yesterday, Father?" said Tymber. "You would have chopped our heads off if we had done that."

"Yes I would have," Pred said, grinning. "I will go first. There aren't any glow rocks so it will be dark until your eyes adjust."

Pred lowered himself through the top of the shaft, Tymber followed and then Jait.

To their surprise it wasn't very far down. When they landed on the floor below they could feel warm air coming through an opening in the wall. To the right they could see a red glow shining through a corridor that connected two chambers. That peaked Jait's and Tymber's curiosity. They had not seen a red glow in the cavern.

Pred moved towards the red glow. The closer they got, the warmer the air became.

When they turned a corner, Jait and Tymber stopped in their tracks as they saw a river of red hot glow on the opposite side of the chamber.

"Don't go too much farther," Pred said. "It gets very warm, very fast."

They moved another few steps closer to the red stream. The red liquid rock passed from an opening in the chamber wall on the right and slowly flowed through a similar opening to the left. The entire length of the red rock flow was no more than twenty feet.

"What is that?" Jait asked.

"I'm not sure. My best guess is that it is a stream of melted rock. And, no I don't know why there is a river of melted rock here in the cavern."

"Tymber," Jait said, not being able to look away from the hot red river, "remember last night when I said that nothing in these caverns would surprise me anymore. Well, I was wrong."

"Now we know why the caverns are so warm," Pred said, "and why the water is so hot in places, and why there is a steam chamber."

Tymber started laughing, mostly because everything just seemed so amazing.

"Jait had found a special chamber yesterday that we were going to show you, but it doesn't compare to this."

"What did you find, Jait?"

"We found a rain chamber," he said, still not looking away from the river of melted rock. "The chamber is about fifteen feet high and from the ceiling drips a shower of water."

"It really looks like its raining in there," Tymber added.

"We have found both rain and fire yesterday here in the cavern."

"You wanted me to bring my bow and arrows with me," said Jait. He adjusted his bow over his shoulder. "I was expecting that you found some sort of animal that you wanted me to shoot."

"Well I do want you to shoot, just not an animal. See that bright white rock up above the red river? I will cook supper the rest of the time we are in the forest if you can hit it."

Jait looked at his father like he was crazy. He could hit that rock with his eyes closed.

He strung his bow with an arrow, looked at his father again, and shot the arrow. As the arrow traveled through the air of the fire river chamber, it burst into flames and landed in the river without hitting the rock.

Jait and Tymber stood there in disbelief.

"That is one hot room," Tymber finally was able to get out. "Well Jait, looks like you get to cook supper tonight."

They worked there way back up the small and narrow passages to First Chamber.

When they left the cavern to cook lunch, they were surprised to find that it was already getting dark.

"I was expecting to have some time to fish today," Pred said, looking out at the moon rising over the sea.

"Well, we'll fish all day tomorrow and probably have as much as we can carry back," said Tymber.

The guys nodded in agreement.

They made a fire on the ledge of the opening to the cavern. They looked out onto the sea as the moon started rising. Pred commented on how nice it was to look up and watch a friendly moon.

As they sat and ate, listening to the sea surf coming on shore, they could not think of anything that would be as peaceful as that moment.

FIFTEEN

Fishing the sea turned out to be an exciting adventure. Not only did they catch fish of all sizes, they caught fish of species that seemed very strange to them.

Some of the fish had long noses and mouths that looked like they could eat fish hiding between rocks. One species looked like a rock and probably hid at the bottom and waited for fish to swim by to eat. Pred threw those back, they didn't look too appetizing.

Occasionally they would catch fish that were quite dangerous to handle, either because of the very sharp fins or their very large and sharp teeth. Pred had to struggle to get the hook out of their mouths.

A number of times the fish that got hooked were too large to bring to shore and broke the line. They were lucky that they brought as many hooks as they did. Pred had to re–shape a couple of hooks that got bent from the weight of the struggling fish.

Most of the time, Pred did the fishing, Jait did the cleaning, and Tymber did the blanching and curing in the cavern. She used the hot water pools for blanching.

She kept each species separate to sample each kind during their meals for taste. They didn't want to carry fish back that no one would eat. They threw away about a third of the fish. They learned which ones didn't taste good and Pred would throw them back when he caught them.

The day to head back to the village came. The previous day was very fruitful in producing a large quantity of fish. The fishing, cleaning, and curing system worked so well that they weren't sure they were going to be able to carry all the fish back.

Jait couldn't bare the thought of fish again that morning for breakfast, so he left the cavern at daylight and hunted a couple of tree squirrels. He didn't like shooting his arrows into the air at them, in case he missed he would never find them, but he just wasn't going to be able to eat fish for breakfast. Luckily he didn't miss and lose any arrows.

After breakfast, they packed up to leave.

"I want to go back by Hantfel on the way back to the village," Tymber told Pred and Jait. "I want to bring Goshenta and Aliptis fish in return for their hospitality to us. They said they had not eaten fish all season."

"That will take an extra half day at least for us to get back," Jait responded. "With all this fish we will be weighted down, too."

"Well I was thinking that you two could go directly to where we will camp tonight on the river. You could get the campsite ready and supper cooked and I'll go up the river to Hantfel, leave the fish with them, and meet you back on the river at the campsite."

"Tymber, I don't think that's a good idea," Pred answered. "We have not separated yet while in the forest."

"Father, if I take only the fish I will give them I will be able to travel fast and maybe even beat you to the campsite. Of course the other option is that we all go to Hantfel, which seems like wasted effort just to deliver fish."

"Tymber your mother..."

"Father, I know what you're going to say and we both know that I am very capable of taking care of myself. You would let Jait go by himself."

Pred just stood there looking at his girl. He wanted to show her that he trusted her and that she will make a good hunter, but if something were to happen to her... He just didn't want to even think about that. And she was right, he would let Jait go, but he is older. But that wasn't the reason. He hesitates because she's a girl.

"I'm sure Jait wouldn't mind taking them fish and..."

"Father!"

"Okay, Tymber, I will let you go. Take your water bag, your bow, and two wrappers of fish and hand me your backpack."

"Thank you so much for trusting me, Father," she said, kissing him on the cheek. "I will tell them hello for both or you, or greetings, as they say. Don't worry I will see you guys tonight."

And off Tymber went at a full walking gait up the bank of the river and out of sight.

Jait looked at his father somewhat surprised that he let her go by herself. Then he decided he better show support for his father's decision.

"She will be just fine, Father. Believe me, I know, she can take care of herself. I have the bruises to prove it."

He smiled trying to get his father to smile, too.

Pred just slightly grinned, maybe not even hearing what Jait had said. He continued to look at the last spot he saw Tymber heading into the forest alone.

"We certainly don't want Tymber to beat us back to our campsite," Jait told his father, while he divided the extra weight of the fish. "We would never hear the end of that."

They picked up the backpacks and headed toward View Hill.

Tymber finally reached the trail that led to Hantfel from the river. She stopped and got a cool drink of water from the stream and rested for a few moments.

It was midday and she was getting very hungry, but didn't want to take the time to eat. She wanted to make sure she got to the campsite well before dark and before her father started to worry too much.

She had been sitting there for a short time when she heard a roar in the distance. Well at least she thought it was a roar. She sat silent for some time to see if she would hear it again. She tried to ignore all the other noises trying to hear just the roar. She did not hear it again.

She felt for her bow, arrows, and knife, and felt more secure knowing that they were there. In fact, she took the time to take her knife out and once again admire its beauty and history.

She got up to continue her trip, but felt dizzy. *It must be time for lunch*, she told herself, and sat back down. "I really don't want to take the time to eat," she said, out loud.

A humming noise was in her ear. It was getting lower in pitch. She tried to find the direction it was coming from, but each way she turned her head, it sounded like it was coming from that direction.

Standing up, it felt like the ground was giving way and that she was on soft ground, but rock was under her feet. She had stood up, but why she could not remember, and sat back down feeling dizzier.

She put her head between her legs thinking that that may help but it did not. Then she realized it was not just her, it was a groundshake.

The birds squealed and took to flight; she looked up and saw deer run by and then run back looking for an escape from something they could not understand, either. The noise was getting louder and she saw the water in the stream begin to ripple and then turn to waves in erratic patterns, not caring about the direction of water flow.

A boom was heard in the distance as lightning flashed from the sky. The thunder was strange because there was no rain. The lightning continued as it appeared that the sky was attacking the ground as punishment for shaking.

The noise became a screech and rumble at the same time. The stream stopped, and then the ground vibrated, the ground shook, and the ground rocked.

She didn't know if she sat down or was knocked down, but found herself sitting and watching everything move in erratic waves—the water, the ground, and even the trees.

She wasn't sure of anything that was happening. The air itself seemed to break apart, re–collide and then split again as she attempted to breathe.

Tymber wanted to scream, but then wasn't sure if she did, or if she even tried. The surrounding noise became waves that slapped her in the face.

She didn't know how long the shake lasted. There was no such thing as time, only this vibration, and it seemed like it had always been this way.

She found herself on her hands and knees sinking into the solid rock bank. The rock would no longer support her weight.

In her confused state, it seemed like a year had passed since she had been home. She wondered why she was there all by herself in the forest when she knew her mother needed help at home. It seemed like she could remember that she had two sisters, but wasn't sure.

The vibration continued seemingly without end. It made everything have a blurry existence. She looked up, but that just made her dizzier and she didn't really like what she saw when she tried. There didn't seem to be individual things, just a mass of stuff. In the distance, she could hear many trees and tree limbs that could not take the strain, fall to the ground.

Slowly the noise became less intense and the vibration slowed to slight jerks, and then was gone. She stayed on her hands and knees for awhile almost expecting for it to start again.

The pleasant sound of the rapids of the stream started again as the stream once again began to flow. She had not realized how much the sound of the rapids was missed during the groundshake.

Her thoughts turned to her father and Jait, hoping they were okay, and then to her mother and her sisters. Maybe the groundshake was local and not felt there, but it had felt like the whole world had shook.

She sat up trying to regain her bearings on reality. She was feeling better, the dizziness was subsiding. Looking around she could see things that had fallen in the shake, but most things looked normal again. She remembered the soft rock and looked down. It was hard. She thought she had imagined it softening, but she could see the imprints of her hands and knees in the rock.

What just happened? Reality left for a while and became a terrible nightmare. Everything that was anything had been gone during the shake. Groundshake just didn't seem like a strong enough term for that event.

Feeling better, she stood up. The birds began to complain in a definite angry manner.

"This fish is getting heavier by the moment," Jait complained to his father, as they started down View Hill on their way to the campsite. "I think Tymber wanted to go the other way just to keep from carrying all of this."

Pred smiled knowing that Jait was just idly complaining and not really mad at his sister.

"She will probably want to stop and give Drel a fish or two also. We will wind up with one small fish by the time she gets done giving it all away."

Jait just finished talking and looked towards where his father had been walking beside him. But he was not there so he stopped and looked back at him.

"What's the matter, Father?"

"I just feel a little dizzy. Do you hear that?"

Jait stood still and tried to hear what his father heard. He started to feel dizzy as well.

"Sounds like distant thunder," he offered.

About that time they heard and felt a hum.

"It's the beginning of a shake," Pred said, looking up the hill.

Pred saw a couple of small stones vibrate and tumble down the hill as all the birds in the area squealed and took flight.

"Run!" shouted Pred. He continued down the hill with Jait running in front of him.

The sound became louder as they ran. They both fell from a surge of dizziness. Jait got up and looked back at his father who was trying to get back up. Jait was trying to get back uphill to help, but his father shouted for him to head for an outcropping farther down the hill. On their hands and knees, they both eventually got there.

Glancing up the hill it looked like the whole top of the hill rocked back and forth like rubber. Now larger rocks broke loose and headed downhill.

The noise became a screech and rumble at the same time.

They lay behind the outcropping hiding from the fall of the hill. At times it appeared to be water flowing and the large rocks were large waves passing them. Then the flow slowed as the vibration increased. The surface of the hill was slowly flowing past them, or maybe they were moving up the hill.

Jait looked at his father and asked the man he didn't recognize what was happening. The man appeared not to understand the question and Jait didn't remember asking it.

A worried look was on the man, as if he had lost someone or something. He looked at the boy that was next to him and knew he didn't belong there.

Why was the sky attacking us? Was it the moon that was attacking? Lightning flashed without end but there was no rain and there were no clouds.

Lightning struck very close to where they laid. The thunder crash knocked Jait out with the impact. Water began to ooze out of the side of the hill where they were laying. The rock became soft as Jait vibrated down within it.

"I am rock," the rock said. "But I can see—and I can breathe, yes, how wonderful to breathe."

Spikes of water jumped into the air from the vibration and didn't have a great desire to fall back to the ground. Slowly the high-pitched noise and the vibration eased off and then finally stopped. Jait opened his eyes and found it hard to remember how to move.

Pred looked like he couldn't wait to stand and did so, but then sat down next to Jait when he realized Jait couldn't move.

"Are you all right, Jait? Are you hurt?"

Some time had to pass before Jait could regain reality and answer his father.

Pred's thoughts turned to Sella, Ispis, and Janna, and worried at how they made it through the shake. He was glad that Drel was there to help. Pred never wanted to be back at his cabin any more than at that moment.

"Father, what happened?" Jait said, as he remembered how to talk and sit up.

Pred smiled at Jait's question because he knew Jait would be okay. He looked up at the large intruding moon hanging overhead.

"Its force on us was strong that time. It's shaking the life out of Adentta. Can you get up Jait? We need to go to the campsite and then go look for Tymber. We are still a long way off."

Jait tried to remember Tymber, and then he could in a rush of regained reality.

He got up and said that he now felt fine and was ready to go. However, he actually felt weak and wondered if he was actually going to be able to remember how to walk. A strange thought about rocks walking passed swiftly through his mind and was never thought of again.

"At least they could have chopped the wood before they left," Drel muttered to himself, as he chopped a couple days worth of wood.

He brought the chopped wood in and laid it by the stove.

"I just about have lunch ready, Drel," Sella said, putting the fried potatoes on the table. "The hen's eggs will be done shortly.

Thanks for chopping the wood for me; I don't know where Jait's mind is sometimes. He knew the wood needed to be chopped before he left."

"I'm very glad to do it for you, Sella," Drel said. "Jait has a lot on his mind these days; don't be too hard on him." Drel would gladly trade doing a little wood chopping for being served meals any day.

"I guess everyone is worried and scared and thinking too much these days," Sella said. "Girls, come eat!"

Sella laid the rest of the lunch on the table, which included fresh bread, jam, hen egg salad, herd meat, and a bowl of blue drop berries with fresh cream poured over them.

"Wow, Sella, this is a lunch made for a leader. Pred is a very lucky man."

Drel looked at Sella as she sat down and realized that she was starting to show her age. Drel guessed that she was probably fifteen years or so older than him. She was still the most attractive lady in the village, he thought.

Ispis and Janna came running in from the other room and stopped short when they saw Drel. They wanted to be on their best behavior while he was around. Ispis smiled at Drel as she sat down to lunch. Drel could just barely see Janna's head above the table. She looked up at Drel and then back at her food, embarrassed that she got caught looking at him.

"Mother says that Father will be home tomorrow night," Janna said, still looking at her food.

"Eat your food dear," Sella told Janna, helping her with the meat.

"You have adorable daughters, Sella," Drel remarked, as he watched them eat their food, "all three of them."

Sella grinned and glanced up at Drel and then back down at her food. She knew that Tymber had an eye for Drel but it was nice to know that it was mutual, even though Drel was a few years older than her. Out of the pick of men in the village, Drel would be Sella's choice for Tymber. He is handsome, smart, and would provide for her well.

Outside they heard the Trelop cow bellowing and the chickens carrying on.

"From the sound of our animals, they are ready to be fed," Sella said. "I will do so when we're finished eating…"

Sella sat back and said she felt a little dizzy. The two girls didn't need to say anything. They were turning pale and put their heads on the table.

A humming sound began and then a vibration. Drel stood up from the table but fell down onto the floor. The glasses and the plates on the table vibrated and some fell off. The noise became a screech and rumble at the same time. The vibration turned into a shaking.

Drel got up to his knees.

"Quick, we need to get outside."

That was not easy. Sella looked green with sickness still sitting at the table as the two girls quickly passed out onto the floor.

The center tower bell started to chime in rhythm to the shaking.

Drel stood, but went back to his knees. He crawled over to Janna and pulled her into his arms. Dust filled the air. Wall hangings left their hooks but danced in midair before falling to the floor.

Drel knew he had to get everyone outside. He first pulled Janna out, then Ispis. As he turned back towards the cabin to get Sella, he heard crashing coming from the kitchen. Sella was at the door crawling out. He grabbed her to help her to get clear of the cabin.

Drel fell again in the yard. The ground was soft, too soft. All four of them were together outside. The two girls were still unconscious, which was probably for the best. Drel held Ispis, and Sella held Janna.

He found himself trying to get air to breathe. It was like the air was only in pockets that floated by and available only occasionally.

The vibration and shaking, the rocking, and the noise increased and Drel wondered where he was. The cabin did not look familiar. "What a pretty girl he was holding in his arms. He wished he knew her name."

Lightning flashed and the thunder rumbled. Sparks shot from a tree nearby as lightning struck it. Drel watched as the sparks didn't fall.

Sella tried to speak to the child in her lap. She could not tell if she spoke or not or remembered if she even tried. She lay back, sinking into the ground, wishing that the world didn't have to end so soon.

The sound was getting lesser and the shaking turned to occasional jerks. Once again Drel could hear the bells. They must have been ringing all along but could not be heard over the sound of the groundshake.

It was over. The bells finally stopped. The endless vibration was gone. Sella sat up and hugged her child as she woke.

Drel sat and rocked Ispis not knowing that she had already woke. Sella asked Ispis if she was all right and she responded that she was.

Janna started to whimper remembering how she felt during the shake and Sella told her that it was okay, it was over. Sella looked over to Drel for confirmation. Drel just shrugged as he tried to stand up. His legs were weak, but he knew he had to start moving.

Sella got up and sat Janna down on the ground, but Janna reached back up to her mother. She understandably didn't want to be out of her mother's arms, so Sella picked her back up.

"I heard a crashing as we left," she said, walking towards the cabin door, not knowing what to expect.

Drel followed her in. The cabin was a mess and the air was full of dust. It appeared like cleaning up was mostly all that was going to be needed.

"This is what made the crashing sound," she said, handing Drel a rock from the chimney.

Drel looked up at the hole where the rock had been.

"That will have to be fixed before we light another fire. I will mix some mud and fix it."

"Thanks," said Sella, looking around to see what she should do first. "I'll start cleaning up this mess."

Of course her thoughts went immediately to Pred, Jait, and Tymber, who, if they were on their schedule, would be somewhere in the forest during the shake.

Sella started to cry from worry. Janna, who was still in her arms, hugged her mother.

"It's okay," she told her mother. "It's over."

"You're such a big girl now," she told her, returning the hug, and kissing her on the cheek.

"Could you please go get the broom for me?" she asked Janna, as she put her down.

Drel came back with a bucket of mud mixed with small stones, sand, and straw. He saw Sella working but also saw her crying as she did so.

"They are all right," he said, as he put his arm around her shoulder, guessing what her tears were for. "I think I'm going to have to stay away from you three."

Sella looked at him in shock.

"It seems like when we are together we have a groundshake," he said smiling, trying to get her to smile.

She did not smile, but she did try.

SIXTEEN

Tymber thought about going straight to the campsite where she would meet her father and Jait, but then being alone in the forest during that shake would have been for nothing. She decided to continue to Hantfel and see Goshenta and Aliptis. She would go see them, if she could walk.

With renewed energy, she headed down the trail going around trees that had fallen in the shake. She hoped that Goshenta and Aliptis and all of Hantfel made it through the shake all right.

She had passed the first trail to the right that went to the stream, and then the first trail that went to the left. When she reached the second trail in the direction of the stream, she heard a squeal. It sounded like it came from down the trail towards the stream. At first she thought that it was an animal, but then she heard a scream. That was no animal; that was a person.

She ran down the trail towards the stream. Again, she heard a scream. She started running as fast as she could, dodging limbs and trees along the way.

She heard a loud growl. This time it was definitely a growl. As Tymber got close she saw a girl halfway sitting and halfway lying on her back, on the ground, looking towards Tymber's right.

Tymber looked in that direction to see a large gray animal with dark spots. It was staring at the girl on the ground looking as if it were about to pounce on her. She looked back at the girl. It was Aliptis!

Tymber stopped and grabbed her bow. She reached for an arrow and tried to string it. She dropped the arrow. She grabbed another arrow and as she tried to string the arrow again, the animal roared so loud Tymber fell backwards. While stumbling to the ground, Tymber got the arrow strung and saw the animal leap for the girl. She shot the arrow as she hit her head on a tree as she fell backwards.

When Tymber came to, many people were gathered around her. She didn't recognize anybody. They had put a wet cloth to her forehead. She sat up and heard someone tell her to sit still. Her head was pounding.

Then she remembered what happened. She stumbled to her feet to look in the direction of where Aliptis had been. She was not there, but what was there was a dead, large, gray–and–dark–spotted animal with an arrow in its neck.

"Aliptis!" Tymber yelled, fearing the worst.

"I'm right here Tymber," Aliptis said, in a soft voice. "You saved my life."

Aliptis hugged Tymber's neck in appreciation. So did everyone else that was there.

Tymber sat back down while she was regaining her bearings. They were slow in coming back. She looked back at the predator laying there with her arrow in it.

She heard a voice she recognized.

"I would not have believed that a tromptaw could have been taken down with just one arrow," said Midton, looking down at her. "You must be an excellent hunter."

"I can't believe it either," Tymber said, in response. "We call them predators. This is the first one I had seen alive. They are huge."

She heard someone running up from behind her.

"Aliptis, are you okay?" Goshenta asked, hugging her.

"Yes I am, thanks to Tymber."

Tymber got up and Goshenta came over and thanked Tymber with a kiss on the cheek.

"Thank you so much for your help," she said. "You are a hero in Hantfel."

"I'm not a hero," answered Tymber.

"Where are your Father and Jait?" asked Aliptis, looking down the trail as if to look to see if they were coming.

"They are headed to our campsite. I just came this way to give you and Goshenta some fish that we caught. I wanted to thank you for your food and drink while we were here."

Tymber glanced around for her wrapped fish.

"I must have dropped them on the trail as I ran here."

A small boy came up to her and gave her the wraps. He said that he found them laying on the trail.

Tymber took them and thanked him, then handed them to Goshenta.

"I feel funny taking a gift from you after all that you have done. Because of your generosity, Aliptis is alive."

"I traveled too far for you to refuse it. You have to take it," Tymber said, smiling at her.

Tymber then remembered the shake.

"Are your people okay after the groundshake?"

"I believe so," Goshenta said. "That is where I was, at home, when this happened. Everything seemed to be okay. I worried that

Aliptis was here at the stream by herself during all the shaking. It looks like it wasn't the shaking I should have been worried about."

"That is probably why the predator, I mean the tromptaw, attacked," Tymber offered. "It was confused and felt threatened."

Goshenta looked over at the tromptaw and shook her head.

"That thing scares me now, and it's dead."

Tymber glanced up at the sun that was now well past midday.

"I need to get going to meet with my father and brother."

Tymber looked back at the predator again.

"I don't want to be late or they will begin to worry, especially after the shake. I had to talk my father into letting me come here alone and I don't want to hurt his faith in me."

"Next time you come to visit us," Midton said, "we will have a feast in your honor. Tromptaw sausage will be the main course."

"Are they good to eat?" asked Tymber, doubting that she would actually want tromptaw to eat.

"I have only eaten tromptaw once, they are a mountain animal and only seldom seen this far from the mountains. They put an excellent taste into sausage."

Aliptis hugged Tymber again.

"Anything you want or need, I will get for you," she said.

"All I want is your friendship," Tymber said, as she waved good-bye to everyone.

"Be assured that you have our friendship," Midton said.

"Say greetings to Jait for me when you see him," Aliptis said, smiling at Tymber, "and your father of course."

Tymber proceeded back down the trail and turned at the fork to go back to the river.

She didn't want to tell Midton and Goshenta, but she really did have weak legs and a headache. She was afraid that they would want to care for her, but she needed to get to the campsite.

"What am I going to tell Father and Jait?" she said out loud, as she walked down the trail.

She got back to the river and looked around. Everything seemed pretty normal after the groundshake, except for the downed trees and the mysterious impressions in the rock. She looked back towards the direction of the sea and thought she could see smoke in the distant sky. But maybe it was just the clouds that looked like smoke at the top of the mountains.

As she turned to travel upriver, she worried about what she would tell her father and Jait. She knew they would worry about the predator attacking and never let her go alone again.

But if she didn't tell them, they would find out next time they saw the Hantfel people. She didn't want to have to try to avoid her new friends. Her father and Jait would not believe that she downed the predator with one arrow as she was falling backwards. It was even hard for her to believe.

She remembered and looked in her quiver. There were two arrows missing. They would notice two arrows missing. Two arrows? Then she remembered that she had dropped her first attempt to string the arrow to her bow. She should have picked it up when she left.

She decided that she had to tell them the story. Maybe not the complete story, and definitely not to her mother, but she had to tell them about the predator attack.

Tymber felt the back of her head where she had hit the tree. No wonder she had a headache. There was a good sized bump on her head and felt like dried blood there too. They certainly would see that.

The way ahead of her was hard. She forgot about the travel between the Hantfel stream and the campsite being so hard, and now there were more trees down that made it harder. The edge of the river had deep sand with trees and limbs scattered to make the walk more difficult. All she could think about was to sit and rest, which she did.

She found a log next to a pool of water that the river left and sat down to rest. She had to keep blinking her eyes to keep them focused. The sand next to her looked inviting enough for her to lie down and take a nap. She wished she had that much time.

When she closed her eyes, all she could see was everything around her shaking. In her mind all the trees fell and the river was drained into the ground. She was starting to think crazy.

As she was looking into the pool of water, it started to ripple. She blinked a number of times but the water still rippled.

"Not again," she said, as she watched the water. She held on to the log she was sitting on and waited to hear the squawk of the birds. But this time the vibration just ended without any shaking. For a moment, she thought she passed out and had missed the shaking.

She longed to sit but couldn't any longer. All she could think about was to get back with her father and Jait. It was getting late afternoon and they would be starting to look for her. She knew what direction to go, but couldn't remember how far ahead the campsite was.

She got back up with renewed determination and started back upstream.

Eventually she found it easier to wade in thigh deep water than it was to walk the deep sand banks and sand bars with all the downed trees and limbs.

Just when she thought she could not travel any farther, she smelled smoke. *Now what*, she thought. *Was the forest on fire?*

Then she heard her brother hoot to her. She looked up to see Jait standing by their campfire. She had never been more glad to see him. Then she saw her father come from behind the tent to wave to her.

It seemed like days since she had seen them. She teared in joy at their sight.

Pred's smile at seeing her gradually changed to a worried look as she approached.

She looked wet, tired, and as she got closer they could see dark rings under her eyes. They could see that she was hurt. Pred and Jait ran through the water to help her to the camp.

"Do I look that bad?" she asked them, as they got to her.

They each took an arm and helped her to the campsite.

"Are you okay Tymber?" Pred asked. "What happened? Did you have trouble during the groundshake?"

"I have had quite an adventure," she said, sitting down by the fire. "Where were you two when the shake hit?"

"We had a little adventure as well that we'll tell you about after you tell us what happened."

"You better sit down," she said looking at both of them.

Pred went to get a wet cloth for the back of her head.

"That looks like a nasty bump," he said, putting the cloth to the bump on her head.

She held the cloth in place and began to tell her story.

"I had gotten all the way to the trail that leads to Hantfel, when I sat down to rest for a moment. That's when the groundshake hit. I was sitting there when the birds and animals went crazy; the stream stopped flowing and ripples in the water turned to waves splashing in every direction. It was like everything rocked back and forth. The air even seemed hard to breathe, like it too was splitting apart. I could hear trees and limbs falling in all directions."

"A limb hit you on the head," Jait said, thinking he had guessed what happened.

"No, actually it wasn't the groundshake that caused this," she said, as she took the cloth from her head to look for blood on it.

"Let her finish, Jait."

"After all the shaking—I think we should call that one a groun-drocking—I collected my thoughts and bearings and proceeded to go see Goshenta and Aliptis. As I was walking down the trail, and I got to where the second trail headed down towards the stream, I heard a scream coming from that direction. I thought at first it was an animal, but it was a person. I ran as fast as I could down the trail to the stream. When I got there, I saw Aliptis laying on the ground and a predator to my right about to pounce on her."

"Please relax, everyone is okay," she continued. "I strung my arrow to my bow, and shot it as it leaped for her. I downed it with one arrow in its neck.

"I know that's hard to believe and I wouldn't have thought that that was possible, but it happened."

"You must have been terrified," Pred said, shaking his head regretting letting her go alone.

"Oh, I was."

"I did notice that there were two arrows missing from your quiver."

"I dropped the first arrow when I tried to string it to shoot."

"That doesn't say what happened to your head," said Jait.

"Just as I was getting my second arrow strung, the predator roared, which scared me and I fell backwards as I was shooting and hit my head."

Jait decided to joke with Tymber a little.

"You are telling us that you shot and killed a predator with one shot as you were falling backwards?"

All she could think of saying was yes.

"Well," Jait continued, "I think you hit your head harder than you think."

"It's a good thing I'm so tired, or you would be swimming in the river right now," Tymber said, smiling at her brother.

Pred checked to see if supper was finished cooking.

"I didn't take the time to eat lunch," Tymber said, "I'm so hungry I could eat a predator."

Jait got up and dished a plate of pork for her.

"We decided to hunt so we could have something besides fish. I hope you don't mind," he said. He knew that she would definitely want a change from fish.

"But it took two arrows," he said, looking at her for a reaction.

As Jait brought the plate to her, he told her he was glad she was okay. He put the plate in her hands and bent over and hugged her neck.

"Thanks, Jait," she said, smiling brightly at him.

"Now tell me the adventure that you two had," she said, with a mouthful of food.

"Well it wasn't near the adventure that you had," Pred said, sitting down with his food. "We were just caught up in a rock slide."

Tymber stopped chewing and looked over at them.

"During the groundshake we were on View Hill, on this side heading down when it hit. When we felt the ground shaking, or as you say rocking, we looked uphill and saw the top of the hill moving back and forth. It looked like it was made of jam. All at once the rocks at the top wanted to come downhill. About all we could do was run. We ran downhill as fast as we could and found an outcropping in the hill and hid there as some of the hill came down."

"And that's what it seemed like, too," added Jait. "The whole hill seemed to want to come down at once."

"We found it hard to breathe too," said Pred. "After the hill settled back down, we stuck our heads out and continued down to here. We need to leave as early as we can in the morning. I know that Sella and the kids are fine, but I can't wait to see them."

"I know what you mean, Father," Tymber said. "But can we not tell her about my adventure with the predator? I will never be able to enter the forest again."

Pred smiled and looked at Jait, "We may not be able to keep it from her, but we will try."

Drel had just finished mending the chimney when they heard many people outside on the trail. He recognized many of the voices to be leaders so he went out to meet with them.

"Drel, we have a big problem," said Herder, as he stopped to talk. "During the shake, many of our fences in the fields have fallen. The herds are loose and many of them are heading for the forest. They seemed to be as frightened as us during the shake."

"We must get them before they enter the forest," said Farmer.

"I will help as much as I can," Drel said. "How is the rest of the village?"

"Most of the damage to the village has been to the chimneys, windows, and other miscellaneous things," said Builder. "We did lose two cabins; luckily, old Groomer's place was vacant. The other cabin is Seeder's. His family is moving in with Storer. Since Storer's children moved, he has the room."

"Keeper, how is your cabin?" asked Farmer, gesturing in the direction of Drel's cabin on the other side of the village.

"Well to be truthful, I don't know and I haven't had much time to think about it. Hunter is still gone and I have been caring for his family."

"We are going that way to look for some of the herd. We sure could use the help if you want to come, and you could check on your cabin."

"Let me go see how Sella and the kids are doing and if they think it would be all right to go help. The groundshake shook them up pretty bad."

Drel came back to the group telling them that he would go with them but would have to return before dark. He didn't really want to leave, but he was anxious to see how his cabin fared the shake and he wanted to help the village get back the herd. The last thing that Pred would want is any reason to have to hunt even harder because the herd was lost.

By the time Drel got near to his cabin, it was starting to get dark. They had rounded up about half of the herd. Men with ropes would catch them and then lead them back to a field that had a fence up.

"The rest of the herd must be in the forest," said Herder, looking in that direction. He did not want to go into the forest to retrieve them. He had never been in the forest before.

"We've done as much as we can today," he said, glad that he didn't have to make the decision to continue. "Let's go look at your cabin, Drel."

Drel's cabin had some damage. Most of the windows were broken, the chimney needed repair, and the porch was sagging on one end.

Drel went inside to get some of his clothes, looked around briefly, didn't see any major damage, and left. He knew that there wasn't anything he could do right now and he promised Sella to be back by dark.

SEVENTEEN

"It looks like the stone cabin held up to the shake pretty well," said Jait, as they passed by on their way back to the village. They didn't bother to stop; in fact, they had not stopped to rest all day.

They were nervous about Sella and the girls. Thinking about it again made them quicken their pace.

"Remember I had Drel stay with them while we were gone," reminded Pred, trying to relieve the tension as they walked back through the forest. Tymber was going to tell her father that that was probably the tenth time he had said that, but decided not to.

"I couldn't sleep last night," she said, instead. "I don't know if I was imagining it or not but I kept feeling little vibrations all night."

"It was not your imagination," Jait and Pred both answered.

With the additional limbs and trees down from the shake, it seemed to take much longer to travel. They were nearly to the edge of the forest when Tymber, who was in the lead, stopped short and ducked down.

Pred and Jait followed her lead, but did not know why.

"Listen," Tymber whispered, as she turned her head to see if that helped her hear.

They heard the noise that Tymber heard. It was definitely a large animal that was walking ahead of them. They strained their eyes to try to see, but there was too much brush in the way. It sounded like it was getting nearer, but at a slow deliberate pace. Jait started imagining the monsters from the stories of his childhood, especially the one with the bright red glowing eyes.

All three of them pulled an arrow from their quiver and strung it to their bow. The walking noise was getting closer.

"Remember," Tymber reminded them in a whisper, "the forest animals may be more aggressive and more confused than normal because of the shakes. We can't wait any longer for it to leave. It will soon be on us."

"At the count of three," whispered Pred, he held up three fingers, "we will get up and shoot."

"One, two, three."

They all got up and aimed.

"Wait!" yelled Pred.

But it was too late; Tymber had already shot her arrow. Pred and Jait lowered their bows before shooting.

The animal in front of them was a big fat cow. Obviously, the animal was from their herd and had gotten loose.

"Nice shot, Sis," said Jait, trying to keep from laughing.

High above the animal, stuck in a tree, was Tymber's arrow.

"Maybe you have to be falling backwards to hit anything."

Even Pred had to start laughing. In fact, all three were laughing.

"It's even too high for us to get back."

"Don't make me laugh anymore," said Tymber, holding her head. "You're going to make my headache come back. I saw that it was a cow and couldn't stop the shot in time so I just jerked it high to avoid hitting it."

"I'm sure that's what happened," Jait said, still smiling.

About that time they heard another animal, and then another.

"The fences must have come down in the shake," Pred said, looking around for other animals.

"Tymber, take a measure of rope and collar the animal. We will take it with us when we go. Jait and I will each get one too."

Tymber roped the cow that she missed with her arrow. Somehow she felt that was insult to injury. She knew that no matter how many predators she felled with one shot, she would never live down missing a cow at point blank range, whether on purpose or not.

Pred found a few more cows and tried to turn them around by swatting their rumps. He roped one and brought it with him.

When they got to the edge of the forest, some men were there standing looking into the forest trying to decide if they should go in or not. Jait got to them and without saying a word handed them his rope.

"I want my rope back," he said, changing is mind. He took the rope off the cow and walked off.

Tymber saw that they were afraid to go into the forest. The men saw a female leaving the forest and seemed embarrassed by their own fear.

"There are more cattle in there," she said pointing to the forest. "You can find them just past the third monster."

Tymber was the only one that was smiling.

Pred, following behind, heard what Tymber had said, and just shook his head and looked at the ground as he approached. In all fairness, Pred thought, it really wasn't a good idea to go into the forest without a bow, arrow, and a hunter to pull it.

He told the men that there was more of the herd in the forest and if they wanted to wait until the morning, he would go in the forest and help them.

"You really shouldn't go in without a bow and arrow."

They looked towards the forest and then looked at Pred and said they would wait for him to return tomorrow.

"Bring some measures of rope with you and bring my rope back."

Pred turned away from them and he, Jait, and Tymber hurried off towards their cabin. Along the way they saw the damage that Drel's cabin took and they were almost running at that point. They wanted to get there soon but they had to slow down. None of them had eaten or rested since breakfast.

It was late day when they reached their cabin. It looked like heaven to the travelers. It was still standing and looked in fair condition. They heard hammering from inside.

"Sella!" Pred shouted, as he approached the cabin.

She came running outside and the two girls not far behind. Hugs and kisses for everyone, and then seconds and thirds, all around.

"Tymber, you're hurt," said Sella. "Let me see to that bump."

Tymber had just realized that she had not taken the time to rinse the dried blood out of her hair like she should have before their return.

They went into the cabin and found Drel working on a shelf that had fallen in the shake.

Pred gave Drel a pat on the back in thanks for staying with his girls while he was gone.

"You wouldn't believe how much it helped knowing that you were here with them."

"This is where I needed to be," Drel said.

"Welcome back everyone," he said, looking at Tymber.

Tymber smiled at him, which made Drel smile.

"We saw your cabin on the way here and you have some damage," Pred said, looking around his cabin.

"Yes I know," he answered. "I was there for a short time chasing cattle."

"We did a little of that too on the way back. We found some in the forest and brought them out. Some of the guys took them back to the fields. Needless to say, they didn't want to go into the forest to get the rest. In the morning I will go help them retrieve more of the herd, and then we can start on the repair of your cabin."

"It's mostly window damage," said Drel, as he finished hanging up the shelf he was working on. "We may be able to clean up a little and repair the porch, but we will have to wait on the glass. From what I have been told, probably half the windows in the village have broke or cracked."

"If nothing else, we will be able to board up the windows so rain and the cool nights won't get in," Pred replied.

"I'm a little worried about the village keepings on my shelves," said Drel. "We don't want them to get damaged. My shadow dials didn't make it through the shaking though. Two fell over and one sunk into the ground."

"Sorry."

"These days they are useless anyway I guess. The sun, when you can see it past the Lost Moon, doesn't register anything closely resembling normal."

Tymber sat down at the table to rest.

"On the way back today," she said. "Jait decided we needed to call the Lost Moon, the Intruder."

"That's really more what it is to us."

The next morning Pred and Tymber went to help with the cattle in the forest, Drel went straight to his cabin to begin his clean up, and Jait stayed at the Trelop cabin and continued fixing things that came loose.

The men of the village that were at the forest's edge to help didn't really like the fact that a female was there helping them with cattle, an obvious male thing to do. Tymber understood how they viewed such things, so she stayed mostly in the forest. There were a couple of bulls that did not want to turn around and leave. Tymber didn't want to make them mad at her to provoke them charging, so she left them.

According to Herder, they retrieved all but ten head of cattle. That seemed to be better than he had hoped for. Pred and Tymber looked for cattle nearly halfway to the stone cabin, but could not find anymore. Pred told Tymber that they could go back to the forest's edge and follow each set of tracks and find every head, but he was anxious to get back to help Drel with his cabin.

A lot of the cleaning–up at Drel's cabin had been done by the time they reached it. Pred decided to start boarding up the cabin's windows.

Tymber swept and dusted.

Drel was meticulously packing the village keepings into leather sacks. In the sacks, they would be waterproof. He didn't want to risk them to the unknown of shakes, wind, and rain.

When it became late in the day, Pred, Drel, and Tymber sat at the table resting, drinking root tea. Tymber made Drel swear not to tell anyone, and when he did, she told him the adventure that she had with the predator and how she got the bump on her head. As she told him the story, he just sat and shook his head.

"You are a very lucky young lady," he told her at the end of the story, "and apparently very skillful."

She didn't tell him much about the groundshake; she didn't like talking about it.

"I don't understand something, Drel," asked Tymber, changing the subject.

Pred and Drel chuckled a little over that statement.

"There are many things I don't understand," Pred said.

Tymber decided to ask Drel, anyway.

"The Intruder is no longer covering any of the sun. Does that mean that it is now past us?"

"No it doesn't. It won't be past us until it goes by the midday sun position when the sun is not in sight. It seems to be moving fast now. It will be by us in a couple of days, I hope. I can see it well enough now to understand why we call it a moon with its similar markings as our moon. It looks to be bigger than the sun now."

"It is bigger than it got five years ago," said Pred. "I'm still a little confused because as it went by us the last time, it was night and now it is going by in the day."

"I believe it is going on the opposite side of Adentta this time, the side facing the sun."

"Listen!" Tymber said. "I hear a hum and feel a vibration."

"Me too. Let's get back," Pred said, as he stood up to leave. "Come back with us and stay at our cabin Drel. There is no reason to be alone during these times."

"Believe me, going through a shake by yourself is not pleasant," Tymber added. "I will sleep with the girls and you can have my room."

"Thank you," said Drel, smiling at Tymber. "I think I will take you up on that offer."

All Tymber could do was smile back.

On the way back to the Trelop cabin, they had to walk the long way around the fish pond because Lake Simpton and fish pond were way out of their banks, and flooded the trail.

"I've never seen the lake and the fish pond so far out of its banks before," said Pred.

"We need to hurry," said Drel. "I've noticed that when they leave their banks, we have a shake. I feel one is close at hand."

On cue, they felt a stronger vibration under their feet. They ran the rest of the way to the cabin.

When they got there, Sella and the kids were already outside in the yard sitting on the ground waiting for the next shake. Janna had tears in her eyes and Ispis and Sella looked like they had been crying too.

Ispis got up and ran to her father to be held. Pred picked her up and sat down next to Sella. Tymber felt dizzy and dropped to her knees. Drel knelt next to her and put his arms around her as they sat down.

"Where is Jait?" Pred asked. "He needs to come outside too."

"He went to see Storer to get meat for supper." Sella could hardly speak. "He has not returned yet."

The ground jerks began. The center bell began to ring again as if it was warning everyone what was to come, but everyone knew what was coming.

They found themselves lying on the ground. Pred tried to lift his head to watch what was happening, but his head was too heavy.

And then they passed out. What happened during that time was never completely understood by them. The only sounds were the extreme screeching and banging of the ground underneath them. It was probably just as well that they did not witness the intense sound and vibration that took over all things on Adentta.

Adentta shook.

For days Adentta vibrated as the Intruder came it's closest. The moon in the sky grew so enormous that all the crater edges on its surface appeared as large as the mountains on Adentta. The sun was behind the large moon so its dark side was facing and if it had been watched at that time, it would be said that the craters and other formations on the moon formed a dark sinister smile.

All the lakes, seas, and rivers reacted to its presence by overflowing their banks. The wind howled, in this direction and then in that direction, trying to find a way of escape. Mountains rumbled and some exploded at the Intruder. Not a living thing on Adentta was able to remain conscious during the moon's close passage.

Finally, the Intruder had come as close as it would. As it left, it pulled on Adentta to follow. As close as it was, it was stronger than the sun and Adentta had no choice but to follow in its wake. The Intruder sped along in the sky but at last it grew smaller and began losing its influence.

At a very gradual pace, the vibrations eased, the water subsided, winds calmed, and the mountain's complaint became only a rumble. The people on Adentta had not yet gained consciousness, but as they lay where they fell, their minds again became active with a mixture of fears, memories, and what would seem to be random thoughts.

Jait lay unconscious in a field. His mind searched through dreams, fears, and memories as it sought to understand reality once again.

Jait was not surprised to see the stone cabin still standing as he approached. In fact, it looked like the vines had fallen away from the outside walls during the shake and he now could see the beauty and strength of its construction.

The steps up to the door looked well used and the rocking chairs on the porch were inviting to a weary traveler. He did not find it odd that the door was open as he went inside.

He went over to the mantle under the head of the tromptaw and lit a couple of candles and a lantern. It was now dark outside and the night kept him from seeing out the windows. The reflection in the glass showed a tired and weary hunter. He did not remember it being dark on the way there.

He looked around the room in an attempt to remember why he had traveled all this way. He took the cup of hot root tea and sat in a very comfortable chair by the blazing fire in the fireplace. The cabin was very cold for a summer night and he found that the fire didn't help at all. A cold breeze came from that direction and blew in his face. Still thirsty, he looked down and found his cup of tea was empty.

Remembering the door in the floor in one of the small rooms, he got up to investigate. He almost fell over it from the floor being very uneven. He opened it and saw the brightness of the glow rocks from the cave below.

He looked at the narrow ladder that led down to the floor of the cave. It was so far down he couldn't really see the bottom, but he knew the floor had to be there. With the confidence of an explorer like his father, he proceeded down the ladder.

Down he went, a very long way. Still, he was sure of a floor to the cave. He hoped there would be a stream of cool water for him to drink from. His mouth was so dry it made him choke.

The further down he went, the heavier he seemed to feel. At one point he thought he could no longer hold on to the ladder.

When he reached the floor he stood in the black sand of the cavern's dried–up streambed. He looked around and knew that it had not been long since water had flowed there, he could still hear its echo.

He had to find the water.

The next chamber upstream did not have water, nor did the one after that. He left the stream bed in search for the water that belonged to the stream. He had a sharp pain in his side that made him double over.

The sound of water flowing only made him thirstier. A cold breeze blew in his face and it seemed like the cavern was getting colder. He didn't remember cold winds in this cavern before.

He stumbled and again felt heavy. He had to use all his strength just to move. He pulled himself along trying to find the way they had come. He knew he would never be able to climb back up the ladder.

The chambers did not look familiar as he crawled in search for the ladder. None of them did. He was weak, injured, thirsty, and lost in the cavern.

Pred's semi–conscious thoughts began where his conscious thoughts ended, in search of a solution. He was lying with his family, and their protection from the Intruder was at the forefront of his thoughts.

He knew what he had to do. He didn't understand why he hadn't thought of it before. He grabbed his bow, arrows, and knife and headed for the door. He did not want to wake his family, so he left quietly in the dark of night alone.

Tymber and Jait would want to go with him, but he knew that this was a job he had to do by himself. Simply put, it was himself and Adentta against the Intruder. Adentta depended on him. His family depended on them. Why else would he have been chosen to be Hero?

He was no fool and he knew that he could not kill the Intruder. The best to hope for was to make it leave and that's exactly what he was going to do. He had to get closer to it. He climbed to the top of a tall hill. A place that did not seem familiar, but he knew why he was there. From the top of the hill he could see a great mountain, the only place on Adentta close enough to the Intruder. This is where it had to take place.

As he stood on the hill, looking up at Pointer Mountain, he knew there wasn't much that he needed to do. Adentta knew what to do all by herself. He just had to be her eyes and tell her when the time was right.

Pred looked west over the field of beasts as clouds were building in the sky. Lightning flashed from cloud to cloud, yet too far away to hear the thunder. A cold wind hit him in his face. Pred watched as the clouds boiled in preparation.

The storm moved closer and Pred could begin to feel and hear the power in the storm. Adentta was generating the power that she would need for the battle to come.

The clouds parted and Pred could see the Intruder move across the sky exactly as he had anticipated. It hung over Pointer Mountain in a fearless manner, like the ruler of the sky. Pred didn't like the dominating attitude of the Intruder.

He stood up tall with his arms out wide.

"It is time," he called out.

He lit the torch arrow and shot it into the sky in the direction of the mountain. It soared brightly in the night sky. Lightning shot from the arrow to the top of the great mountain.

That signal from Pred was understood by Adentta. Pred could feel the vibration of Adentta's anger beneath his feet. For too long Adentta had allowed the Intruder in her sky. It was time for it to leave. Adentta will make that very clear.

As lightning struck the top of the great mountain, a small stream of smoke escaped, and then a plume of smoke, and then explosions started softly and grew in power and intensity. Melted rock and ash spewed from the top of the mountain aimed directly at the Intruder.

Lightning bolted into the air from the top of the mountain, seeming to ignite the gases and smoke as they bellowed up to the Intruder.

The Intruder turned red from anger and fear. It soon was smothering in a cloud of smoke and ash.

Pred fell to his knees under the pressure of the intense noise and shaking. He knew his job was done. He continued to watch the spectacular show of force from Adentta on the Intruder. He knew now that the Intruder would not stay.

Pebbles of fire fell around him. The Intruder tried to fight back with the call for falling stars. They lit up the sky, but was no match.

A shower of ash fell on Pred as he watched the night sky turn red and yellow in the attack. The smoke bellowed up to Intruder in the shape of fists on fire. The Intruder was no longer visible through the cloud of smoke, but Pred knew it must be in agony from the assault.

Pred could not look away. Vallend seemed unconcerned. He stayed until the end.

Some of the Trelops began regaining consciousness and Sella patted Pred's hand as she lay beside him. Her hands were as cold as the air around them. Ispis hung on to him and Janna held on to Sella as tight as they could and trembled from the fear and cold. Pred was glad to be back with them again after such a long journey.

There was no shaking or jerking and the bell was not ringing. All they felt was a cold wind in their face, which probably helped them to wake.

Pred and Sella sat up when they got enough strength. Both were shivering from the cold dark night air. Pred slapped his clothes to shake off the ash that wasn't there. Neither knew what had happened except that they passed out during a shake. He could not see anyone else in the dark so he called to Tymber and Drel to see if they were okay.

Tymber did not answer.

"I believe she is alright," Drel said, as he tried to wake her. "She is just not awake yet." He stroked her face as he laid next to her in the dark.

Before Tymber woke, she wondered why she had vibrated down into the caverns. Nobody else came. She was sitting on the sand watching the cold water flow by. She looked closely at the water to make sure it had no ripples from vibration. It no longer did. The silver glow of the rocks shimmering on the water seemed like a wasted invitation to drink.

She was so thirsty, why could she not get up and drink from the stream? She did not feel hurt, just unable to move.

The rocks were wasting water as they dripped down and splashed in the stream. Don't they know they should absorb any water that they find?

A sudden fear came to thought. Jait was lost in the caverns.

"Jait," she called. "Jait are you there?" She did not hear an answer, only the echo of her voice in the chambers.

She took a deep breath and it was good to breathe again. The air was sweet with the scent of the flowers at her cabin. She looked around but could not see the flowers she smelled.

The warm air from the melted rocks in the chambers below seemed to seep up through the sand. She had been cold but was warm now. She could feel his warm hand on her face, closed her eyes, and laid back to enjoy his company.

When she opened her eyes again, she found that he was still not there.

"He must be waiting for me," she whispered.

The travel back to him would be long.

"It seems like you could come here instead and sit with me," she said to him. Then she realized he didn't know the way to the cavern and he would not be coming.

"Tymber," she thought she heard him say. She grabbed sand in her hands in hopes that would keep her there.

"I told you to come here," she said, in a weak voice. "I was waiting for you."

"I'm sorry Tymber, I don't understand what you are saying," Drel said, helping her sit up and lean against him.

"The glow rocks have gone dark."

Confusion came over her and a chill. She was outside sitting on the ground in the dark with a blanket on her, sitting up against Drel.

A lady came out of a cabin with a lantern and asked her how she felt and kissed her on the forehead.

Tymber opened her clenched hands to empty them, but they were already empty. She turned to Drel and thanked him for coming to her when she needed him.

He didn't know what she was talking about. He touched her face and looked down into her eyes and said that he would gladly go anywhere that she wanted him to go. He bent down and kissed her and she kissed him back.

He told her not to talk, just sit and rest until she felt better. He kept his arm around her and comforted her and again she felt warm. She sat and enjoyed his company.

Everything went dark when Jait opened his eyes. Jait was laying face down on the ground in the middle of a field in the middle of the night. He just laid there as he tried to gain his senses. Not really remembering what had happened, he wondered if he was hurt. He felt no pain except for his lips, tongue, and throat, from being dry. He moved his waist to see how bad his side hurt, but it did not.

He moved his hand along the grass by his side and he felt the dew. He pulled a hand full of grass up and rubbed it on his lips for moisture.

He lifted his head to look around and could see only things that were even darker. He thought they were probably trees. He could hear no noises, no animals, no crickets, so he grunted to make sure he could hear.

Pulling himself up to kneeling position, he realized he couldn't remember which field he was in when the shake started. He wished now that he went the longer way to Storer's using the trail.

He looked around to see if anything looked familiar but he could not see in the darkness. Even the stars were confusing and seemed out of place. He had no clue as to the direction of the cabin.

"I got to get back," he croaked, not really able to talk.

He was kneeling in a field not too far from his cabin, but he was lost.

"Jait?" he heard Tymber say. He turned his head in the direction of the voice.

"Are you there?" He looked for a landmark in that direction. He saw three stars in a group in the direction of her voice and started to walk towards them. His attempt to answer her call just fell to the ground as a whisper.

Tymber was feeling better and surprisingly she was able to get up.

"Where is Jait?" She looked around in the dim lantern light and still didn't see him. "Where is my brother!" she demanded.

"We have not seen him since the shake," said Sella, as again she became worried about him. "He went to Storer to get meat for supper. I am so sorry I sent him."

"I will find him," said Tymber, as she grabbed her bow off the ground. She was actually more determined than she was strong. She had to go to her knees as she bent over for the bow when the blood left her head.

"I appreciate you wanting to save me Sis, but it is quite unnecessary," Jait half whispered a croak as he walked up the trail to the cabin.

Sella squealed when she heard his voice and ran to hug him.

"I must have passed out. I just came to and found myself in Forger's field in the dark. It took time to realize what had happened and where I was."

"We all passed out, son," said Pred, also giving Jait a hug.

"I'm glad I didn't have to go get you and drag your butt back," said Tymber.

Pred went to the well and brought out a bucket of water for everyone to drink.

"I don't think I have ever been so thirsty in my life," he said. The bucket emptied quickly with everyone being thirsty, so he went back to refill it.

Drel was away from the lantern looking up at the stars. Tymber went over to him, handed him another cup of water and asked what he was looking at.

"I have been looking at the stars most of my life and they seem to be out of place. I can not tell if it is just now dark or if it will be light soon."

Tymber put her arm through his as they stood there. He looked down and smiled at her, but he was not sure she could see him.

"Look at all the falling stars," he said. "All outer objects seem to be disturbed tonight."

"Look towards the light," she said, turning towards the lantern on the porch. "I would not have thought it was cold enough to snow. See the snow flakes?"

"It looks more like ash falling," Drel said. "It seems a little odd, but probably ash from the chimney."

He really didn't believe his explanation but couldn't explain the ash any other way.

"Mother is trying to cook supper, I should go help her. She said that the meat that Jait brought back is spoiled. It looks like it had been butchered a week ago."

"That doesn't sound like something Storer would do. But actually, that might help confirm what I've been thinking. Believe me, I don't know, but I think we may have been unconscious for days."

Drel could feel Tymber twinge at the thought of laying on the ground unconscious for days. In fact, she started leaning on him a little heavier since her legs were still not strong.

He turned her around and started towards the cabin door.

"That would explain why everyone is so thirsty and hungry," Tymber said, as they walked into the cabin.

They ate like they had never eaten. Each had multiple plates of grain cakes.

After the young girls left the table, Drel told the adults of his theory about the multiple days of being unconscious.

"We could have been eaten by animals," said Sella, looking at Drel in disbelief.

"I would think that most of the animals were in about the same shape as us, Sella. I think that is why we all were so hungry and thirsty when we woke."

"How long until daylight Drel?" Pred asked, looking out a window that no longer had glass.

"I'm not sure. None of the stars look to be in the right place for at any time of night."

Sella got up to check on the two girls. She came back surprised that they were asleep.

"It looks like they have gotten some color back in their faces. I was worried during supper that they were sick."

"What we went through was probably harder on the younger," Pred said, looking carefully at Tymber to see if her color had come back.

"I don't know about the younger thing," Drel said, teasingly looking at Tymber and smiling. "Tymber was the last to wake up."

Tymber just stuck her tongue out at him as she got up to get another cup of water. She was glad she could move to get a drink and thought how strange that was.

Sella asked Jait just out of curiosity how he found his way home in the dark after being unconscious, waking, and then not knowing where he was?

Jait looked around like everyone should know that answer.

"I heard Tymber call out my name and I followed the direction of her voice," he said.

"All I heard her say was a bunch of mumble," said Drel. "She was unconscious until just before you got back."

Tymber came back to the table and everyone was looking at her.

"What's the matter?" she asked.

"Nothing," said Drel. "Jait was just telling us about something he thought he heard."

They sat, ate, and drank for what seemed to be an endless night.

After many meals and naps, the sun still had not risen. They began to wonder if the world would ever be light again.

EIGHTEEN

It was still dark.

After the length of three days and nights, Jait was outside trying to chop wood for the stove with just the light from a lantern, when he noticed a faint lightness in the east.

He called for everyone to come outside.

Cheers all around as they saw the signs of a sunrise about to happen.

Their cheers died down to extreme silence when they saw the sun clear the horizon. The sun was small and dim.

"What happened?" asked Sella, as she turned to Drel for an answer.

Drel was sitting on the edge of the porch with his head down. He suspects what has happened; one of his greatest fears appears to be coming true. When asked the question he looked up.

"We need to make the most out of our day," was all he could say.

As the small sun slowly rose, the light of the day was not much better than a cloudy day even though there were no clouds. The dim light didn't cast much of a shadow and the air did not want to warm. The cool breeze was chilling to the bone.

The Trelop family did the only thing they could; busy themselves with the chores of repair from the shake.

When they stopped to rest, Pred, Drel, Jait, and Tymber were sitting around the table.

"Drel, why is the sun so small?" Tymber asked.

"I didn't know it could happen so fast, but it looks like Adentta has moved away from the sun at a very fast pace. I believe the Intruder has pulled us away from our sun, the way it pulls the water out of the lake."

"Will Adentta move back towards the sun?" Tymber asked.

"To be truthful, Tymber, it is unlikely," Drel said, hesitantly.

Everyone sat in silence.

"What do you think will happen now?" asked Pred.

"I think that we will continue to drift away from the sun, and we will be left in darkness. It will be like a continuous cold dark winter."

The town bells chimed and everyone braced for the shake. But it never came.

"That's the signal for the leaders to meet," Pred said, after he realized that it wasn't another shake.

"I've been waiting for this meeting to happen since dawn," said Drel. "They want to ask me the questions that I don't want to answer."

Pred and Drel started down the trail to the village center when Tymber came up from behind them.

"May I come with?" she asked.

"Of course," answered her father.

"Father," Tymber said. "We need to move to the cavern."

All three people stopped.

"You know I'm right."

"We don't even know if the caverns have survived the shakes," he replied.

"I will go and see."

Pred looked at Tymber and he knew she would go by herself if she had to.

"Drel just said that we soon may be in the dark, a long, cold winter dark. In the cavern, we don't need the sun to live."

"We need to see what the village wants to do first," he answered.

"It is large enough for the entire village," she said.

They continued to walk and talk about living in the cavern.

"I planted some vegetables when I was there last time," she said, when they talked about food supply.

"For some reason that doesn't surprise me," Pred said.

"We will see if they will grow there," she said, shrugging and holding her hands up in wonder. "I think that the caverns are warm and moist and if it is light enough, they will grow well."

"Let's not talk about living in the cavern at this meeting. We need to see what the leaders want to do."

They walked up the steps of the Fendal Betalum Community Center. The building looked like it had been through a couple of groundshakes. There were boards missing and all the windows were broken.

"Tymber, wait in the foyer as I ask permission for you to come into the meeting."

"Okay, and don't feel bad if they don't let me in," she said, "I really just wanted to talk to you two on the way here."

The meeting went as Pred had expected, except it was shorter. Drel was asked many questions about the length of night and the size of the sun. He simply explained what he believed to be true. He had believed for some time that Adentta has been moving away from the sun. The appearance of the Intruder seems to have increased the speed of that happening. He then was asked about the future of the sun. He told everyone not to expect for it get better, but he really didn't know for sure.

There was only one thing that Drel said that was good. There was no longer any sign of the Intruder.

Leader asked all the leaders to hurry in their tasks and to expect an early and harsh winter. Farmer was asked about the harvest and he said they were only ten days away from the beginning of harvest.

"If we have sun to harvest by, we will complete it soon after that," he said. "The harvest will be better than expected because of the added planted fields. Some of the plants in some of the fields, however, did lose their fruit because of the shaking."

Leader dismissed everyone knowing they had much to do to repair the village. When Tymber saw her father come out, she thought that he came to get her to join them in the meeting, and was shocked to learn it was already over.

Before going back to the Trelop cabin, Drel asked them to stop in the Center square on the benches and talk about what they needed to do. They were the only people in the square; everyone else was busy in repair of the crafteries.

"I am not sure the leaders understand the situation," Drel said, talking low to make sure no one else could hear. "I don't believe that things can be fixed. It is without a doubt that Adentta is moving away from the sun. I think it will continue to move away and eventually not shine as a sun on Adentta again.

"I think what Tymber has suggested about living underground in the caverns may be the only way to survive. Without the sun, we will have no light or heat. It will be like a dark cold winter, colder than any and it will be for always."

"Father, we need to go to the cavern, and if it is still there, we need to prepare it for us and the village people. Well, actually, we need to prepare it for two villages."

"They will not want to leave here," said Pred, looking around at the people working hard on their crafteries and their cabins.

"Maybe not now, but they will."

"How long do we have?" asked Tymber.

"Now that I don't know," he responded. "The days will be much longer. It is almost the time for sunset and the sun is only but one–fourth of the way up the sky. Of course, that means that the nights will be very long as well."

Pred looked at Tymber.

"If the cavern is no longer there, we will have the length of four nights in the forest to make our way back."

"The cavern will be there, Father. I know it will be. It feels like I have just been there."

"Well let's go back and talk to your mother."

Pred got up to start walking and looked back at Drel.

"You of course will be coming with us, won't you?" Pred asked.

"Of course, I will go wherever Tymber goes," Drel answered.

Tymber put her arm in his as they started the walk back.

Pred stopped and went back to them and put his arm around them both.

"Sella and I are very glad you two are together. It makes both of us very happy."

"Thank you, Pred."

"Thanks, Father."

The walk back to the cabin was not long enough for Pred. His job now was to convince Sella to give up what she has here and take her and the kids through the forest and live in a cave. It seemed like a much better idea in the center square than it did in his cabin looking at Sella.

Pred took Sella by the hand and walked with her to the kitchen table.

"Girls, you need to go to bed," he told them. "It has been a full day even though it's still light."

Ispis and Janna complained about going to bed while it was still light, but they did go.

Pred and Sella sat down at the table. He knew this was going to be the hardest thing he ever talked to her about.

Pred looked at Sella.

"We have to talk."

Tymber took Jait by the arm and whispered to him that they needed to go outside and talk too.

"Come with us," she said to Drel.

Outside, she led Jait away from where anyone from inside the cabin could hear and sat down under a tree.

"First off, I wanted to tell you that Drel and I are now together as a couple."

"I think you two were the last to know that," Jait said, laughing.

Tymber stuck her tongue out at him and told him that wasn't the main reason for her to come outside.

"Jait, Drel doesn't think that the sun will ever be the same. He thinks that Adentta is moving away from the sun and that the sun will only get smaller."

"Adentta will be in a constant dark cold winter," Drel said, as he sat down next to Tymber and Jait.

"Father is inside asking mother to move to the cavern to live. Hopefully, we will go and prepare it for the whole village to live."

Jait did not seem surprised by the notion. He loved the cavern as much as Tymber and had given that some thought himself.

"I don't know that mother will agree to that," he said. "She has always been spooked to think about being in the forest. Giving up everything here will be hard for her."

"And for all of us," Tymber said. "But we really have no choice. The dark winter will come whether we are prepared for it or not."

"I will not leave you and the girls here alone again," Pred said. The three outside overheard the conversation from inside the cabin.

"That was the part where she told him to go and prepare for them and then she and the girls would go, and that, was his answer," Tymber said.

Drel and Jait knew she was probably right.

"Is there room in the cavern for a herd to graze?" asked Jait.

Drel looked at Jait like he was crazy; Tymber didn't even flinch at the question.

"We have not even investigated much of the other side the rain room yet. There could be enough room there to have all the animals graze. We already know that grass grows well in the cavern."

"We will have to build a ramp to get people and cattle up to the ledge," Jait said, talking out loud, but mostly to himself.

Thinking about the cavern made Jait thirsty.

"We will bring with us everything that you want," they heard Pred say. "We don't have to take it all in one trip. Jait and Tymber can come back to get the things we leave behind."

"Sounds like Father is having trouble convincing Mother," Jait said, after hearing another part of the inside discussion.

They sat for a little while to see if they could hear anymore of the cabin conversation. They did not so they continued their thoughts.

"Looks like you may get your wish to see if things will grow in there," said Jait.

"We will find out when we go back to the cavern. I planted corn, tomatoes, squash, and potatoes last time we were there. "

"Always thinking ahead," said Jait. "You know, I never thanked you for calling out to me when I was lost in the cavern last night."

"I didn't know if you were in the caverns, too, or not. It felt like you were there and you were lost and I needed to call out to you."

Then Jait and Tymber sat in silence as they thought about last night. They knew that had happened but also knew that it couldn't have.

"I meant to say when I was in Forgers field," Jait corrected himself. "I heard you call for me as I searched for the direction back."

Tymber looked confused. She remembers calling for Jait, but in the cavern. It couldn't have been last night, but it was.

Drel saw Tymber fighting with reality.

"Last night during the shake was very confusing for everyone. Where reality started and dreams ended was not clear for anyone. And when we all woke, it was to a reality that seemed like a dream."

Tymber looked at Drel not really believing his explanation nor believing her memory.

"It must have been a very realistic dream," she said.

"Well I know one thing," said Jait, standing back up. "I was not asleep when I heard Tymber calling to me."

"Do you think if she called out your name from here, you could hear her in Forger's field?" Drel asked Jait, in a teasing manner. Drel knew that it was impossible to hear Tymber all the way to Forger's field.

"Well I did."

Jait was about to go back inside the cabin when Tymber asked him to stay for a moment.

"Jait tell me if you don't want to, but I think that just you and I should go to the cavern before it gets dark again to check on it. That way Father can stay with mother and the girls and we can find out if it's worth the time to plan to live there."

"I think that's a good plan, Tymber. We need to tell Father that we will leave soon so we can get there by dark."

"I will come, also," said Drel.

Jait looked at him wondering if he really wanted to go to the cavern or just spend some time with Tymber.

"I have heard so much about this cavern I have to see it for myself." Then Drel hesitated for a moment, and said, "I want to go see my new home."

All three went back into the cabin. Pred and Sella were still sitting at the table talking but told everyone to come in.

Jait decided that he was going to be the one to tell his mother and father about their plans to go to the cavern. Surprisingly, they both took it pretty well. They knew that before a lot of work went into moving they needed to know if there was somewhere to move.

"I will be going also," Drel said. "I want to see the cavern for myself."

"Drel, are you not worried about going into the forest?" asked Sella.

"I have Tymber to protect me."

Everyone laughed at that, but it probably wasn't that far from the truth.

"Just to be safe, I will let you take my bow and arrows," said Pred. "Tymber and Jait can show you how to use it if you need lessons."

Jait couldn't help but tell Drel that he was the one who needed to teach him how to shoot. Tymber couldn't hit a cow at point blank range.

Tymber told Jait to make sure he brought an extra change of clothes on their trip just in case he fell in the river.

Drel had to smile at Tymber. Jait was nearly twice her size, but she was still able to get her way with him. Of course, that was only possible because Jait let her.

The next few hours Pred and Sella were preparing things for the trip while Jait, Tymber, and Drel rested. Tymber moved the girls over, got into bed and fell to sleep immediately. Jait didn't have much trouble sleeping in the light either, but Drel slept very little. He had many things on his mind, least of which was the condition of his cabin, which he hadn't seen since the last shake. He kept telling himself that it didn't matter, he was going to be moving anyway, but that didn't seem to help.

When the three woke, everything had been packed and was ready for them to leave. It was what would normally have been thought to be noon, that is to say the sun was directly overhead. It would seem like they had two normal days in time length to get to the cavern before the long night, if Drel's estimates on day length were correct.

Sella cooked food to be packed, but also food for a meal before they left.

"What I want to know is if this is breakfast, lunch, or supper?" Jait asked, as he sat down at the table.

"Well it looks like noon so we'll call it lunch," Sella replied.

They sat and ate without much conversation.

"Are you excited about finally going into the forest, Drel?" asked Pred, just to see if he could start a conversation.

"The forest is something I always wondered about, but going into it wasn't one of my goals. This time though I am looking forward to traveling and experiencing some of the adventures that you three have been talking about. I am very anxious to see the stone cabin and the caverns. They really seem like amazing places."

"I'm looking forward to exploring the Sea Cavern more," Tymber added, "and showing you the spray room and the melted Rock River chamber. I can't wait to see if my vegetables have grown too."

Drel smiled at Tymber's excitement about the cavern. He loved her excitement about things she discovers and finds beautiful. How could he not have seen falling in love with her? She quickly had become the most important thing in his life.

When they got up to leave, Pred looked like he wished he was going with, but he knew his place was with his wife and his young daughters during such strange times.

A round of hugs and they walked out the door. Pred handed Drel his bow and arrows.

"Thanks," Drel said, as he took them from him.

Pred teased Drel and told Jait and Tymber to make sure they stayed behind Drel if he shoots.

"I hope I don't have any reason to try and shoot this."

"You may change your mind after days of eating fish and would like a little pork or deer meat instead."

They took off from the Trelop cabin heading towards Drel's cabin. Drel told them that they didn't have to take the time to stop, but when they reached his cabin they stopped anyway.

The damage to his cabin was extensive and a large tree limb had gone through the roof. The chimney had almost completely collapsed and every window had broken and was scattered on the floor.

Drel went inside to check on the village keepings. They were intact in the leather bags. He covered them additionally with blankets for additional protection and left.

Tymber gave Drel a hug for sympathy.

"It is good that you were not here during the last groundshake," Tymber told him. "You may have been hurt."

Drel nodded, but it really didn't seem to help his spirits.

After another quick look around, off they went into the forest.

At the forest boundary line, Drel hesitated when he entered. He took a deep breath and followed after Tymber. He tried not to show his nerves, but it was obvious to both Jait and Tymber, who tried not to show that they recognized Drel's apprehension.

Just moments after they entered the forest, the sky grew cloudy and they could hear thunder ahead. With the dimmed sun, it became not much lighter than the night.

"Just great," said Drel, as they stopped to try to let their eyes adjust to the dimness.

In the confusion of the sudden darkness, the animals started to react by howling and squawking. A hoo owl sat high in a tree above them along their trail. They could just make out its silhouette against the clouds in the sky. It peered down on them like they were to blame for the sudden darkness.

Hooooo, hoooo, eerk. It swept down just over Drel's head as if to warn him to return the way he came. It circled around through the tree limbs and landed where it had sat before, continuing to stare down at them.

"Not quite the reception into the forest I was hoping for," whispered Drel, laying on the ground and looking around in the sky for other possible attackers.

"It looks like the owl is sitting by a nest and probably has chicks that she is trying to protect," Tymber whispered back. "The animals are just as confused by the shakes, dim light, long days, and long nights, as we are. She thinks it might be us to blame."

"We may want to respect her territory and walk around," Jait said. "We don't want to make her anymore mad at us than she is already."

"Her eyes seem to almost glow in the dark," Drel said, looking back up at her as they walked around her area. He was successful in hiding a sudden shiver.

"Has that ever happened to you before," Drel asked Tymber, after they had gone around and was back on the trail.

"No, not in the forest, but one time in the village I had a hoo owl wanting to protect her nest by the fish pond. She didn't swoop down on me, but she did make a lot of chatter because I was there. So things like that just don't happen in the forest. Even in the village animals will protect what is theirs."

The wind started to pick up and the thunder seemed to get closer. The clouds in the sky were moving at a fast rate in the direction they were going.

Tymber turned to Jait and said that they may have to spend a little time in the cabin again because of rain.

"We had to do that once already," she told Drel.

"Of course I wanted to stop at the stone cabin anyway. I want to see it for myself, along with the head of a predator."

They walked slower than normal because of the dim light even though they wished they could speed up. Seeing the next marked tree was not always easy and often Jait had to walk ahead and find them as they progressed.

After what seemed to be twice as long to get there, they finally reached the orchard by the stone cabin. Drel saw the orchard before Tymber had a chance to point it out.

Of course Drel was on a travel adventure, so he wanted to investigate the orchard. Tymber saw yellow fruit on the ground and some still in the trees. It looked like many had fallen from the shakes.

Tymber bent over and picked one up. She drew her knife in a manner that made Drel realize she could handle it well. She sliced it in half, smelled it, and then tasted it.

"Lemon," she said, smiling. "If I had honey I would make you a very delicious drink."

Drel took half of the lemon and took a bite. He cringed with the sour taste.

Tymber and Jait had to laugh at the faces that Drel made.

"You would need a lot of honey to make a good tasting drink with that," he said.

"Believe me, it's really good."

"I saw a honey hive near where we will be camping tonight... I mean later," said Jait, still smiling at Drel.

"We can collect some honey there and I'll make you a delicious drink. Help me up into the tree so I can pick some fresh lemons."

Drel lent Tymber a hand to get up into the tree. She threw down to him more than he thought she should carry.

She jumped down on her own and surprisingly was able to put all the lemons in her backpack.

"I saved some room for them in case they were ripe enough to pick. Come see the stone cabin," Tymber said, leading the way.

As they approached the cabin, Tymber commented on the vines that had been climbing up the sides of the cabin had fallen away. Tymber looked at Jait for a reaction to that, but Jait didn't seem to be too surprised.

"What a magnificent structure," Drel said, as he got a good look at it. "The outside doesn't seem to be injured at all from the shakes."

Drel went up to the stone wall at the front of the cabin.

"The builders seemed to use a harder substance than we do to bond the rocks together. I wish we had a chance to learn from them."

"That's pretty much what Father said, too," Jait said. "The people of Hantfel said they would be glad to show us how. It looks like they make their mud in a similar way."

Inside, Drel went through the same amazements that the Trelops did when they first went into the stone cabin, but he spent most of his time in front of the head of the predator.

Jait remained by the door feeling like he should know something, but couldn't remember why he should know it, or what 'it' was.

"I can't believe you faced one of those in the forest by yourself," Drel said, as he put his arm around her. "I would have been scared to death."

"Oh, I was. I just lucked out as to what I did."

"Luck had nothing to do with it. You saw what had to be done and you did it. I'm very proud of you."

"Thanks." She gave him a kiss. Feeling a little embarrassed doing that in front of Jait; she turned around to realize that Jait was not with them, so she went to find him.

He was still standing in the doorway, half in and half out of the cabin.

"Are you all right?" she asked.

"I'm fine," he answered. "I just think we need to get moving. We need to get to the cavern by dark."

"That won't be for a day and a half," she said, as she pushed Jait out of the doorway so she could leave.

"That's just an estimate, Tymber," Drel shouted after her to make sure she heard it.

On the way to the front of the cabin Drel saw the shelves where Pred found the writings and maps. He looked into a drawer and found many wrappers of writings. It took Drel somewhat by surprise. They looked like a village's keepings. He put what he could find into his backpack to look at later.

As Drel went outside, Jait looked inside one last time and attempted to close the door. It would not close. One of the hinges broke in a groundshake, so he just left it half open.

The sky still looked like rain, and the thunder now seemed to come from every direction, but they knew that Jait was right. They couldn't stop for the night this far from the cavern. Daylight may run out before they got to the Sea Caverns.

The stream bed was still dry so they used it again to move down to the river. Tymber wanted to go in the other direction in the stream to show Drel the Stone Cabin Cavern that they found, but Jait again said that they needed to keep moving.

Lightning flashes were getting closer, but still there was no rain.

"How much farther is the river," asked Drel, wondering if they had enough time before the rain started.

"It's going to take a while longer to get there," answered Tymber. "If it was light enough to see, I would show you were we are on the map."

A cold wind followed the stream bed and blew in their faces as they traveled. They started to appreciate the nearby lightning because it was the only time it was light enough to see. Even the larger rocks in the streambed were hard to see in the darkness.

"I hope the sun didn't fall in the sky and turn night on us already," Drel said, as he fought to see where to walk.

"Not funny," answered Tymber, knowing he was just joking. "I'm getting hungry, Jait. We may need to camp soon."

"I was hoping to get to the river and catch fish for supper. I didn't want to eat what was packed for us too quickly, but I'm getting hungry too."

"We could have had owl for supper," Drel said, smiling at Tymber, who decided to ignore that remark.

"Without the sun it's hard to tell how long we've been traveling," Tymber said, catching up to Jait when he stopped to look around.

"Father would stop now and camp," Jait decided. "We are tired and hungry and we need to rest."

"I agree," said Drel, who had been ready to stop for some time. "Remember, this is my first travel. I am getting pretty tired."

Tymber moved over to a sandy area of the stream bed and took the tent out of her backpack.

"Drel, gather wood for a fire," said Jait. "We need enough to last us the whole time we are camped. Hopefully, it won't rain and put it out."

Jait continued down the stream in hopes to find game to harvest for supper. Drel piled the wood near where Tymber was putting up the tent.

"Do you need some help?" he asked.

"I just about have it done now," she answered.

"It looks like it may be getting a little lighter."

"Yes it does," she said, knowing that he was just looking for things to say.

He got out his striker and started the fire, which took awhile to get burning good in the damp air.

They both moved a log over next to the fire and sat down to warm up. Drel put his arm around her and she put her head on his shoulder. They both watched the fire and sat mostly in silence waiting for Jait to return to see if he found supper.

It wasn't long when he returned empty handed.

They got out one of the meals that Sella packed for them. Drel found a flat rock and heated it up to put his grain cakes on to warm them. Tymber and Jait used it too.

That 'night' the sky stayed fairly dark from the low clouds. They had only received a slight sprinkle of rain.

Drel woke a few times when he thought he heard strange noises. Seeing that the other two were still asleep, he decided he was imagining them. He didn't want to tell Jait and Tymber, but this was the first time he had ever slept outside of a cabin.

He didn't particularly like the fact that his first time was in the middle of the forest when the animals seemed to be in unrest.

Just when he was getting more nervous, the fire outside the tent popped loudly and he almost squealed. It was then that he decided he was being silly and worked at falling back to sleep.

Jait and Tymber woke up first and restarted the fire for warmth before Drel came out of the tent. They simply had a quick breakfast and again began their trip. It looked like the sky was finally going to clear up; however, it didn't get very light. The small sun was low in the sky and was not very bright. The lower it got the more orange in color and dimmer it became.

They did not stop until they got to View Hill, except at the honey hive between there and the river, where Tymber emptied her water bottle into Drel's and filled hers up with honey.

The view on the hill was spectacular even though it was faded and dim. Drel said he had never seen anything so beautiful. The valley with the river below, the sea, the Guard Mountains, and even the small orange sun was beautiful as it lowered to set behind them.

Drel stood and looked at the wonders.

"This really must have been beautiful in the bright sunlight," he finally said.

Tymber was wishing he had not said that. It brought back the fears of what their destinies might be—the destinies of all the people of the villages. When the sun sets this time, will it rise again? She didn't want to find this view and then lose it to the endless night.

Jait woke her up from her thoughts by saying that they had to get moving.

They hurried along their trail to the Sea Cavern, stopping only briefly to eat.

It was nearly dark from the night when they climbed up on the ledge leading to the cavern. They moved slowly, almost afraid to enter, afraid that they couldn't enter.

They peeked into the cavern opening. All looked okay.

As they walked through the cavern, they found that besides a couple of openings between chambers having more rubble, the cavern seemed the same as before the shakes. They all shared a sigh of relief. From what they could see, the caverns were indeed still open and usable.

Tymber and Jait showed Drel around the areas that they had already explored. The first, of course, was First Chamber and the stream running through it. They stooped down to drink from it.

"I can now see why you two have fallen in love with this place. It is amazing."

"You haven't seen anything yet," Jait said, as he motioned Drel to follow him.

They took him to Spray Chamber and then down to the melted rock river. Jait shot an arrow into the melted Rock River Chamber to show Drel how hot the chamber was.

After they left that chamber, Tymber couldn't wait any longer to inspect her planted vegetables. They climbed back out of the lower chambers, and she nearly started to run back to where she had done the planting. Jait and Drel were only barely able to keep up with her.

When they next saw her, she was standing at the entrance to the chamber that she had used for the planting.

"I can't believe you hadn't entered," Jait said, as they approached her from behind.

Then all three of them stood and looked at the vegetable plants that were in front of them. To Tymber, it looked like all that she had planted was growing.

"This is more than I had hoped for," she said, still in shock. She turned to Drel with a tear in her eye.

"The soils must be good for growing," she said.

"I would think that is an understatement, Sis."

They walked around the small area that Tymber had planted. The plants seemed to be doing very well. They all had a nice dark green color to them.

"Like we hoped, we will be able to live here," Tymber said, hugging her brother. "We will have very good news to tell Mother and Father when we get back."

"I'm hungry," said Drel.

"Do you think it's too dark to go out and fish?" asked Tymber.

"We can go see."

They went back outside and stood on the cavern ledge. All they could see were the stars in the sky. They could hear the sea, but could not see anything except an occasional sparkle on the water.

"I'm guessing it's too dark," Drel said, trying to lighten the mood.

"I haven't seen our moon in the sky since the long nights," said Tymber.

"I haven't seen it either," said Drel, "but it can be there. It doesn't have a bright sun to shine on it so it may stay in the dark. One way to tell is if we still have the high and low waters that the moon causes."

A cold wind was blowing off the sea and with disappointment they went back into the cavern to prepare a meal.

"I won't have enough food for the time we will be gone," she said. "We will have to fish and hunt while we're here and on the way back."

"After we rest, we can build a fire on the beach and fish by firelight," said Jait.

Sitting around after they ate, resting from their travel, they were discussing what they should do first. Jait said take a nap. Tymber said she meant after they rested. Jait said that was correct, a nap after they rested.

"Jait," Drel asked, "the Spray Chamber seemed like it was sea water, right?

Jait nodded.

"That water obviously comes in somewhere and then is heated to a boil and then sprays through the hole in the spray chamber."

"That's pretty much how we have it figured," Jait responded.

"We need to find out where the water comes in from the sea. There may be sea fish that come in as well."

"And fish there," Jait perked up.

"Yes," said Drel, smiling. "If we can find where the water comes in, and we can get to it, we may be able to fish in the comfort of the cavern."

They quickly ate more grain cakes and got up to go look for the water entrance.

"You two go ahead," said Tymber. "I brought more seed and I'm going to start planting the rest of that chamber."

"It's been a long day, Sis, and you are tired and should rest. I will help you tomorrow."

"I will just work till I'm tired, which won't be long I don't think. And besides, I'm not really sure when tomorrow is with no sun to tell us."

"I've been working on that problem," said Drel. "I may end up talking to Moment. I have tried to avoid that, but we are going to need something to tell us when days go by. He had worked on a device to tell the time of day. It didn't work well, but maybe he can try again. I don't know what we will do, but we will need something to tell us that it is morning, midday, or suppertime."

"I know when it's suppertime," said Jait. "I get hungry."

Jait and Drel headed towards the spray chamber. They decided that that would be a good place to start looking for the sea entrance. Tymber went to the Grow Chamber, as she named it, to do some planting.

They entered Spray Chamber just as it finished spraying. Drel went to the spray opening and tried to get a feel for how far up the spray was coming.

"Let's go back down to Melted Rock chamber and look around more down there," said Jait. "All I've ever seen down there is the one chamber, though."

They were about to climb back down to the lowest chamber when Jait noticed a small opening, about half his height, over to the side.

"Let's crawl through there and see what's in there," Jait said, already stooping down to look through it.

"Let's go," answered Drel.

They didn't have to crawl long, the passage ceiling raised back over head–high. There were areas however where there were no glow rocks, so at times they had to move slowly and feel their way along. They had not brought a torch or lantern with them.

"I can smell the sea," Jait said, excitedly.

The glow rocks returned and they found themselves going downward. The corridor opened up into a small room and the passage ended in a drop–off. There were no glow rocks beyond the drop–off, so what was at the bottom of the drop–off could not be seen.

Jait picked up a stone and threw it over the ledge. In a second or two they heard a splash.

"Well, we found water," said Drel.

Jait got on his stomach to try to see down into the pool of water, but could not.

"I don't think that the rope on my net is long enough to reach down that far.

"Let's go back and call it a day and tomorrow we can come back with additional rope and see if anything lives in there."

"I'll put a longer rope on the net tonight," Jait said, throwing another rock over the drop off and waiting for the splash.

When they got back to the main chamber, they found Tymber sound asleep in a dimly lit corner. Jait and Drel grabbed their stuff and lie down next to her and fell sound asleep.

NINETEEN

"I can't do this, Pred," said Sella. "How can you expect for me to pack up everything we own and leave where we have lived all of our lives?"

"I don't believe we have a choice to make," Pred responded. "It is move or live in a cold dark winter. Have you been outside since it's gotten dark? It is just now the beginning of autumn and its almost freezing."

"Has Leader asked you to start hunting yet?"

"No, in fact, he did ask me if we would help Farmer with harvesting during the next light cycle."

"Light cycle? Is that what we call days now?"

Sella sat down in her rocking chair by the big window that Pred had replaced after the first shake. She looked out at nothing. It was too dark to even make out any shapes.

"This is the only window we have left to look outside and you can't even see anything," she said.

Pred sat down next to her in his comfort chair.

"After we are finished harvesting, I will be going to Leader and tell him that we are moving to the caverns. That is, of course, if Jait and Tymber come back and say that the cavern is still there and livable."

"For all we know, they may be in the middle of the forest in the dark."

"Sella, you shouldn't think of all the worst things that can happen. And if it did, they would simply make a large fire and wait until it got light again."

"Speaking of fire, we could use a couple more logs in the stove," she said, after a slight shiver.

Pred got up and went outside to retrieve a few logs and against Pred's wishes, Sella sat and thought about all the worst things that could happen.

He returned and put the logs in the stove and stirred the coals to get it blazing. He put the poker down and sat back down with Sella.

"That's something that I won't have to do in the cavern," Pred said, smiling hoping to cheer her up a little. "The cavern is self-heating. There are a few places we will want to hang lanterns, but not that many, so we won't have to do that much, either."

Pred saw that Sella was about to cry. He was going to tell her that she won't have to sweep floors because they would all be sand and rock, but wisely decided against it.

"The cavern is really very nice," he said, trying to comfort her. "Remember, Tymber wanted to live there before we realized that we may have to."

Janna came into the room and stood in front of Sella until she was recognized to speak. "Mother," she said with a smile on her face, "Ispis told me to tell you that she's getting hungry."

"Janna!" They heard Ispis shout from the other room when she heard what Janna had said. Pred started smiling. He knew that Ispis told Janna what to say, and that wasn't it.

"I'll make us something to eat right away," Sella answered.

Janna smiled and left the room.

Sella got up and realized that she didn't know if she should be cooking lunch or supper.

"It's been dark outside so long I don't know what I'm doing. I'm letting my children starve."

"It's not that serious Sella," Pred told her.

Sella busied herself with cooking which cheered her up. She didn't have to think about the dark outside or that two of her children were somewhere out there. At times she thought that her family might be better off in the cavern, at least they would be together.

She didn't want to live in a cave. She didn't want any of this to be happening, of course no one did.

They all sat down to eat.

"Father," Ispis said. "When will it get light again?"

Pred realized that his young daughters didn't know much about why it was dark so long or why it stayed light. It always seemed right, or maybe just easier, to avoid their questions.

He looked at Sella to confirm that it was time to explain things to them. She nodded.

"Our sun has changed. You've seen how much smaller it is now. For some reason that I don't really understand, it takes longer to go across the sky during the day and takes longer to come up when its night."

"It is now just the beginning of autumn and you can feel how cold it is outside," Sella added.

"We think that the sun has changed so much that we may have to go to where Tymber and Jait are right now, the cavern, to live. In the cavern it will be light and warm and a very nice place to live."

"Tymber has told us all about the wonderful things in the cavern," Ispis said, as she put jam on her biscuit. "I don't know why we have to live there, though."

"We think that it may get so cold because the sun is so small, that this cabin will not keep the cold out. In the cavern we will stay warm."

"Why is Tymber at the cavern now?"

"She has gone to prepare the cavern for us to move to. Just kind of getting things ready."

"Can I take my smile doll with me?" Janna asked, as she held up her doll.

"Of course you can, Janna," replied Sella, smiling at her. "We are going to try to take as much of our things as we can. In fact we may have to make a couple of trips to the cavern and back to get everything."

"Are Tymber and Keeper getting married?" asked Janna.

"Janna!" Ispis said, shaking her head. Everyone knew that the reason she had asked that was because she and Janna had talked about it.

Pred and Sella smiled at her bluntness and relieved that the subject had changed.

"We don't know, Janna," Sella answered. "We really like Drel, but they will have to decide that."

"When is Tymber coming back?" Ispis asked.

"Well let's see," said Pred, as he pretended to figure out when they should be back. He knew very well when they should return.

"We have about two days of dark left so they won't leave the cavern when it's dark. When they leave the cavern it will take about two and a half days of light to get here. So, they should be getting here about the next time the sun is overhead."

Janna looked sad.

"That's a long time," she said.

"I hope you girls are going to help me weave baskets to help us carry our things to the cavern," Sella said, to help them lift their spirits. "We can go down to the lake and cut hemp to weave."

Their eyes lit up. A trip to the lake sounded like a lot of fun to them. Skipping stones was one of their favorite things to do.

The girls got up from the table talking about who was going to skip a stone the furthest.

"When you weave the baskets Sella, make them so they can hang off of Bossy. We will have her do as much of the work of carrying as we can."

"That old cow isn't going to like that very much," Sella said, getting up to clear the table.

"Actually I plan to take a bull with us also."

"Is there a field around there for them to graze?"

Pred didn't know exactly how to answer that question. If he understood Drel in his forecasting of what will be coming, they would not survive outside. He just realized what Sella still didn't know.

"In another section of the cavern, we are thinking about putting some of the cattle," he finally said. "Drel doesn't think that anything will be able to live outside during the dark winter."

"We are going to have to live with the cattle?"

"They will be far away and you won't even know that they are there."

"I find that hard to believe."

"After you see the cavern and see how massive it is, you will understand better. And, if that doesn't work, we can give up meat and milk and set them loose outside."

Sella could tell by Pred's answer that he was getting a little upset by all the doubt that she had towards this move. She decided not to press any further and just hope that Pred knew what he was doing.

"I will work on weaving straps to the baskets to hang over the cow. We can balance weight so they will carry better."

"I'm going to design a double seat so the girls can ride when they get tired of walking," Pred said, to show that they could really get there without that much trouble. "I think Herder will give me an old bull to take with us. He has said we need more cows and fewer bulls."

"Is the rest of the village going to live in a cave too?"

"I hope so Sella. I would hate to think that they were left here in an endless winter night."

Jait was sure that it was his imagination. Certainly he didn't really smell cooked pork and hen's eggs? He opened one eye and, yes, he was still in the cavern like he remembered and yes, he still smelled the pork.

He rolled over to see Tymber setting down a couple of plates of food on a flat topped rock outcrop. Leave it to Tymber to find a good place for a table.

Jait got up and walked over to her.

"Morning," he said.

"Morning, I guess," answered Tymber. "I got up because I was hungry, not because it was morning. I have no idea how long I slept."

"We may have slept the whole night and it's light outside," Jait said, teasingly.

Tymber looked at him and shook her head.

"Nope, I already looked."

"I didn't know you had brought this food with us."

"I brought enough for one meal, so this is it. Mother was running low on food since all the time we have had in the dark. I didn't want to bring food that they needed."

"Drel and I think we found where the sea water comes into the cavern. It smelled like seawater, anyway. It is a chamber that has filled with water. The entrance to the chamber is pretty high and the net rope wouldn't reach down that far. It was dark so we really couldn't even see how far down the water was. We may find some fish in it. If we don't, we will just build a fire outside and fish."

Tymber handed Jait his plate of food. She looked over to where Drel was sleeping.

"Do you think I should wake him up?" she asked.

"He would want to get up, I would think, to eat such a great breakfast."

She looked over towards him hesitantly while she decided if she should wake him.

"Drel! Breakfast!" she shouted towards him deciding to try that.

"I'm awake," he answered. "The smell of that breakfast would wake the hungry dead."

He appeared out of the shadows from across the cavern and sat down next to them.

"Tymber, this breakfast smells great."

"Thanks, I hope you enjoy it."

She just realized that this was the first meal she had made for Drel. It was just her luck that it would have to be a meal thrown together and cooked on a hot air vent in a cave. All of a sudden she got a little nervous hoping he really would enjoy it.

"Tastes great," he said after his first bite.

"Thanks."

"Did you go all the way down to the hot air vents to cook this?" he asked.

"Yes, but I found a quicker way there. Just takes a moment."

"Did Jait tell you that we may have found a fishing place down in a lower chamber?"

"Yes, he did."

"Are we ready to go see if there are fish in it?" Drel asked Jait, after he finished his meal.

"I will be after I weave the ropes together."

"I thought you were just going to replace the shorter rope with the longer."

"After I thought about it, I decided to weave them together. We really don't know how deep the water is and how far down the net will sink."

"True."

"I'm going with you two so I can see where it is," Tymber said, picking up the empty wooden dishes that they brought on trips.

"I have already planted all the seeds that farmer would give me. He, of course, couldn't really understand planting anything this time of year."

"Time of day and time of year don't seem to matter here in the cavern," Drel said, as he examined the cavern as a whole again. "It may have been like this for thousands of years."

That comment made everyone look around the cavern and appreciate it that much more.

"Drel," Tymber said, tilting her head to the side like she does when she is confused about something. "We talked before about Adentta moving further away from the sun and how that would make the sun look smaller and the year longer. I think I understand that, but you never said anything about the days and nights changing too. I may not have paid enough attention."

"The long days and nights I never expected," said Drel. "The only way I can explain what happened is that when the Intruder came past us, its influence pulled us further from the sun and slowed the spinning of Adentta. It would seem like it slowed the spinning down to about a fourth of the speed it was."

Everyone sat in silence for awhile. They were trying to imagine what exactly that all meant to them. No matter how long they sat, they couldn't guess at all the changes that might take place.

"Drel, will all these changes ever go back the way it was?" asked Jait.

"I don't think so," he responded. "If it changes back, it may be very gradual."

They again sat for a time without talking.

"I feel the need to go outside to make sure that this isn't a dream," Tymber said, breaking the silence and getting up.

"Why don't you two go outside or whatever and I'll fix the net rope," Jait said. He got up to get what he needed to begin the work.

Drel and Tymber jumped at the chance to be alone for a little while.

They walked through the tunnel that was the entrance to the cavern. When they got to the outside ledge, they stopped when they could no longer see the ground.

"It amazes me how dark it has become," Tymber commented.

"I have looked at the stars all my life," he responded, "and they all seem to be in the wrong place. I am thinking now that they look wrong because I am seeing them from a different angle.

"Look at the falling stars," he said. "It may be that all the outer objects have changed, and not just us."

"It's so cold."

Drel stood behind Tymber and put his arms around her to try to keep her warm.

"I didn't think about bringing my jacket out here."

"Tymber, look!"

In the dark Tymber had no idea where he was looking.

"Straight ahead."

Tymber still couldn't tell where he was looking.

Drel held the sides of her head and moved it in the direction he was looking.

"Can you see it?" he said.

"All I see is a lot of dark and stars."

"Look just above where the stars end at the horizon. Can you see that dim circle?"

"Not really."

"It is a round area just above the horizon that doesn't have any stars and has a very faint circle around it."

"Yes I see it."

"I think that is our moon."

"It's not very bright."

"The sun is on the other side of Adentta and can't shine on it. We may actually be able to see it on occasion. I was afraid it was no longer around. To me, this is very good news."

"I'm glad you think so, Drel, but I'm just a little tired of moons," she said, smiling although he didn't know it.

"Our moon had not done us any harm. We are supposed to have a moon in the sky."

"Is the Intruder gone for good?"

"Gone for sure, for good, I don't know."

"I'm freezing!" Tymber said, shivering.

"The last thing we need is for you to get sick," he said, moving them back inside.

When they returned to the chamber where they ate, they found Jait just finishing the weave.

"You two ready to go fishing?" he said, when he saw them come back in.

Drel saw the fishing net and the longer rope attached and was amazed at how well Jait was able to weave the two ropes together. They looked like one rope.

"We're ready," Tymber said.

Jait grabbed the net, Tymber got the fish basket, and Drel picked up a torch.

"Fish and potatoes sound good for lunch," Tymber said, as they started for the seawater.

"It sure would be great if there are fish in that water," Jait said, ducking down to go through the opening in the chamber that led downwards to the water chamber.

"It's very cold and dark to be outside fishing," she said. "But we will do it if we have to. That's what we expected to do."

When they reached the end of the passage, Drel used his strike box and lit the torch to see into the chamber. It was much larger than they expected and was nearly square in shape. Jait didn't think he would even be able to throw a rock all the way to the other side. The walls of the chamber close to the torch were dark gray and had streaks of lighter gray running through them. They were not able to see the walls on the other side of the chamber well enough to tell their color.

The water was dark and far below. It had a little swelling action and occasionally they could hear the swelling break on the wall of the chamber just below them.

"The slight wave action is a good sign that it is directly linked to the sea," said Drel, looking over the ledge. "It looks like the water level goes up and down too. See how the edge of the wall is wet up a ways. It must go up and down with the moon too."

"The moon?" Jait asked.

"Oh yes, sorry Jait, we forgot to tell you. We could see the faint outline of Adentta's moon. It has been so long since we have seen it, I was not sure it was still around."

"That's good," he said. "At first I thought you meant the Intruder."

"I think it is gone, for now."

"Well here goes nothing," Jait said, throwing the net into the water. They watched as the rope slid through Jait's hands as the net sank into the water. The end of the rope was wrapped around Jait's wrist and all the rope was out before he began to pull it in.

"It looks like we needed all the rope," Drel said, bending over the ledge with the torch. "I hope to see what we caught before we bring it all the way up, in case it has big teeth."

"Big teeth fish taste better," Tymber said, smiling.

It did not appear that Drel shared in her humor.

When the net got to the surface of the water, it became fairly heavy.

"I think we got something," Jait said, needing to use his strength to bring it up.

"I don't know what it is but it doesn't look harmful," Drel said, straining to see what they caught.

"Woohoo," Tymber reacted, when she saw the catch. "That's the fish we call Red Head. It is very good eating."

"Lunch today will be Red Head with baked potatoes," Jait said, holding up his catch.

"That fish looks big enough for a couple of meals," Drel said, joining in on the excitement.

"Looks like the remainder of the dark we will be catching, cleaning, and curing," Tymber said, grabbing the Red Head fish from the net and putting it into the basket.

The next couple of days were spent fishing, eating, and exploring the cavern waiting for the sun to rise. Drel in his normal 'Keeper' ways started making a record of what has happened and started a map of the complex arrangement of chambers in the cavern. He had an idea that every chamber needed to be named and a sign put up as to what chamber it was. To him, they looked mostly alike.

Tymber and Jait both wanted to explore the cavern on the other side of Rain Chamber. They left Drel to himself making his sketches in First Chamber and they headed out to explore. As they hoped, there was another massive series of chambers on the other side. The trouble was getting completely wet going through Rain Chamber.

They hoped to find another way to that section of the cavern so getting wet was not necessary to get there.

Jait and Tymber sat down on a dry ledge on the other side of the large rain room. Jait was deep in thought when Tymber asked what he was thinking.

"If what I think is true," he started, "this side is heading in the direction of North Guard Mountain. We just crossed the river and we will soon be exploring an area that we really have never been to above the surface. We never crossed the river this far east. Just seems strange some how."

"We have done a lot of things that seem strange," she replied. "Would it make you feel better if we crossed the river and explored on the other side when we leave?"

"I don't think so, Sis," he said, getting back up to continue their exploring.

In the new section of the cavern, on the 'other side' as they liked to refer to it, they went through a number chambers of all shapes and sizes.

They found a number of hot air vents coming up from below. One of them had a bad smell to it so they avoided that area. Luckily, it was set off by itself and it wasn't necessary to go through that chamber to continue.

They found cool and hot pools of water and the streams that fed and emptied them. They never followed any of the streams to their end, but they were all heading toward the direction of the sea and assumed that they ended there.

What wasn't expected, was finding a number of large chambers that were dark and had no glow rocks. They looked like the chambers that grew the glow rocks, so they couldn't understand why they didn't grow there. They decided to ask Drel the reason they were dark. They didn't enter any dark areas because they didn't have any lanterns or torches with them.

There were many lighted chambers that had grass and weeds growing in them. They could be used to keep animals in, if they needed to do that.

After a lot of exploring, they still did not get to the end of the cavern. They wondered if there really was an end to the series of chambers.

Occasionally, one of them would go check to see if the sun had risen. Time was very hard to judge in the cavern and they weren't really sure how long they had been there.

When the sun finally did start to rise, it wasn't very dramatic. It simply got light enough to barely see. The heavy fog was going to make it hard to travel.

"It feels like it's been dark for a season," Drel said, as they left the cavern on the way back to the village.

A chill ran through Tymber as she climbed off of the ledge. It was a good thing they brought heavy clothes to wear. The air seemed nearly freezing and the fog made the cold stick to them. Tymber wished she had gone by the clothier before they left to see if he could make her a new coat.

Tymber said that she would love to go by Hantfel on the way home and bring them some fish.

"I would be glad to go there alone and meet you two at the river campsite."

Drel and Jait looked at each other, and almost as if it were rehearsed, they took off their backpacks and grabbed Tymber by the arms and pretended to be bringing her to the river to throw her in.

Tymber knew of course they were just playing around and she didn't particularly want to go to Hantfel by herself again anyway.

"We will visit them on the next trip to the cavern," Jait said, after letting her go. "We want to make sure they know what we expect to happen with the sun and help them prepare. Don't worry, we haven't forgotten about them."

The fog was so thick that Sella could see it coming into the cabin from under the door.

"It must be getting light," Pred said, watching Sella put a cloth under the door to try to keep the cold and fog out. "I can see dark gray out the window now instead of complete black."

Sella shivered when she thought about Tymber being out in that cold fog.

"I need to leave to help Farmer with the harvest," said Pred. "He is expecting Drel and Jait, also, but I will just tell him that they are not coming for a couple of days.

"We will have a village meeting when they return. I hope they have good news."

"We could use some," remarked Sella. "Maybe they will come back and we decide that we won't have to move."

"Good news will be that the caverns are still there and we will be able to move."

Sella looked at Pred in dismay, but then realized he was probably right.

It seemed like the entire village, men, women, and children, were in the fields helping with the harvest. They couldn't see far because of the fog, but they could hear many people in the fields as they worked. Even Sella and the girls came to help out.

By start of the third day, the sun was high in the sky and the fog was only a wisp, but the light was still poor, and it was still very cool.

Sella kept looking off expecting to see the travelers. She knew that this was about the time that Pred expected them to return. She kept looking up knowing they would have to walk by this field on the way back. She was getting tired of her family being gone all the time. Moving to the cavern would be worth it if all of them would be together everyday.

She had just looked up from digging potatoes when she heard a teasing voice behind her complaining that all the potatoes that Sella was digging were small.

"I must have gotten into a row that didn't grow very well," she responded. Then looked up and saw that it was Tymber who had said that.

Sella jumped up and hugged her as fast as she could move.

"Tymber, I have missed you so much. How was your trip? Where are Jait and Drel?" she asked, looking out from the direction that Tymber had appeared.

"Jait and Drel are over talking with Father. The trip was good, we learned a lot more about the cavern, which was pretty much in the same condition it was the last time we were there. And I missed you, too, mother," she said, and kissed Sella on the cheek.

Sella put her arm around Tymber and they both walked over to where Jait and Drel were talking to Pred. Jait saw his mother approach and went to meet her.

"Hello Mother," he said, giving her a hug. "How are you?"

"I am fine Jait. How are you and how was your trip?"

"The trip was good and worthwhile. We learned a lot about the cavern on this trip. After all, we had plenty of dark time to fill."

"It's good to have you back too, Drel," she added, as they walked up to him and gave him a hug.

"Thanks, Sella."

"They have been telling me good news," Pred said, smiling at Sella hoping she would think it was good news too.

"That's good, Pred. Tell me all about it over supper. I'm starving and I bet they are too. Let's go back to the cabin. I cooked a roast and potatoes today before I came out into the field. I have it keeping warm on top of the stove."

"I've never seen so many people in the fields at one time," said Tymber, as they walked back to the cabin.

"People have been taking turns during the light helping with the harvesting," said Pred. I think they got the crops that are real sensitive to frost and freeze finished. These potatoes are not as sensitive to the weather."

At the cabin they ate and talked about the cavern. The most exciting news to Pred was the Sea Chamber, as Tymber named it.

They had just finished a very enjoyable meal when the center bells started ringing. Everyone instinctively sat still to see if it was a shake, which it was not.

"Leader must be ready to have a meeting to discuss how to live in the dark," Pred said. "I know he doesn't know there is an alternative. I just hope he will listen to ours."

Tymber looked at her father a little surprised at what he said.

"You act like he will completely reject living in the cavern," she said.

"I really don't think he will ever tell anybody that they should go to live there."

"Maybe not."

Pred wanted Tymber and Jait to come along to the meeting. He thought they will be able to help Drel and him explain what their plans are about moving to the cavern, and try to convince Leader that it is the best thing to do for the whole village.

Pred knew however that it would not be an easy task. The best he could hope for was to show them that there was an option to living in the village. Of course, it would all work best if everyone moved to the cavern. That way they would not lose any of the crafts or craftsman. They would need the crafts people that know how to do things in the cavern.

It would probably take a few seemingly endless freezing cold nights to convince them to move.

They got to the Fendal Betalum Community Hall almost before anybody was there. Shodder, Farmer, and Storer were the only ones.

Tymber, thinking that it was going to be like the last meeting when she waited to be called to the meeting, sat down in the foyer. Jait followed her lead.

"No, I want you two in the meeting from the start," said Pred, when he saw what they were doing. "You two have done a great service to the village. I want you in there and I want you to speak when it is appropriate."

Drel took Tymber by the hand and helped her to her feet showing total agreement for Pred's decision.

Shodder was the first to welcome them.

"Well, if it isn't my good friends Drel and Pred. I haven't seen you two since the beginning of summer, I don't think. Come over here and sit with me."

Neither Drel nor Pred wanted to go sit up front but they did as Shodder requested.

"Certainly that can't be little Tymber there with you. She has sure blossomed into quite a pretty young lady."

"Thank you," she responded. She didn't really think of it like a compliment. She thought that he could have complimented her on a lot of things that were more important than looking pretty, but she did like him saying it this time, since Drel was there too.

They sat down in the row just behind Shodder and Storer.

"I think that's the first time I ever agreed with Shodder," Drel whispered, leaning over to Tymber's ear.

Tymber smiled back.

Leader entered the room and sat up front with Farmer without any acknowledgement of anyone else in the room. He looked like he had the weight of all of Adentta on his shoulders.

"Hello Leader," Pred finally said, when it seemed like a long enough time for him to settle in.

"Good morning or afternoon or evening, Hunter, "Leader returned, without even looking up from his paperwork. "Whichever you think fits the time best."

Farmer leaned over and whispered something in Leader's ear that did brighten his spirits some, in fact, he even smiled a little.

Leader looked up and saw that Hunter and Keeper were there and also that Tymber and Jait were.

"I see we have all the travelers here today," he said, as he smiled at the meeting newcomers.

Pred unexpectedly stood up and asked Leader if he and the other leaders could meet before the meeting.

"We have made very exciting discoveries on our journeys into the forest and I would like to share them with the village leaders before the meeting."

Leader looked back down at his paperwork thinking of his answer.

"This meeting will be directed to the remaining time we have to harvest, the need for rapid production of sapburn for the lanterns, and generally how to survive the long nights. You know we have had a few people lose their breath from burning the lanterns so long without opening any window or door for fresh air.

"We can hear about your travel stories sometime at night while we are all sitting around the campfire."

Hunter turned red in the face, sat down, and Keeper stood up.

"Leader, long winter nights are ahead and we may not be ready. You have seen how cold it is getting already and it is just now autumn. I believe winter will be unbearably cold."

"Yes, yes Keeper, we too believe that the winters will be very dark and cold. That is why we are having this meeting."

"We know of a place that is light all the time and will remain warm during the winter," Pred said.

"Are you talking about your caves?"

"They are bigger than caves we call them caverns. They are huge, have water and air, hot and cold water, and most of the areas are light."

Leader laughed lightly and shook his head. "Hunter and Keeper, our history says we lived in caves. My dear travelers, we have grown past the days of living in caves."

Pred and Drel looked at each other and sat back down.

Tymber wanted to jump up and shout, *Okay you big ox, I did think you were one of the smartest men around, and now I think you're being an idiot. We are not sure what the winters will actually be like or if we can even survive.*

Father did say he wanted us to speak when we thought it was appropriate, she thought to herself.

At that moment, almost as if Drel knew what she was thinking, he put his arm around her shoulders. She was not sure if it was to hold her, or to hold her down. Drel looked away from her when he caught that suspicious look in her eyes.

As they talked, other people had entered the hall. Some of them had no chance to clean up from being in the fields and came in with their clothes very dirty. The additional people in the room made Pred hesitate, but he got up and told Leader that his family will be moving to the cavern by the sea. Drel got up and said that he would be moving, as well.

A silence came over all the people there. No one in memory ever decided to leave the village. After all, there was no reason to move. Everything that was needed was right at hand, or within a short walking distance.

"My family will finish the daylight time helping in the fields with the harvest," Hunter continued. "We only ask for a bull in return. I have a cow, but would like a bull as well."

"I also will help in the fields," added Keeper. "In return I would like some seed from the crops."

Leader could hardly believe what he was hearing.

"Drel, Pred, certainly you need to reconsider your decision to move away from your home. You have lived nowhere else. We are your neighbors and your friends."

Pred looked at everyone that was present.

"It is true we are your friends and neighbors. And we will always be your friends. This move is not to get away from you, but to go to our new life. We will need your help in having what we need to survive.

Leader looked at Keeper and Hunter for a few moments.

"You will always be part of this village whether you live here or in the cavern. You do not have to earn your bull and your seeds. Please feel free to take with you what you will need, within reason."

"Keep in mind," Pred scanned all that was present, "the cavern is a very big place that can hold our whole village and everyone that wants to come with us is very welcome to do so. And we will come back to visit in the spring if the sun will let us." Pred smiled at everyone and sat back down.

"Are you guys about ready to leave?" Jait whispered across Tymber to Drel and his father. There is no talking reason to these people."

Pred shook his head no. He wanted to see what was on the agenda for the village to do in the times ahead.

"We may not be here, but I want to know what they are planning," he whispered back.

So they stayed and listened to the rest of the meeting. Nothing was really decided except to make more sapburn and open the windows or doors more often so they don't choke.

Confused by the undecided attitude of the meeting, the travelers tried to sneak away without much more discussion about the cavern.

Smith did stop them and ask if he could go see the cavern. He would then be able to decide if living there is what he wanted to do. Pred said that he would be glad to take him with on their next trip.

For the rest of the daylight time, people came up to the travelers in the fields and asked about the cavern. Some of them thought they were betraying the village by asking questions about it, so they pretended to have something else to discuss. They weren't real sure about moving there, but were interested in knowing more about the cavern by the sea.

Except for a few minor fields, the harvest was finished by dark and as the sun set, everyone hustled back to their cabins. Everybody was extremely tired and nobody wanted to be out in the dark.

The Trelops went back to their cabin to rest and prepare for the move. Drel went back to his cabin to do the same. They knew that they would have to spend a few light cycles to get ready. They did what was necessary inside during the dark of night and outside during the day light.

Pred wanted everything done before they left. He knew that it would take more than one trip, but wanted it prepared before the first trip.

Sella had been weaving baskets to carry things and Timber, Ispis, and Janna were packing them with their possessions. They tried to pack the things that were most needed but would not be needed until they got to the cavern. The pots and pans would probably be the last things packed.

TWENTY

The light of the new day finally came, if it could be called light. With each light cycle, the sun became smaller and less bright and the days and nights much colder.

Drel came to the Trelop's cabin and told them that he was more or less ready to go. Tymber gave him a hug and told him that she missed him. Pred gave him the list of things they needed to get from Storer and Farmer before the move to the cavern.

"Not much time for romance around here so it would seem," Drel said, with a smile on his face.

"We will have all the time we could dream of at the cavern," Tymber said.

Jait came into the room with two backpacks and two belt baskets of light belongings.

"As heavy as we have packed, it will take forever to get to the cavern," he said.

"Jait and I are about to leave," Tymber said in a hurry knowing that Drel didn't know that she was leaving. "We want to go to Hantfel before going to the cavern."

"We also need to build a ramp up to the ledge before mother and the cow get there," Jait added.

Jait looked towards his mother hoping she didn't pick up on the accidental analogy.

"We were going to stop by your cabin on our way," she said.

"Well you won't have to do that now," Drel said.

He was disappointed that she was leaving so soon and that he wasn't going with them to Hantfel. He had never met anybody that wasn't part of the village and would love to meet those people.

"I just have to go see them to make sure they are all right," said Tymber.

"I know, Tymber," he replied. "I just wanted to go there as well."

"It is closer to the caverns than it is from here. We can go and visit them sometime."

"Actually I would rather they decide to live in the cavern too," said Drel.

"That would be great. They seem to be very nice people."

"Let's go sis," Jait said, handing her the backpack.

"I'll see you in a few days at the cavern," Tymber said to Drel.

"Take care out there. It is very cold, the fog is thick, and I think the ground is frozen in places."

"Just perfect for traveling in the forest," Sella said, sarcastically.

Pred looked at everyone in the room.

"Tymber and Jait please be careful on your trip," he said. "Say greetings to the people in Hantfel for me. Drel it's time to get our supplies."

Everyone looked at Pred. He seemed anxious for everyone to get busy. So everyone got busy.

Tymber went to her father and whispered:

"Be on the look out for an owl when you first go into the forest. One swooped down on Drel."

Jait and Tymber got hugs from everyone and went out the door just before Pred and Drel left to go to Storer's.

"Let's make one last giant meal that will last until we leave and have some for our trip," Sella told her two young girls when they were left alone in the cabin. "That way we can pack the pots and pans."

"I can't believe that we are actually doing this," Sella said, looking at the edge of the forest.

She looked behind her and saw Pred holding the leads of a bull draped in baskets of their belongings. Drel was holding the leads of Bossy with baskets hanging from her and Sella's two little girls sitting on top. She didn't believe that she would ever see such a sight, and to top it off they were heading into the forest.

She shook her head at Pred and told him to lead the way.

"Isn't she beautiful when she's mad?" Pred said, smiling at Drel. "I know one thing, she must love me."

"I guess Smith decided not to come with us," Drel said disappointedly. "He said he would meet us here if he decided to go. We are going to have to come back a time or two just to lead the village to the cavern."

"I hope so, Drel," Pred said, as he started to walk into the forest. "But now is the time to get our family settled."

The bull didn't seem to want to enter the forest. He stood his ground and didn't want to move.

"That bull is the only one here with any sense," Sella said, smiling at Pred.

After slapping the bull on its rump and pulling on its collar, the bull finally gave in and followed Pred into the forest.

"I'm not going to have to do that to you too, am I," Pred said to Sella, hugging her as they started walking.

"Don't forget to look out for that owl," Sella said smiling.

Of course Pred didn't realize that she had heard Tymber.

The fog was heavier in the forest, or at least with the shade of the trees it was darker. They could only see half dozen trees in front of them.

The limbs of the trees were dripping water from the condensation of the fog. Occasionally, they would hear the rustle of leaves ahead as a small animal moved out of their way, but the forest seemed unusually quiet.

At times it seemed like the entire world existed of only what they could see, and the rest of the world had been absorbed by the fog.

Sella stayed pretty close to the side of Pred. Her thoughts were on the edge of sight looking for danger. She wasn't really sure what danger looked like, but was sure she would recognize it. Pred could tell she was uneasy and knew that she would be.

"Don't you think you should carry your bow in your hands just in case?" she asked him. "No farther than we can see, I think something could get us before you would be able to respond."

In one errorless and swift motion he pulled his bow, strung an arrow, and shot a tree exactly in the middle trail marking.

Looking impressed she called him a show off.

Pred looked back at his two daughters and saw that they seemed a little nervous as well and Pred had scared them by pulling and shooting his bow. He handed Sella the rope to the bull and went back to talk to them.

"Ispis and Janna, I'm going to need your help it would seem. I want you to look ahead and tell me what trees have the three hatchet marks on it. See this tree here? Trees with this marking will show us the trail. I need you two to look ahead and help me find those trees."

They seemed to get excited to be able to help which made them less nervous. Once in a while, Pred pretended not to be able to find marked trees to give them something to do.

The travelers moved slowly along the trail. Pred silently worried that at the rate of travel they may not get to the cavern by dark.

"This is where I was during the shake when I was alone," Tymber said, as she looked around the area and shivered with the memory of that day.

"Are you cold, Sis?"

"No not really, just had a chill is all."

"It seems like the shake was extremely violent here," he said, looking around at the damage. "There are many trees that have fallen since I was here.

"Show me where you killed the predator?"

"Up the trail more," she said, as she suppressed another chill.

They began up the trail to Hantfel.

When they got to the trail that went to where Tymber killed the predator they stopped and looked down it.

"I still can't believe you were able to do that."

"I can't either. I thought both Aliptis and I were going to die."

"It just wasn't your time yet, Sis," Jait said.

"No, I'll probably die from something foolish and all alone."

They both laughed as they continued down the trail to the Hantfel cabins.

When they arrived at Goshenta's cabin, there was no one in sight. If it wasn't for the smoke coming from the chimneys, they would have thought that Hantfel was deserted.

The cabins didn't look too bad, but like the village, most of the windows had been broken during the shakes and the window openings boarded up.

They could hear some movement in the cabin.

"Goshenta," Tymber called out. "Are you there?"

The door flew open and Goshenta came running out.

"Tymber! I can't believe you are here! Greetings my friend."

Goshenta, a larger lady, almost knocked Tymber off her feet when she grabbed her for a hug.

"Greetings, Jait," she said, when she realized that Tymber's brother was there too. "You know of course that you have a hero for a sister?"

"Yes, she has told us the story."

"We promised Tymber a feast next time she was here. I will begin preparation immediately."

"We really can't stay too long," Tymber responded, not really knowing how to react. She had never had a feast prepared in her honor.

"Oh, don't worry Tymber," said Goshenta, "It won't take us long to prepare the meal. We have a gift for you as well. Come inside and sit and rest."

Her cabin was very nice inside. Tymber and Jait sat down in the comfort chairs by the stove.

"Bareback," Goshenta called for him and leaned over to Tymber, "we call him that because we couldn't keep a shirt on him when he was younger. "Go tell Midton that Tymber has returned and that I have started preparing a feast. On the way, tell Aliptis that Tymber is here and that Jait is with her this time."

Goshenta looked over at Jait and smiled. "She will be very happy to see you too, Jait." She winked at Tymber.

"Let me make the two of you hot root tea. You must be cold to the bone being out in this weather. I bet you never had any hot root tea with lemon in it."

"Let me help you," said Tymber, getting up from the chair.

"Don't be silly, Tymber. The feast is for you."

Many wonderful smells came from Goshenta's kitchen as she cooked. Jait and Tymber sat and rested and occasionally talked to people as they came in telling them of their adventures.

Aliptis came in and stayed the longest. She hugged Tymber, but sat next to Jait. She talked in great detail about the tromptaw attack and how Tymber had saved her. It was easy to see that she was still quite upset over the incident. Aliptis got up and told them that she would see them at the feast and left. That was the first indication that the feast was not to be held there.

Goshenta came out of the kitchen and asked for Tymber and Jait to help. They were each to carry a dish of food with them.

"Follow me she said, we are having the feast in the Gathering Hall. The entire village will be there to welcome you."

Goshenta smiled because she knew that would make Tymber nervous.

"You have many friends here Tymber, some you have not yet met. Come and enjoy yourself. We are having a party."

As they walked to the Gathering Hall, they passed many stone cabins. Hantfel had many designs of cabins from small to large. None of them looked the same, except each had a porch with rocking chairs.

Some people were leaving their cabins as they walked by. They waved and joined them in the walk, each carrying a pan or dish of food. Goshenta introduced them to Tymber and Jait as they walked.

Ahead they could see what appeared to be the main area of Hantfel. Their buildings were arranged around a square much like Lake Simpton Village center, except around the center's edge was a stone walkway with sections that led to each building.

The Gathering Hall was in the middle of the main buildings in Hantfel Center. It was a massive building built with carved rock of every color imaginable. The windows were of course boarded up but it was still a very beautiful building as were all the buildings in their village.

Inside the Gathering Hall was impressive, as well. The two main walls on either side were the inside of the stone walls and the other two walls were made of light wood. All around the hall there were lanterns lit for the occasion. There were also two multiple lanterns hanging from the ceiling. How they were lit, Jait had no idea.

The hall was full of people gathered around many tables. When Tymber and Jait walked in, everyone became more silent, looked at them, and then started to clap. All Tymber knew to do was to wave and turn red in the face.

Goshenta led Tymber and Jait to the front table to seat them. Midton was there to greet them and to offer them their chairs to sit. The clapping stopped when they sat down. Beside Tymber sat Aliptis and beside Jait sat Goshenta. In between Tymber and Jait was Midton.

Midton held up his hands and everyone became silent and found a chair in which to sit.

"People, it has been a long time since we had reason for a feast," Midton began. "The days of late have been weak in light and the nights have been cold and dark. The trembles may have made our buildings weak, but not our people. Today with our recent bountiful harvest, we gather to pay honor to a very heroic young woman. Many of you have met her before when they visited us. If you have not, I would like to introduce you to Jait, to my left, and Tymber, on my right."

The hall became loud with clapping and cheering.

"I am sure I do not have to tell you what Tymber has done for us. She not only saved Aliptis from a great danger, but has saved us all from great sorrow. For these reasons we are having this feast.

"In honor of this, we are serving tromptaw sausage from the same beast that Tymber had downed. And I would like you to know that Butcher himself made the sausage. And thank all of you for bringing dishes of food to this feasting.

Again everyone clapped.

"As everyone here in Hantfel knows, Aliptis is an outstanding clothier. She has made many of the fine clothes that we are wearing today. She had decided to make Tymber a most beautiful gift.

"Aliptis, could you bring out the gift please."

Aliptis got up from the table and went to a side room. In just a moment, she came out with something draped over her arms. When she got to Tymber she revealed her gift.

She held up the most beautiful coat. It was dark gray with darker gray and black spots. It was from the fur of the tromptaw.

Tymber quickly put it on. The coat came down to mid thigh on her and fit perfectly.

Everyone started clapping when they saw the gift.

"It has a hood and the buttons are made from sellicta wood," Aliptis said. "The inside and hood are lined with rabbit fur."

"It is so beautiful," Tymber said, trying her best to hold back the tears, which she wasn't completely successful in doing.

Tymber and Aliptis embraced for a long time and then they sat down when the clapping ended.

"Everyone, come, lets eat our feast," Midton said.

They let the head table go to the food table first and then everyone else got their food.

Both Tymber and Jait thought the tromptaw sausage had an excellent taste.

Jait and Midton talked during their meal about the dark and extremely cold nights that would be coming this winter. Jait told him of the caverns and how they would be welcome to live there too.

The only thing that Midton said was that it is something to consider. At that moment, he reminded Jait of Leader.

Tymber had a little bit better luck with Aliptis. Goshenta came and joined in on the conversation. They seemed amazed at all the marvels of the cavern, and said that they would love to come and visit.

"Leader," Tymber said, "Please have your people come and live with us in the light warm comfort of the cavern."

Midton either did not hear Tymber or decided to ignore her request. Aliptis told Tymber that she would love to come and see the caverns.

After eating their fill and accepting some tromptaw sausage to take with them, Tymber and Jait told everyone that it was time for them to continue on their way.

They shook everyone's hand and hugged many of them as well. Again they thanked everyone for everything and continued on their way to the cavern. Tymber proudly wore her coat as she left Hantfel.

The fog didn't subside. All day they walked in the cold, dull, dripping wet forest. Sella was getting concerned about her young daughters being in the cold and wet so long. Pred seeing that she was constantly rewrapping the blankets around her daughters tried to start a conversation.

"In just a little while we will come to an orchard, the one we told you about, with the lemon trees," he told Sella and the girls. "Just past the orchard is the stone cabin. You will see how amazing that place is. We can start a fire in the fireplace and sleep there. It will be warm and dry with comfortable furniture."

"That sounds better than sleeping on the wet ground," Sella said.

Drel walked a little faster so he could move up next to Pred.

"I'm not sure you want the girls to see the predator over the fireplace," Drel whispered to Pred.

Pred nearly stumbled when he heard that.

"Do you think you can get there before us and take it down?" Pred whispered back. "I'll stall them at the orchard."

"Why?" asked Sella.

Pred and Drel looked around at her.

"I want to see what a predator looks like," she said.

"Now you see why I can't keep any secrets," Pred told Drel, rolling his eyes.

"I want to see a predator, too," added Janna.

"No, you girls just think you want to see what one looks like," Drel said, shaking his head.

"Is it the one that Tymber shot?" asked Ispis.

"Now how did you know that Tymber shot a predator?" asked her father.

"I have good ears, too," she said, giggling.

Pred knew that it probably wasn't a good idea to let them see what a predator looked like, but it would seem that he had no choice. Little girls, or anybody for that matter, could have terrible nightmares about such things. It was a very beautiful, but deadly looking animal.

Pred had a little shiver again thinking about his daughter confronting one by herself.

"Well if you girls want to see the predator, you need to know that it is a pretty scary animal. It's dark gray with darker gray and black spots with thin streaks of white. The scary part is the size of its teeth. They are as long as my little finger and as sharp as needles. The head above the fireplace looks like it is still alive."

"I want to see a predator," Janna repeated.

Ispis didn't say anymore.

In a short while, Pred pointed out the outline of the stone cabin lemon orchard.

They looked almost mystical standing tall in the fog with countless numbers of yellow fruit hanging from their limbs.

"I left room for lemons in the rear basket on Bossy," Pred said. "Let me help you girls down and you can go collect as many as you can carry."

The girls were very happy to get off that cow. They had only been down a couple of times all day. They ran along looking for low branches that they could reach to pick the lemons. There were plenty of good lemons on the ground, but they were no fun to get.

"I'll watch the girls," Pred said, when the girls couldn't hear him. "You take Sella to the cabin to see if the girls should see that animal."

"No need for that, we will go there as a family. If there are true dangers, they need to know them and know what they look like."

"I'll never figure you out, Sella," he said shaking his head.

The cabin door was half open and Pred had to push pretty hard to open it the rest of the way.

He climbed up into the doorway and went in first to make sure it was safe, lit a couple of lanterns, and then went back to the door to help them come in. Drel went about the business of getting firewood for the fireplace. He figured he didn't want to see the reaction of the girls to the predator. So he made himself busy outside.

The girls looked cautiously around the cabin for a few moments. Pred picked up Janna and walked into the living room where the predator head was hanging, the others followed.

They all sucked in air as a response to seeing it, but really didn't seem as afraid of seeing it as he would have thought. He expected to hear screams.

"Those *are* big teeth," Janna said. "Its eyes are looking right at me."

Ispis stood behind her mother and just peeked at the predator from behind her and said nothing. Being a little older than Janna, she seemed to have a little more fear for it but didn't want to look more scared than her little sister.

Pred then showed them the rest of the cabin. Sella loved the carved wood figures on the shelves. She told him that somebody that lived there truly was an artist.

Drel came in with the wood for the stove and had it lit before Sella got to the kitchen. She made herself at home and prepared their meal of grain cakes and pork. She added a couple of vegetables to the menu as well.

Pred took down the head of the predator. He knew that everyone was going to have to sleep in that room by the fireplace to stay warm and didn't want the girls to have to look at it all night. After they ate and went back into the main living area, no one seemed to even miss it.

They all had a good sleep before they started out again. They didn't wake the girls up until it was time for breakfast. They both looked like they could use more sleep.

As they packed their backpacks, Sella quietly asked Pred if there was really two more days of travel before the cavern. Pred just nodded his head.

Pred re–hung the predator head before they left.

They made it down to Dry Stream with no problem, but getting down into the streambed seemed to be more of a challenge than was expected. Neither the cow nor the bull wanted to go down the bank. They had to travel through the brush on the bank until they found a low enough spot where they would go down. Pred knew that was just another delay in getting to the cavern.

"That tree is too large, Sis, we have to keep them smaller so you and I will be able to move them. Try chopping that one and I'll get this one."

They began constructing the makeshift ramp. All they needed for now was to have a ramp that mother and girls could go up. The cow and bull will stay tied up outside.

After felling and removing the tree limbs, Jait and Tymber dragged the small trees to the lowest point of the entrance ledge of the cavern. They arranged them so the fat end of every other tree faced towards the ledge.

Jait climbed up onto the ledge while Tymber stayed below to tie a rope onto the logs. Jait pulled each up, arranged them into a flat ramp about an arms width wide, and started binding them together with twine.

Tymber got two forked limbs to stick in the ground with a cross member to support the middle of the ramp and she tied them together.

When they finished, both were quite pleased with their rushed ramp. They walked across it, jumping to make sure it would support the family.

"We should have done this a lot sooner," Tymber said. "This ramp makes it so much easier to get up and down."

Jait decided to tie off the ledge end of the ramp with climb rope to make sure it didn't slide to the side or off the ledge. He made it so the ramp could easily be lowered if they wanted to. He didn't want to give animals an easy way into the cavern.

Tymber looked out from the ledge to where they first started chopping down the trees. "Jait, can you see my coat from here? I hung it up on a branch near the first tree I cut."

"No," he answered. "It must have fallen."

"It hasn't fallen. It took me a long time, but I can see it now."

After Tymber did some explaining as to where it was, they both commented on how camouflaged the coat was.

"You could be right next to me and not see me."

Jait watched her as she retrieved her coat. When she slipped it on, she almost disappear. He wondered to himself how many predators watched them pass in which they were never aware.

"I can't believe that I'm hungry after all I ate at the feast," Tymber said, when she got back up to the ledge.

"That's been more than a half day ago."

"Well, that explains why I'm tired too."

Tymber and Jait put everything into the cavern, did a few things in the Grow Chamber, and then made a fire by the sea and sat, fished, ate, and talked until it was nearing the time that their family should be arriving.

Jait and Tymber moved to the forest side of the cavern ledge and watched in the direction of the trail when it was time for them to get there.

"The sun will be setting in a little while," Tymber said, in a very concerned manner.

"I know. It seems like they should have been here by now. It must have been more difficult to travel with the cattle, the family, and with the fog."

"As foggy as it is, we will probably hear them before we see them. We should light a fire to help guide them."

"The light from the fire would not reach very far in the fog," said Jait, as he stood up. "I have an idea."

Jait ran along the ledge and into the cavern. Moments later he came out with their hatchets.

"Did you decide to cut wood for a fire?" she asked, when she saw the hatchets and torches.

"No. Come with me."

They walked down the ramp to the ground below.

"Tymber, light two torches and stick one in the ground at the base of the ramp."

Tymber followed his request.

"Remember that large hollow tree that we pass along the trail?" he asked. "Well I think we can make a lot of noise with that tree to help guide them. I'm afraid they had to leave the trail because of the cattle and may like help in finding the way."

By the time they got to the tree, it was completely dark. Tymber stuck the torch she carried in the ground and they tapped the tree to see where the most noise would be.

Using the flat end of the hatchets, they took turns pounding the tree. It did make a loud noise. In fact, it made many birds and other things they couldn't see, scurry away.

"As quiet as the night forest is, I think the village could hear this beating," Tymber said, as they continued to thump away.

A long time passed. They continued to pound on the hollow tree. The air was getting very cold and the fog seemed like ice crystals floating in the air. When Tymber moved, Jait could see the fog swirl around her in the orange torch light. When they stopped to rest they could hear the iced fog fall and make tinkling sounds on the few leaves that were brave enough to remain on the trees after all the freezing weather.

"We will need to leave soon, Tymber," Jait said, as he stopped to rest.

Tymber looked at him like he was crazy.

"Just long enough to get a couple more torches, and then return."

She picked up the pace of the pounding, but then she stopped. Jait was about to say something but Tymber cut him off.

"Listen," she said.

Jait turned his ear to the forest. He could not hear anything. He looked over at Tymber to see her smiling.

"Jait! Can you hear that?"

He listened again.

Tymber hooted as loud as she could.

Jait heard the response. It was the hoot of his father, still at some distance. It was Jait's turn to hoot.

Tymber played a rhythm on the tree in delight.

They continued to drum until their father was in sight.

Tymber and Jait ran to them when they saw them. Tymber hugged them all and gave Drel an extended kiss that made the girls giggle.

"We were getting worried," she said, to her father.

"I think we were all getting worried," said Pred, looking at his wife. "The pounding on the tree sure helped us find our way. We had to leave the trail at the river because of Bossy and Brute. They couldn't climb the bank where we normally cross the river so we had to go farther down river and then in the fog, we could only guess at our way."

Sella still had her arm around Jait.

"The drumming noise came just as we seemed to be heading in a wrong direction," she said. "We turned and headed towards it."

"It did come at just the right time," Pred admitted. "If we continued the way we decided to go, we would have been back at the village before we got here."

"Well it was Jait that had the idea of pounding the hollow tree," Tymber said.

"Tymber, where did you get that coat?" Sella asked.

"It was a gift from the Hantfel people," Tymber said. "Aliptis made it herself."

"It looks like it was made from a predator."

Tymber looked at her mother in surprise for knowing that.

"We stayed in the stone cabin and I saw the one over the fireplace. Is that the one you shot?"

"Yes." She didn't know exactly what to say. Her mother knew about shooting the predator? "It is very warm..."

"And a very pretty coat," her mother added.

"The people of Hantfel had a feast for Tymber, for her saving Aliptis," said Jait.

"Now I really wish I had been there," said Drel.

"Let's get to the cavern so we can rest," said Pred. "We can talk about our travels after we have eaten."

"I have supper already cooked," said Tymber. "All we need to do is warm it up."

Tymber lifted Janna from her seat on Bossy and Jait took Ispis. They carried the girls as they led the way to the cavern ramp.

The torch was nearly burned out when they walked up the ramp to their new home. Sella, Ispis, and Janna heard the crashing of the waves of the sea for the first time. They strained to see in that direction but could see nothing in the dark and fog.

Janna held on to Tymber tightly as they walked along the ledge. She seemed somewhat nervous about the powerful sound of the sea. The waves did seem loud as they crashed onto shore. Tymber thought that it might be good to stop and explain the noise.

She explained to her mother and sisters the view of the sea from where they stood. She told them of the shore of sand and waves they were hearing. She will enjoy showing them the sea when it again got light.

"Don't worry Janna," Tymber told her. "You can't hear the sea in the cavern."

"Sister?" Janna said.

Tymber almost dropped her when she said that. She never called her sister.

"Yes, Janna." Tymber could feel a slight shaking coming from her and heard a quiver in her voice.

"How did you become so brave?"

Tymber smiled at her sister's question.

"You will grow up to be brave too," she said. "Being brave is simply knowing that things scare you, but doing them anyway."

"I'm not so brave yet."

"I've got a good idea," Tymber said, as they entered the cavern. "Why don't we sleep next to each other tonight? That way we can talk together about our new home."

"That would be great."

Janna turned to look into the cavern holding on to Tymber tightly.

TWENTY ONE

Sella was amazed at the cavern. She had not realized how nice and comfortable it would be. She was surprised that it was so warm even a sweater wasn't needed. Pred was happy how she seemed to want to know as much about the cavern as she could.

Tymber had picked out a chamber that she thought would be the best for making their home chamber, but Sella found one she liked better, so that is where they placed their possessions and called home.

Ispis and Janna were told to stay within a few chambers of home unless they were with someone, but seemed to find plenty of things to do, including helping Tymber tend to the vegetables and clean fish.

Jait took the time to show Sella around. He brought her to the garden chamber first to show her how well all the vegetables grew.

"Those tomato plants are only about twelve days old and they already have a few green tomatoes," he told her.

Sella spent a lot of time in the rain chamber. She sat with Jait and they talked about the rain coming from the ceiling. In the middle of their conversation Jait realized that the purpose for the tour of the caverns wasn't only to learn where everything was, it was because she just wanted to spend some time with her son. Spending time with her son has been difficult now that he was an adult. He was glad she wanted to spend the time, he enjoyed it as well.

Tymber and Ispis were in the garden chamber tending to the vegetables. Even with her successes at growing vegetables, she was worried and concerned about what she saw.

"Ispis, could you go find Drel and ask him to come here. I have questions I hope he can answer."

In just a short while, Ispis and Drel came back into the garden.

"Drel, I have a couple of questions," Tymber started, looking over her plants. "Why are the potatoes growing so well, the tomatoes are doing okay, but some of the squash and cucumbers plants are growing well but are bearing no fruit? The corn isn't doing as well producing ears as I would think as healthy as the plants look."

"I don't know, Tymber," he said. "The plants look healthy and they are blooming."

"But some of them haven't been making any vegetables."

"When I make the next trip to the village, I will ask Farmer or Crops for the answer to your question. I'm sure that one of them would certainly know."

Tymber seemed a little disappointed. She was hoping Drel had the answers and would not have to wait on an answer from the farmers.

On a happier note, she took Drel's hand and led him to a side cavern of the garden. It was a smaller but taller chamber and it was obvious that Tymber had things growing in there.

"This is the chamber where I'm growing nut and fruit trees. There is not room for very many but I wanted to show you the latest that have sprouted."

She pointed to eight small tree sprouts.

"Those are my lemon trees," she said, smiling.

When Sella thought that the dark cycle had passed and it would be starting to get light, she told Pred that she wanted to take a walk outside to see the sea.

They both put on their coats, hats, and gloves and headed to the cavern opening. As they approached the opening, they could feel the temperature getting progressively colder.

They walked out into ankle deep snow on the ledge and found the dim orange sun just above the horizon of the sea.

Sella shivered at the cold. The air was so cold it was hard to breathe so they breathed through their scarves.

She stood still so she didn't slip in the snow, and looked out onto the sea for the first time.

"What a beautiful place, Pred."

The rhythm of the waves breaking on the beach was a peaceful sound. She wished it were warm and she could walk barefoot through the waves in the sand.

"The sun is getting so small," she said. "We live in a continuous dusk."

"A very cold dusk," said Pred, with a little shiver.

"The cavern will make a nice shelter for our family, Pred. I don't know what the future holds, but I know we are safe and warm and we will be together."

"I'm glad you think our new home will be good." he said, as he stood behind Sella and held her in his arms.

"This big old cave isn't really so bad."

She looked up at him and he saw her smile in the dim orange light with the sea in the background. Now it really was a beautiful sight.

Through the next couple of light cycles, Drel and Jait returned to the village to retrieve chairs, beds, and dressers. They knew that they would have to disassemble Sella's weaver to get it into the wagon and then into the cavern. One of Pred's major requests was for them to bring every board they could find, even if they had to disassemble the cabin. Wood was something that he knew the cavern wouldn't grow and harvesting trees in this cold would be nearly impossible.

Their plan was to clear a way through the forest large enough for a small wagon to travel. They were to hitch it onto Bossy and Brute to bring the rest of their things. One good thing about the cold weather, the river was frozen and they could drive the wagon down the frozen river.

At the end of the second light cycle, they returned to the cavern. This time they brought many people from the village with them. To the dismay of Pred, none of the leaders came.

Baker seemed to be the most impressed with the cavern. He said he should have been living there all along. Tymber was the most delighted about Baker coming. She hoped he would continue to bake. She was determined to find a way to make the grains grow.

Smith said that he was just going to stay for the winter. He believed that when spring came a large sun would rise in the east and he would move back to the village.

Drel said that the farmers did not want to come. They saw no reason for a farmer to live in a cave. Fisher on the other hand said that the sea would bring new fishing challenges and brought his family there to live.

Surprisingly, Shodder and Slippers came with their family. Tymber found them a larger chamber to live.

It took Jait, Drel, and the other men a long time to get everything into the cavern, and when they did, it took them nearly a whole long night to get everything back to the chambers. They had plenty of help with all the newcomers that came.

The women were not allowed to help and found the situation almost comical at times to watch. The men made a lot of mistakes and had to try things many ways before they could get everything into the cavern. They even had to take some things apart and reassemble them when they got the pieces to the proper place.

But when it was all completed, it almost seemed like home.

During the next light cycle, Tymber received a big surprise when people from Hantfel came to live in the cavern for the winter, including Aliptis, Goshenta, and surprisingly, Midton. They seemed to understand the situation that Adentta was in better than the people in the village.

The Hantfel people brought many things with them to the delight of everybody, including very large pots and pans to cook for many people at one time. They also brought a very generous supply of food and seeds, including grains, fruits, vegetables, meat, and the rest of the tromptaw sausage.

Perhaps the best of what Hantfel brought were their village's craftsmen. People of knowledge in construction and crafting that were needed for a community to survive.

Tac, the Hantfel herder, brought cows, chickens, sheep, and pigs. It took a long time to get all the animals through the passages and back past the living chambers to where Pred had said for the animals to graze.

The people of Hantfel didn't have much trouble deciding which chambers they wanted to live in. They almost all went to live on the other side.

As Goshenta and Aliptis were settling in where they had chosen to live, they told Drel and Tymber how difficult it had become to live in the cabins.

"There is no going outside during the long night," Goshenta said. "Just stepping outside is forbidden. Many of our people, including my father, froze to death in attempts to go out at night. The frozen night air is nearly impossible to breathe, even through a scarf."

"The light of day is not much better," Aliptis said, putting her pillows on her makeshift bed. "The light is dim and it doesn't warm up much."

Pred and Sella walked through the cavern and visited all that had come to live there. It made them happy to see all the crafts that were now living in the cavern.

"It would seem like the cavern is going to be very self sufficient with all the various craftsmen available and plentiful supplies of food," Pred told Sella.

Sella found the people from Hantfel extremely interesting and fun to be with. They had a hard work and a playful attitude. The people in the village always seemed too absorbed in work to have fun.

Tac was put in charge of all the animals. He had said that he thinks the chambers that already have weeds and grasses growing will be enough until he can get better grass to grow in the larger north chambers and move them there."

Pred, to his dismay, was voted as leader of the cavern. At least for the time, the things he wanted he got, but he wasn't very demanding. It was time to learn from each other and become friends.

He was very happy that so many people came to live there, and for the most part, everyone got along with each other. It was hard for some of the people to share living space with another family or two, but they did find if they worked together on problems they were solved quicker.

The Builder from Hantfel put everyone that wanted a rock wall built down on his list. Pred made a request that a wall could not block the way to another chamber or passageway.

When Tymber caught up to Drel, she asked him if he had asked Farmer why some of the vegetables were not bearing fruit.

"Yes, I did," said Drel. "You may not like the answer though.

"Farmer said that it was probably a couple of things. One is that here in the cavern there is no wind to help pollinate. Many vegetables rely on the wind to carry the pollen. Another thing is there are no bees in here to pollinate the blossoms of the vegetables. He also said that many of the fruit and nut trees require wind but mostly bees for pollination."

Tymber looked sad. She had not figured on those things to make fruits and vegetables.

"I'm sure everyone would love for me to bring bees into the cavern," she said sarcastically.

"They would if they wanted those things to eat," he said, in response.

Tymber looked at Drel with an 'I've got a plan' look.

"We need honey too," she said.

"You won't find any bees outside in this cold."

"Actually, we know where a hive is, don't we." She was grinning from ear to ear. "The bees are inside the hive and are dormant in this cold. The whole hive will be easy to get."

"Traveling there and getting bees may not be possible in this cold."

Tymber didn't hear what Drel had just said and got excited about getting the bees. She would dig a hole in the Garden Chamber wall to place them.

Realizing that she didn't know if it was light or dark outside, she went to go look. It was dark, so she made plans to leave and get the beehive when it turned light.

She saw no reason for more than one person to suffer the extreme cold. Her coat was the warmest coat in the cavern so she would get the bees by herself. With a little bit of luck, she could be there and back before anybody even knew she was gone.

The first chamber was starting to get a little cold from the extreme cold outside air coming down the entrance corridor. The builder from Hantfel requested that at the beginning of the entrance corridor, they build a stone wall with a wide wooden door so the corridor could be closed off from the outside cold. Pred agreed.

Everybody in the cavern was extremely busy with making the cavern home.

The women, along with Smith, were setting up the hot and warm chambers with cooking abilities by setting metal plates over hot air vents.

The large pots that the people of Hantfel made were needed in food preparation, which was done mostly as an entire group cook.

A couple of families wanted to do their own cooking and they were more than welcome to do so.

The stone builders of Hantfel were very busy carving and fortifying rock to make people more comfortable. They were also teaching anybody that wanted to learn the rock wall building craft.

Tymber went to the cave opening and watched the building of the wall for the door. She made sure she knew how the door was going to operate in case it was finished and closed when she returned.

When she looked outside, she thought at first that it was still night, but it was a very dark day.

She went out on the ledge to make sure that she could see. The snow on the ground helped make it look lighter outside than it really was.

How could I have been so stupid not to remember the need for bees? she thought.

She went back into the cavern to get supplies. She needed a lined basket to carry the hive, and she found a cooked chicken leg, baked potato, and a tomato to bring to eat. Of course she always carried her knife, but got her bow and hatchet to bring with her.

Tymber knew she needed to tell somebody she was going, but she also knew that everyone would try to stop her. They would think it is too cold to travel. They were probably right, but she was the one who forgot about bees, so she had to try to get them.

She told Ispis that she was going to get honey. Ispis thought that was a great idea. She loved honey on her mother's biscuits.

Tymber knew that if Ispis said anything, Drel would know what she meant and Jait would know where she was.

Tymber stood at the entrance to the cavern and looked out onto a very unfriendly day. She carefully walked along the ledge to make sure she didn't slip in the snow. Looking ahead she took a deep breath and with renewed determination, she headed down the trail.

The bee hive was on the sea side of their river camp, just on the other side of View Hill. It would take a little more than a day to get there and back, if she hurried. It wasn't easy to hurry. The snow on the ground helped light the day, but made it slippery to walk.

The climb up View Hill was a difficult challenge. It seemed like every step up she took, she slid down two. Nevertheless, she got to the top and going down hill to the hive was then an easy walk.

She got to the hive in what she thought was a very fast time considering the snow. As expected, the hive was completely dormant and the honey was nearly solid. All she had to do was hack a little at the opening with her hatchet and pull on the inside of the hive. It slipped out of the hollow tree and fit nicely into the basket.

Before she started her return trip, she stopped to eat her chicken leg and ate the potato like an apple. It was almost frozen from being in her backpack, but as hungry as she was, it tasted delicious. The tomato was frozen so she decided to put it inside her coat to try to thaw it as she walked back.

Just as she got up to continue it started to snow. The day was just slightly lighter than night now, but still the snow on the ground helped her to be able to see.

"It must be getting colder," she said, out loud with a shiver in her voice. "I shouldn't have sat down. It's made me cold."

She continued her way back as the snow fell with increasing speed. The harder the snow fell the more the wind blew it around.

Tymber had to slow down her travel home as it became harder to walk in the deeper snow. Her tracks from her trip there could no longer be seen through the fresh snow. She began to lose the trail marks as the wind blown snow stuck to the trees.

When she got back to View Hill she knew she had to walk up hill and then back down. She could not see the way, just guessed at the direction.

She had to rest, she cuddled behind a tree that blocked the wind and sat for a little while. She had no idea that it could get this cold.

As she sat resting, Tymber heard a snarl in the distance. It wasn't exactly a snarl, but more of a meow of a small animal. She thought for sure she was hearing things. She pulled on the side of her hood just enough so she could listen. Again, she heard it. She got up and grabbed her basket and went to where she thought she heard the noise.

She didn't see anything. Again she heard it but only louder. There were two meows now. She looked around and behind trees for the sound. Behind a large tree there was an opening at the base. The tree was hollow and inside huddled together were two very small predator cubs. They were only a little larger than Tymber's hand not including their tail.

She could barely see them in the light but they did not seem afraid of her. She held them in her hands as they shivered in the cold. She stuck them down inside her coat and they immediately started to purr in the increase warmth of Tymber's body. She hoped their mother was not around. They seemed abandoned.

She tied her hood to her head so only her eyes were showing. She breathed the warmer air inside her coat.

The excitement of finding the cubs somewhat warmed her up, but she really didn't know which way to head. All she knew was she had to keep moving. Her guess was to head into the wind which most likely came off the sea. She walked and walked not knowing if it was the right direction. As she walked she would talk to the cubs and decided to name them. She named one Moonshadow and the other Foggynight.

Tymber's legs were so cold they were turning numb.

"Okay guys, I'm going to have to rest," she told the cubs. "I can't walk any further without a rest."

She took off her frosted bow. Actually, it mostly fell off when the frozen string broke. She sat down in the snow with her back up against a tree.

"I have never been so cold and tired and sleepy. I have to rest. I was hoping to save you two, but it looks like you may have been better off where you were," she said, looking inside her coat at the cubs.

Almost as if Moonshadow knew what she had said, the cub reached his head up and licked Tymber on the chin.

Tymber tried to get up to continue but couldn't. Her legs were completely numb.

"I can't seem to move," she told them.

She sat in silence. She started to tear in sadness.

"Yes mother I will do the dishes when I return home," she said, but then realized that she was dreaming.

"The door is closed and I can't get in."

She awoke when Moonshadow meowed and lightly stuck his claws into her.

"I can't stay awake."

"Yes, Jait, yes. I am here, come and get me."

"Father, it was the only way to have vegetables to eat, she mumbled into her coat.

Again she woke when the cold wind pierced through her pants.

"I always thought that I would die in a tremendous tragedy or during the worse of all shakes or as a hero. Not die in my sleep, frozen to death."

She thought about what she told Jait, about dying alone from something stupid. This seemed to qualify.

On a cold, snowy, dark, windy day, Tymber's frozen tears sealed her eyes shut as she fell asleep.

Drel found Sella in the kitchen chamber helping the other ladies cook breakfast. He could smell the grain cakes, hen's eggs, and sausage many chambers before he got there.

"I'm so hungry I could eat a predator," he told Sella, jokingly.

"Well you will get your chance. That sausage is made with predator and pig meat. It is the predator that Tymber shot. It came from the people of Hantfel."

"Where is Tymber? I was hoping to find her down here. I have some time to help her in the garden chamber. It would seem that we have the job of being the wind and bees."

Sella briefly looked at Drel with a confused frown but then realized it was probably something that Tymber had suggested. Pretending to be the wind and bees sounded like her.

"She may still be asleep," she said. "I tried not to wake anybody when I left to come down here"

"I may go get her up," he said. "I have to meet Storer in a little while and I wanted to help her first. We have found some very high chambers that are getting very cold. We think it's because they are close to the surface. Storer thinks that chambers up there would be perfect for storing our foods.

"Well, sit down and eat first, before the food gets cold."

"Drel, we need a way to tell if it is day or night. It is not too important except for eating and sleeping. Most of the ladies here are helping with breakfast but some are making supper. We are very confused. Also it would be quieter if all the families slept near the same time."

"I know, Sella," he said. "You are right. I will talk to Moment as much as I hate to. We need a way to keep track of our days. If we don't develop some way, I won't even know how to label my writings."

"Mother," Ispis called. "You need to come. Jait has fever this morning. I have been putting a wet cloth on his forehead, but he is still moaning."

"Thanks Ispis, I will come in a moment."

"Feel free to get more food if you're still hungry when you finish with this."

Sella put down a large plate of food for Drel and followed Ispis.

When they got to Jait he was moaning and shouting strange things. Mostly things they could not understand.

Sella went to him and put another wet cloth to his forehead.

"You have done well, Ispis. You did just what you should have done."

Sella sat with Jait until he woke, sweating from the broken fever. Still dazed he just lay there for a time.

"How are you Jait?" his mother asked, as she wiped the sweat from his face.

Aliptis heard that Jait was sick and entered the chamber to see how he was doing.

"I am doing okay now," he said, looking at both his mother and Aliptis. "I think I tossed and turned the whole time I slept. I feel like I just made a trip to the village and back."

"You have had fever, but I think it has broken."

"You were talking crazy, Jait," Ispis smiled at him. "You kept shouting for Tymber."

"I must have been dreaming she was pushing me into the river again. I never have repaid her …"

Jait sat up.

"Mother! Tymber is lost outside!"

"You had fever, Jait. It was just a dream," she said, as she tried to get Jait to relax. "Just lie back down and try to rest."

"No mother, when I called for her she answered. She wants me to come and get her."

Realizing that it had been quite awhile since she had seen Tymber, she turned to Ispis.

"Ispis," Sella said nervously, "where is Tymber?"

"I don't know mother. The last time I saw her was after break-fast, yesterday. She said she was going to go get some honey."

Jait jumped up to get dressed.

"You can't go out, you have fever," Sella told Jait.

He ignored that.

"Ispis," he said, "go get Father and Drel and hurry."

"Drel is in the kitchen," said Sella. "I will get him, go for your father. He is with Builder."

In no time Jait, Pred, and Drel were dressed in coats and were running for the cavern entrance. When they reached the entrance the cold air smacked them in the face. Drel gasped for air before he started to breathe through his scarf.

They too could barely see. The snow was still blowing but luckily the wind was at their backs. They stumbled in the direction of the hive as quick as they could go, which wasn't very fast.

They tried to call for Tymber, but their voices seemed to simply fall on the snow.

It was not very long when Jait heard a snarl in the distance. Well, it wasn't exactly a snarl, but more the 'meow' of a small animal.

He ran to the spot he heard the noise, but didn't see anything. Pred and Drel followed. This time they all heard the 'meow.'

Pred almost fell over Tymber before he saw her. She was in a sitting position up against a tree covered in a light snow. It took all three of the men to carry her and her basket back to the cavern.

In the cavern other people helped them get her down to the warm chambers. She was still alive but unconscious and breathing only slightly.

They took off her clothes and laid her in a pool of slightly warm water. They worked her legs and arms to help regain her circulation. After a long time taking turns, her body temperature seemed normal again; however, she still had not waken up.

They brought her back up to the Trelop chamber, laid her in bed, and wrapped her in blankets. It seemed like days had past and Sella never left her side. She dripped water into Tymber's mouth to try to keep her mouth moist.

Tymber knew that she should not be sleeping. She no longer felt cold. Numbness must have spread throughout her entire body. She had to wake or she would certainly freeze to death if she didn't. She struggled to wake up. The numbness she thought she felt was actually warmth. She laid there confused.

She felt a pressure on her chest. It made it hard for her to breathe. She attempted to open her eyes. She let out a little scream when she finally got them open. It scared her at first, but just for a second, for when she opened her eyes, a predator was nose–to–nose with her, staring back.

Tymber relaxed.

"Hi, Moonshadow."

Sella ran over to her when she realized she was awake. Moonshadow didn't like the quickness of Sella and snarled, but then allowed Sella to approach.

Sella put her hand on Tymber's face as Moonshadow snarled his disapproval.

"How are you feeling?" she asked, glancing at Moonshadow and Foggynight to make sure they were going to stay where they were.

Tymber moved all her limbs, fingers, and toes.

"I seem to be fine, Mother."

"Your friends here don't seem to like anybody getting near you."

Tymber smiled at her mother.

Ispis came into the room and Sella told her to get the family, Tymber was awake.

"They are allowed to be in here," Sella said to Tymber, but looked at the predator cubs, "because Jait said that they saved your life. He said he heard the beasts' growl."

"Mother," Tymber said, "surely you can't call those cute little cubs beasts."

"Another reason they are here is because they would not agree to leave."

Sella smiled down at her daughter.

Tymber shook her head.

"And I thought I was going to save their lives."

The cubs stayed on her chest and started to purr.

"How long have I been asleep?"

"Out in the cold forest covered in snow or in here?" Sella answered sarcastically.

"They need to be fed."

"We tried, but they would not eat."

"Bring me a bowl of milk and let me see if they will eat for me."

"Don't you think you should eat first?"

"I will in a little while after they do. You can get me some water; I'm mostly thirsty."

"Well, I will get you a lemon juiced drink and the cubs a bowl of milk.

"I am so glad you are all right." Sella smiled through her tears. She leaned over and kissed Tymber on the cheek as the cubs meowed at her.

When Sella turned to leave, Pred, Drel, and Jait came into the chamber.

The cub's snarl turned into meows when Moonshadow and Foggynight recognized them.

"They are very protective of you," Pred said, leaning over to give Tymber a hug.

"And they have very sharp claws," Jait said, showing scratches on his arm. "We had quite a shock when we opened your coat and out popped two predator cubs."

Tymber started laughing.

"I'm sure you did."

"And a tomato," he added.

"You had us scared to death. You should be spanked for doing such a thing," Drel said, jokingly and came over and kissed her.

"You would have to catch me first, and then be able to out wrestle me," she said.

"Careful Drel, you may wind up in the river," Jait said.

"My bees!" she remembered.

"I put the hive in the garden chamber in the hole you prepared for them. They have become active and are flying around in the chamber. We may have to fashion a curtain for that chamber door to keep the bees in."

"That may be a good idea," Tymber responded.

Sella came in with a juiced drink and a bowl of milk.

"Hand me the bowl of milk first."

She took the bowl and set it on her chest. She dipped a finger in the milk and touched it to Moonshadow's mouth. He licked it, but made a funny face and shook his head. She put some more milk to his mouth and this time he licked it completely off her finger.

She dipped her finger in the milk and did the same for Foggynight. She licked it off completely.

Tymber held her finger over the bowl and let milk drip from it. In a little while, the two cubs came and licked the milk from the bowl.

Tymber sat up and realized she didn't have on any clothes under the blanket.

"Could you put the bowl on the floor and see if they will go to it?"

Drel looked at Tymber.

"You mean you want me to take food away from predators?"

Tymber laughed, "Yes, it will be okay."

He did, and it was.

A few day and night cycles went by but the sun was never bright enough to light the sky. The new cavern village decided to have a ceremony. The door to the cavern entrance was just now finished and they thought that it should be a day they remember in ceremony.

The cavern village families were all dressed in coats and lined the corridor to the entrance. The Trelops all held hands. Drel held Tymber close and Jait held hands with Aliptis.

Pred, as leader, said a few words of encouragement, of change, and of survival.

"It is time for us to celebrate our plan to survive," he said.

Everyone was in tears not knowing if they would ever go outside again, but thankful for their new home.

They closed the entrance door as Adentta slowly spun further from its sun.

EPILOGUE

The Sea Cavern villagers work hard at adjusting to life in the cavern. They have begun to learn how to live life without the sun. Most of the crafts needed for survival and comfort had joined the cavern village, so they think that survival is possible.

It is their only hope. It has to work.

Some things, however, they must relearn how to do, not to mention how to record the passage of time without the ability to count days.

Tymber must convince the villagers that the tromptaws should remain inside and sheltered from the intense dark and cold of the outside. Many people do not think that is a good idea. They fear the tromptaws as they grow older. Some villagers ask Pred to have his daughter turn them loose because there is no place for them in the cavern. A continuing thought of Pred is the concern of people in the two villages that did not come to the cavern. Also, were Simpton Lake Village and Hantfel the only people on Adentta? When they found Hantfel, Pred had to change his ideas about the world in which they lived. He had to consider that there may still be others trying to survive. What about Vallend?

The story is not over. There is much left for Pred, Drel, Jait, Tymber and the rest of the Sea Cavern Village to do to survive. Look for their second book in the *To Lose the Sun* series:

THE CAVERNS
OF ADENTTA

Contact the Author at moonshadowcub@yahoo.com
Or don@ToLosetheSun.com

Be sure to visit:
www.ToLosetheSun.com